A chance to shine . . .

The closest Avery Shields expects to get to the music industry is her janitor position at Charisma Recording Studio, and singing secretly in her local karaoke bar. Working two jobs and studying full-time, she's doing all she can to earn her parents' trust after making mistakes in high school. But now a gorgeous stranger is filling her head with dreams of singing professionally—and filling her nights with desire....

Lazarus Kyson's A&R career took a hit after he was wrongfully accused of harassment. To restore his reputation, he needs to discover a new talent. And when he least expects it, there she is—singing while she cleans the Charisma offices. As stubborn as she is talented, she refuses to audition. If he wants Avery—her voice and her heart—he'll have to open himself up for the first time for a love too crazy good to let go....

Visit us at www.kensingtonbooks.com

Books by Crystal B. Bright

The Love & Harmony Series
Crazy in Love
Love Like Crazy

Mama's Boys Series
The Look of Love
Forget Me Not
Head Over Heels

Published by Kensington Publishing Corporation

Love Like Crazy

The Love & Harmony Series

Crystal B. Bright

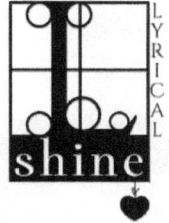

LYRICAL PRESS
Kensington Publishing Corp.
www.kensingtonbooks.com

Lyrical Press books are published by
Kensington Publishing Corp. 119 West 40th Street New York, NY 10018

First Electronic Edition: April 2018
eISBN-13: 978-1-5161-0469-7
eISBN-10: 1-5161-0469-2

First Print Edition: April 2018
ISBN-13: 978-1-5161-0472-7
ISBN-10: 1-5161-0472-2

Printed in the United States of America

This book is dedicated to all those people with a dream in your heart to do more in life but may feel stuck for whatever reason. Sing when you want to sing. Dance when the rhythm hits you. Love and laugh freely and often. Life is too short to live in fear.

Acknowledgments

Thank you, again, to Renee Rocco and Martin Biro for allowing me to spread my wings and fly with this new series. It feels like you're letting me run around with scissors, and no one looks worried. That's a good feeling.

Thank you to my editor, Mercedes Fernandez, who is making me a stronger writer and storyteller. I appreciate everything you do to help me improve my story.

Thank you, always, to Jim Stark, the love of my life. Thanks for always supporting me, through my highs and lows. I love you.

Author's Foreword

After writing *Crazy In Love*, I couldn't imagine writing a sequel to that story. Now that I've been given that opportunity and I have written *Love Like Crazy*, I can't see the series without these characters. My heart pulls for both Laz and Avery for different reasons. Hopefully, readers will feel that same tug in their hearts for these characters. Both have something to prove for different reasons. Question is: will they find harmony in each other? Read on and find out.

Hope you enjoy book two in the *Love and Harmony* series.

Keep reading,
Crystal***

Chapter 1

"I want that asshole fired!" The petite starlet jutted her finger in Laz Kyson's direction as he sat at the opposite side of the table from her in the Universe Records office.

He wanted to react, but he knew timing meant everything. Controlling himself meant he could manage anyone and any situation. Since the company's attorney acted like a mute as well, he figured his reaction worked.

"He…he," she paused for effect, "told me that if I didn't do certain things to him, he would make it difficult for me here." Then the sobbing came…without tears.

Laz shifted in his seat. The heat under his collar started to get a bit unbearable. He began drumming his fingers on the table until he saw Mr. Zinner's stare go directly to his hand.

The man had been salty to him since Laz went to bat for Chantel Woodley, or Shauna Stellar as Zinner continually referred to her when he lamented about the amount of money lost from losing her and Truman Woodley. Zinner had his chance with her, and he had blown it.

Zinner raised his arm like he wanted to pat the young woman's hand to console her, but he stopped as though thinking better of his actions considering what she accused Laz of doing to her. He, instead, spoke in soothing tones. "There, there, Kat."

To punctuate her hurt feelings, she responded to Zinner's sympathy with a protruding bottom lip. Her raven hair along with her sky-blue eyes and pale, clear skin made her a stunning beauty. Yet coupled with her rotten insides, Laz only saw a monster at the end of the table, who had now made it her mission for the summer to get him fired. Not happening.

Music and the music business encompassed every cell in his body until it became all he could think about. He would be damned if some pampered, lip-syncing diva would get him run out with his tail tucked between his cheeks and hide.

"Although I don't want you to relive this traumatic moment again, for the record, I'll need to know what happened. Will you please describe for me and the attorneys present the details of this alleged sexual harassment?" Mr. Zinner leaned back, probably to allow his gut freedom to expand away from the table.

As much as Laz wanted to tune the woman out, he made it a point to listen to each and every word that would come out of her mouth. His livelihood depended on it.

"I was doing my pop-up show at that little venue in Norfolk, Virginia." She wiped underneath her nose with the back of her thumb. "Then he shows up." She pointed at Laz again.

At least Kat didn't say Laz's name. Keep his name out of her mouth and he would be happy.

Kat continued. "I thought it was weird that an A&R rep was there at my show."

"Yes, that is unusual." Zinner cut a harsh look at Laz.

Laz glared back at the man, hoping he picked up his unspoken complaint about doing more for the label. When Zinner returned his attention to Kat, Laz released a long breath. His boss didn't get it.

"He starts showering me with compliments at first, telling me what a great singer I am and all."

Laz tried hard to suppress his laughter but it puffed out. He covered the sound with a cough, and then took a sip of water. He didn't need her stirred up any more.

No way did he think her vocal chops matched that of the great singers out there like Aretha, Christina, Adele, and Chantel. This pop star needed to stay in her lane as far as what she offered to the music industry, and she needed to start being honest. He didn't know how long he could hold out not saying anything while she massacred his reputation.

Kat sniffed. "Then he pulled me into a room."

"Mr. Kyson put his hands on you?" Zinner sat up taller.

So did Laz. He heard his heartbeat pounding in his head and it shook his body. It took every bit of his strength for him to not scream that this woman lied about everything so far except for the fact that he did approach her, but it had been for business, only business.

Kat nodded. "When we got in there, he said that if I didn't—" She hesitated and leaned over to her attorney. "Do I have to say it?" She whispered it to her but said it loud enough for Laz to hear.

The older woman next to her nodded and patted her hand.

"Fine." Kat took a deep breath and tucked a wavy curl behind her ear. "He said if I didn't put my mouth down there that he would make my life miserable." She pointed down in the vicinity of his genital area through the black marble tabletop that covered their lower sections.

A gasp echoed throughout the room. Kat's attorney stared at Laz with her mouth agape. Zinner couldn't even look at Laz now. The studio attorney adjusted his tie, and Laz wanted to scream.

Laz could count to a million in his head and he still wouldn't be able to calm down. He pressed his hands against the cold table while he bounced his knee under it. He had an ace up his sleeve. He needed to wait for his moment.

"That's the reason I haven't been in the studio to record. And because of all this, I'm not sure if I'm up to going in there for a while." She wrapped her arms around herself and shook her head. "I'm too shaken up." With her head down, she peered up at Laz. "That man is a monster. If he's not fired, I'm walking. I have ten million Instagram followers. They'll boycott this studio if I tell them to."

Zinner shook his head, letting the sweat that poured from it fly. Droplets littered the table. "Let's not be hasty, dear. I'm sure there's a misunderstanding." Finally, Zinner directed his attention to Laz. "Mr. Kyson, is there anything you want to say on your behalf?"

The air in the expansive boardroom went still and made it difficult for Laz to breathe. That wouldn't prevent him from responding. He had his name to clear. Before he did that, though, he would have a bit of fun.

"Yes. I have always preferred tea over coffee." Laz took a deep breath, relieved to finally say anything even though the thing he said seemed to not make sense.

"Excuse me?" Zinner braced his meaty hands on the table.

"And I would rather have a cat than a dog. Cats are quiet." Laz, realizing what he had said and the name of the woman across from him, amended his statement. "An older cat though. No kitties." He glared at the pop star.

"He's making this out to be a joke." Kat's pale face turned crimson. "I'm prepared to go to TMZ and *People*."

Laz reached into his front jacket pocket and pulled out his phone. "I'll be glad to help you with your story."

"I think you've said enough." Zinner held up his hand, then directed his attention to Kat. "You can take as much time as you need to record your fourth album. We can push the tour out as well."

Kat leaned over to her manager sitting on the other side of her this time. She whispered something in his ear.

The manager nodded. "For her inconvenience and mental trauma, Kat would also like a ten-million-dollar kicker to her contract."

Hush money. No way would Zinner agree to that. He had kicked out Chantel Evans, a far superior singer and entertainer, when she asked to be fairly compensated.

"Done." Zinner slammed his hand on the table.

Unbelievable.

"Hold on." Laz held up his hand. He clipped an attachment to his phone to project a video on the wall. "I think you all need to see this."

He pressed play and made sure to turn the volume up as high as it would go. Even though Laz had only been in the music industry for less than ten years, he knew enough to cover himself.

The stories about Kat's predatory behavior ran rampant throughout the industry. She played virginal, but she had a voracious sexual appetite.

Laz did not dig Kat's vibe or her aggressive nature. In his world, he ran things, that also included his intimate life. Now, he had his head on business.

The night in question, Laz had set up his phone to record in Kat's dressing room where he had been told to wait for her after her show. He had his phone on a shelf above to look at the full scene below. It showed him in a full suit, pacing back and forth in her room with her hair and makeup people.

When the door opened, Kat walked in wearing her trademark sparkly leotard, sky-high booties, and her hair piled high on her head.

"Get out." She waved her hands in the air to get everyone to leave the room. The people started to go, including Laz, but she put her hand on his chest to stop him. "Not you." She laughed.

"We don't need to see this." Kat started to stand.

"Sit down." Her attorney held her client's arm and pulled her down to sit. "I need to verify if this is authentic."

"He had this video doctored. I told you exactly what happened."

Kat's screeching voice pierced Laz's eardrum. He continued playing the video, especially since Zinner couldn't stop staring at the image.

"Thank you for seeing me. It's great that you want to talk about the progress of your next album. We have a pretty aggressive schedule planned, so it would be beneficial to get the ball rolling on the music. I was fine talking to you afterward on the tour bus with your manager." Laz took a few steps back from her.

"I'm not really down for a threesome, not tonight." Kat pushed Laz down on a couch in the room, and then straddled him.

"Um, that's not me. I think that's one of those drag queen impersonators." Kat pointed to the image on the wall.

In the video, Laz tried laughing off her antics in a polite yet reserved way. "Look, I would be a lucky man to be able to bed the famous Kat."

"Bed, couch, wall. I'm very flexible." She swirled her hips. "Yes, you would be very lucky. I'm really good at what I do."

Laz put his hands on her shoulders. "I'm only here to talk about your album and that's it. I don't want or need anything else." Laz, while trying hard not to touch her anywhere lower than her shoulders, managed to get himself from under her and stand.

Even after he stood, Kat wrapped her arms around the back of his neck. She kissed his neck, chin and cheek. "I haven't had you yet. I think this will be fun."

"Oh, God." Kat hung her head down at the table while the incriminating evidence played.

The video continued. "Wow. You are strong." Laz pried her arms from around him. "Trust me. This would not be a good idea. I'm the jealous type. If I see you talking to another man, whew." He shook his head. "I don't want to think about how I would react. And since *I'm* the idiot for turning down this insane offer, I definitely won't say anything to anyone." He winked. "Our secret."

Kat cocked her head and crossed her arms over her chest. "What? You think I should be embarrassed or something, like I did something wrong? I'm a young woman. I have needs. It gets lonely out on the road."

The group kept their full attention on the video even when Kat tried interrupting their viewing pleasures with her frantic voice and gesturing.

"Stop this." Kat waved her hand in the air.

Laz didn't. He wanted his name fully cleared. Here he thought he had been polite to her, gave her every opportunity to bow out of the situation graciously, even pinned the lack of performance on him. Yet she still tried destroying him.

In the video, Laz said, "All I want to do is talk about your music. You owe Universe—"

"Universe can kiss my ass." Kat punctuated her point by slapping her small ass cheek.

Zinner cleared his throat. Laz enjoyed the slight tingling sensation that took over his body. Vindication felt good.

In the video, Kat's phone rang. "You wait right there. I'm not done with you."

"That's what I'm afraid of." Laz headed toward the shelf area.

Kat answered the phone. "Hello?" She paused. She clicked a button on the phone first. "It's my bitch of an attorney. This will be quick. Don't you dare go anywhere or I'll make your life a living hell." She ducked into a room next to her dressing room.

The end shot showed Laz grabbing his phone. "Insurance just in case." He winked in the camera and stopped recording.

Kat let her feelings be known about the video and her statement by throwing up on the floor. The stench of her vomit stung Laz's nostrils until he had to turn his head away for a moment and breathe through his mouth.

Laz, confident that he got his point across, ended the video. "You want to go to a gossip site and a magazine with your claims?" He pointed his phone to Kat. "May not be a good idea. I don't want to do it, but if pressed, I'll release this video." His gaze dropped down to Kat's hand. "Before you leave, make sure you put your purity ring back on. Fans are standing outside waiting for you to come back out. They want to believe in the image you've created."

This time when Kat cried, real tears rolled down her cheeks. She stood from the table. "Next week. I'll be in the studio next week." She waved her hand wildly in front of her. "No kicker needed."

"Wait." Her manager tried to grab her other hand to stop her.

"No. No more games. I tried holding out to get more money. I tried a lot of things." She glared at Laz. "I'll do what I agreed to in my contract. I'm sorry." She turned to her attorney. "I don't think you're a bitch."

Her lawyer must not have believed her. She collected her belongings and walked out before Kat.

Kat started to leave. When she got behind Laz, she grumbled, "Asshole."

"Hope you're feeling better, Kat." Laz slipped his phone back into his pocket.

When Kat's team vacated the conference room, Laz finally smiled, a first since hearing of Kat's accusations a couple of days go. He turned to the staff attorney, expecting him to share in Laz's delight. He looked more pissed than Kat.

The attorney shook his head. "Should have kept your mouth closed."

Zinner addressed the attorney. "Prepare the gag order." Then he glared at Laz.

"Done." The attorney picked up his tablet and left Laz there with Zinner.

When the attorney closed the door behind himself, Laz faced his boss. Surely this man would have his back.

Wanting to get Zinner's opinion on the situation sooner rather than later, Laz spoke first. "I didn't do what she accused me of doing. I never touched her."

Zinner snickered. "You idiot." He shook his head. "Do you really think you're the first person in the music biz accused of sexual misconduct with the talent? Hell, you're not even the first person Kat has been with on this *staff*. This is not unusual, and you're not special."

At that moment, Laz didn't even feel heard.

"I knew what she was trying to do." Zinner swung himself back and forth in his chair.

Laz nodded. "Yeah, take down my career."

Zinner held up his hand. "Bigger picture, kid. She wanted more money. It's always about money. Nothing more. Nothing less."

"And you were willing to pay her more money for a delayed album and tour?"

Zinner slammed his hand on the table. "Ten million is nothing compared to the revenue we could have generated from her. She is a pop music money machine. The pre-sales for the album she has yet to go to the studio for has already sold a quarter-of-a-million copies. Her tour would have paid us even more, on top of lucrative endorsements for the sweet-as-pie, goody-goody act she puts on so well. We could have gotten her to sign an additional contract with us...until today." He snickered. "Thanks to you, more than likely she'll fulfill her obligations to this contract and then move on to another company or, worse yet, pull a Shauna and put out music on her own."

Laz shook his head. "Paying her for a lie meant that my reputation would have been tarnished, and I would have been out of a job. She wanted me fired."

Zinner didn't blink, didn't react.

Laz was not special.

"I could have talked her out of seeing you let go. I would have made sure to keep her away from you, which, by the way, why did you even approach her? You're A&R. I just need for you to acquire talent. We have people on staff to talk about contract obligations. Those people are managers and attorneys, not you." When Zinner pointed at Laz, it looked like he wanted his finger to be a gun and he yearned blowing Laz's head clean off his shoulders.

"I told you I wanted to do more here. I've been here long enough to go into management. I've heard music from unsigned artists who would be perfect for Universe, like this one named Destiny Starr. I don't know who she is, but if I find her, I would love to sign her and represent her." Laz sat up taller. "I can be used more."

"You could have." Zinner stood. "Not anymore. Pack your shit and go." He pointed to the door.

Laz stood with him. He hoped his towering height would give him a little bit of an intimidation factor. "What the hell? You saw with your own eyes that Kat lied. I never dragged her into a room and asked her for oral sex. She jumped on me. Why am I getting let go if she was the one in the wrong?"

The automatic blinds in the room started to lower on their own, casting a shadow on the scene.

"You're poison to us now. The threat that you may release that video will keep Kat from saying anything publicly, but privately, with other up-and-coming talent, our business will be mud, including this unknown talent you have a hard-on for."

Instinctively, Laz clasped his hands in front of his body to cover his genital region. If Zinner heard this woman's voice, he would want her, too.

"They'll associate Universe with perverts and creeps, whether it's true or not." Zinner strolled toward the door.

"Then I'll sue her. I've worked too hard to be—"

Zinner put his hand on Laz's shoulder. "It's over." Then he blinked. "Unless..."

Laz peered down at Zinner's hand before redirecting his attention back to him. "Unless what?"

"I can have you doing another position. You remember Mable?"

This time Laz blinked. "The older lady in H.R.?"

Zinner nodded. "She's retiring. Or she died recently. I can't remember. Anyway, she used to be over the interns. You could do that. You could wrangle the intern pool here, which will keep you away from the talent."

Laz took a few steps back, which broke the hold Zinner had on him. "With my education, experience, and years of service here, you want to bump me down to a babysitter?"

Zinner exhaled like he needed to, not out of exasperation. "You'll still work for the company."

Laz shook his head. He didn't do this business to have his name associated with a company. He had something to say, something to prove.

"I'll be gone in five minutes." He stormed to the door.

"Not until you sign that gag order preventing you from talking about the whole thing with Kat. One word about it to anyone and you'll be sued for every dime you have and every dime you'll ever earn."

"Believe me. I don't want to talk about this bullshit situation." He continued to the door.

"You won't make it out there," Zinner called after Laz, but Laz kept moving.

From this point on, he would have to do what he could to make his own way.

* * * *

Avery Shields leaned on the mop handle she'd just used on the women's bathroom floor as she peered down to read her statistics book. She needed more hours in the day to get it all done.

"Avery, you done in the bathroom?"

She heard her father's voice, but she had a few more pages to review first. She glanced at her watch and cursed. In a few more hours, she would have her first of many exams. Life wouldn't be life if it didn't include tests.

The door to the women's bathroom creaked open.

"Did you hear me, gal?" Her father came up behind her and tapped her shoulder.

"Yeah." Avery didn't have to look at Clinton Shields to know he disapproved of how she responded. "I mean, yes, sir." She broke away from her book to give him her full attention. "The toilets are cleaned. The mirrors are all shiny. I just mopped. I'm good in here."

As though not believing her, Clinton scanned the room that had a row of about seven stalls and then about five more stalls around the corner. He dropped his gaze to the floor first before proceeding to inspect the rest of the place.

In the meantime, in the quiet, Avery continued reading until she heard that disappointed groan she had heard from her parents before. Each time, it gave her an uncomfortable tickle up her spine to the back of her head.

She heard the sounds of plastic crinkling before she saw her father coming around the corner with a full bag of garbage in his hand.

"*All* of the garbage receptacles. You have to empty them all." He shook his head as he walked by her. "I swear sometimes you don't think."

"I was going to get it." She winced at the lie with good reason.

Clinton didn't make it out of the door. He returned to her and cocked his head. "So you thought it would make more sense to mop the floor *before* emptying out the trash cans?"

"When you put it that way, I guess it doesn't hold any logic." She shrugged. "My name is on this cleaning business."

When Clinton started on his rant, it could wear on a person's nerves. Avery wouldn't dare roll her eyes or cut him off from speaking his mind.

"I know, Dad." She understood the sacrifices her parents had made for the family.

Clinton had driven taxis, cleaned office buildings, and even had his own pressure-washing business at one time. Avery's mother usually worked alongside him until she started taking classes to become a nurse.

Avery really had no reason to complain. She had a job, too many jobs, actually. Her father didn't have to hire her, but he did. That didn't mean she didn't see more for herself like her mother. Her dream, though, didn't involve another high-level profession like nursing.

Clinton's gaze dropped down to her opened book. "The sooner we get this place cleaned, the faster you can get home to finish studying."

"Yes, sir." She slammed the book closed and slipped it into a side pocket that Avery had made to hang from the rolling cleaning cart that housed all her supplies.

Her father carried the same warm honey skin tone color, but on long days like today, he looked ashen and tired. His gray coveralls stretched tight over his rounded belly. The scowl that masked his expression spoke volumes. He, nor Avery's mother, could easily hide their expressions.

Avery bent down to roll the cuffs on her oversized coveralls to keep from tripping on them while she walked.

"You get that end and I'll get this end, and I think that'll be it." Clinton nodded to the area behind Avery.

"Yes, sir." She watched him walk away before she pushed her cart to the end of the top floor where she knew magic had to happen.

Avery scanned her identification badge over a reader to open the door first. As soon as she stepped inside, her shoulders relaxed. The place already smelled like flowers and fragrant candle wax. She loved stepping inside Charisma Music's studio.

She got the studio on a good night. The section sat empty, which lately had been a rare occurrence. On the nights when artists filled the studio space, Avery tried keeping away from the area. She didn't do it out of embarrassment because of her job. She worked and worked hard. However, she didn't like seeing others going for a dream that had been hers at one time.

Avery left her cart in the center of the room so that she could start her work. No use lamenting about what could have been. She dusted the surfaces. When she got to the control boards, she dragged her fingers over the knobs and buttons.

"Maybe." She snickered. "Probably not."

After dusting, she adjusted her headscarf over her hair, styled with two-stranded twists all over. Then she tackled the thick glass panes that surrounded the recording booths. She let her hand rest on the glass rumored to have been smashed with a chair by country singer Laura Smalls. Strange what people will do for love, or even lust.

To make sure she didn't leave any handprints, she examined the glass thoroughly. She didn't need her father catching her slacking on her duties again.

When she got by the piano that sat to the side, Avery hung around it longer than she should have. Like the control board, she danced her fingers over the keys, allowing one to dip down on one key so that the sound reverberated throughout the compact space. When the sound came, so did the involuntary hum that rattled her chest.

Avery peered up to make sure her father didn't pop up all of a sudden. When she didn't see or hear him, she took a seat at the piano bench. She took a breath before tickling her fingers over the keys. She tried doing it ever so lightly, but then she got into playing a Stevie Wonder song and found herself getting into it more and more.

She smiled and her body didn't feel like her own. It felt both relaxed and on autopilot as she played the melody first. Before she knew it, Avery had started singing.

She closed her eyes and imagined her life recording music in a studio like this and with people like Chantel and Truman Woodley. If Chantel could make it out of her humble beginnings to be a major power player in the business, Avery held out hope that maybe one day after finishing her business degree and getting a job her parents would be proud of, she could really pursue her dream. She could finally be Destiny Starr. If she did that, would they still be proud of her?

When the thought hit her, she stopped playing. She hovered her hands over the piano keys. What was Avery doing besides torturing herself? This life could never be hers. She had made up a fake name to go with her fantasy life.

Avery stood from the piano and returned it to the condition she had found it. She vacuumed the carpet and made sure to empty out all the trash bins around the recording studio area. With that done, Avery started to push her cart out to meet with her father. Getting done by two a.m. seemed like a gift. She would have some time to go home, study a bit more, go to work at the diner, and still get to class on time.

Thinking about her schedule had her sighing. She shouldn't complain. At twenty-two, she had time and energy to burn to go without sleep and work hard.

Right when Avery opened the main door to go back out into the hallway, her father met her face-to-face, which startled her. She had hoped with the soundproof walls that he hadn't heard her playing only moments ago.

"All done in here." She smiled to ease his concern and keep the conversation going in a different direction. "I would say you don't have to check behind me, but I know you." Avery laughed.

"I should have had you do the business offices and I should have taken care of this area."

Busted.

The relaxed feeling Avery had felt earlier behind the piano disappeared. She felt her shoulders tense up around her ears. She balled her hands into fists. When she realized the position of her hands, she shoved them in her pockets.

"I didn't—" She had almost said she didn't touch anything, but she couldn't lie to her father…again. "I didn't break anything. Everything in there is fine."

Clinton nodded toward the bank of elevators. "I'll check your work. Go put your cart away and wait for me downstairs."

"Dad, do you want me to—"

He pointed. "Go."

With a single word, her father reduced her to a trembling child again.

On the elevator ride down, Avery thought about the situation. Sure, she had made mistakes as a teenager. Who hadn't? Since her breakup with Kenan, she had done everything she could to get in her parents' good graces with one exception. She moved out and got her own apartment, despite her parents wanting her to stay while she pursued her degree.

Avery realized years ago that she needed to take some responsibility in her life. She no longer needed to feel shame for her past mistakes. She worked hard. She earned her own money and paid her own bills. She hadn't had a serious relationship in six years. She needed to be cut some slack.

She secured her cart in the storage closet on the lower level. Avery removed her coveralls and hung them on the crook of her arm to take home and wash. She tried making the garment smell like something other than bleach and ammonia.

Avery had her arguments ready in her head by the time she heard the elevator doors ding and she saw her father coming out of the darkened location. The sounds of the wheels going over the tile floors echoed off the walls until he got to Avery at the closet.

She took a deep breath before she prepared to tell her father to respect and understand her. Despite past mistakes, she could be trusted. Even though she had her eye on a more professional career, that didn't stop her other loves.

"Dad, I—"

Clinton cut her off. "You want to sing? You can do it in church. You are still going, aren't you?" He shoved the cart in the closet and locked the door before he closed it. "You move out and we don't see you there anymore." He placed his fists on his hips. "This life, the one you desire that involves music, will only break your heart. It's not a business that can guarantee you'll get to eat every day or have a roof over your head." He held her shoulders, which made her gasp. "Promise me that you won't think about pursuing a life in music." He shook his head. "I'm not saying you can't sing. We both know that God blessed you with a voice. This life is something you don't need."

Avery had so much to say. She hated feeling suppressed and raised on fear and regret.

"Promise me," Clinton said again.

She swallowed. Every argument she had running around in her head disappeared. "I promise."

So did her dreams.

Chapter 2

"Lazarus, are you listening to me?"

Never a good thing when Dad used his full first name. No one, not even his mother, still called him Lazarus. That got his attention. In order to keep his schedule, he would have to treat his father like he had taught him to treat the women he dated, think about something else while acting like he cared.

"Listening, Pop." Laz whipped off the towel he had around his waist and hung it over the shower rod.

Laz flew from one side of his small Brooklyn apartment to the other to pack items into a couple of suitcases. As much as he didn't want to ignore his father, Laz had too much to do in a short amount of time. Thankfully, he did this call on speakerphone instead of Facetime.

Laz's father snickered. "Doesn't sound like you're listening to me."

"Really? What do you think I'm doing?" Not that Laz cared.

Running around naked only made sense until he finished packing. Laz had a game plan, although it did seem like his dad had some sort of sixth sense to know when he had lost his job. He hadn't told his nosy sisters, who, even though they didn't live with either parent, still felt the childish need to run to them with all news, particularly about him.

"You're not answering me." Bradley Kyson would not be ignored.

So that Laz's frantic movements didn't translate through his voice, he stopped for a moment to address his father. "I did. I'm traveling. I'm packing up right now."

"You're leaving New York?" Bradley's voice reminded Laz of some excited kid. "Coming down to D.C.?"

Thankfully Bradley couldn't see Laz and watch his son roll his eyes. Laz knew exactly why his father wanted him to visit. It had nothing to do with wanting to see his only son.

"Yes, I'm leaving New York. No, I won't be stopping to come to your home." Laz had work to do if he wanted to keep his name relevant in the music industry. Kat and Zinner wouldn't derail him from his goals.

"You know you can stop here even if you just spend the night." Bradley chuckled, but it came out like a lecherous growl. The man stayed on the prowl.

"Yeah, yeah." He grabbed a few suits from his compact closet and piled them on his bed.

Bradley cleared his throat.

"Yes, sir." Laz ran his hand over his still damp hair. Even through his haste, he had to remember his manners, especially with his parents.

"Where are you going this time? You're traveling for work, right?" The lightness started to return to Bradley's tone.

Laz hated lying to anyone, especially to his dad. "I am traveling for work. I'm going to meet with a record company here in town, and then I'm going to hit some open mics down the east coast, looking for talent."

Bradley snorted. "You're *searching* for talent? Why do that when you have it in spades? You didn't give up playing piano, did you? I hope you didn't waste all those lessons."

Laz felt the same uncomfortable churning in his gut that he used to get afflicted with after each lesson when he knew his parents wanted a show.

"I still tickle the ivories now and then." Laz glanced at the small piano in the short hallway in front of his door. He managed to find it in halfway good condition at a flea market.

After some tuning and dragging it up two flights of stairs, he used the instrument to wind himself down each night. Luckily, he had neighbors who didn't mind his mini nightly concerts.

"And you still sing."

With that statement, Laz had to stop in his tracks when he suddenly felt lightheaded, as though a stadium full of people stood by to watch him play and sing in the buff. He took a deep breath and hoped his father didn't hear him attempting to catch his bearings and calm himself down.

"Only in the shower." Laz had to get off this topic. "It's not about me, Pop. I won't fill seats." No one wanted to see him floundering on stage or, worse yet, hiding behind a large piano. "Audiences want beautiful people with stellar voices. I have a keen eye and ear for both. I have a feeling, though, if I have to go past Virginia to find talent, I'll be in trouble."

The last address on file at Universe for Destiny Starr had the songstress situated in Virginia. With only a post office box address and no social media accounts, he would be hard pressed to find her.

"Or it could be a great thing. You can stop here and—"

"Pop."

"What?"

"If you're still talking about me visiting you, I'm not doing it. I'm not going to be your wingman." Laz distinctly remembered being a little kid when Bradley had trotted him out in malls and grocery stores to get women to come to him.

"Don't call yourself that. I'd like to think that we're just two single men on the prowl." Bradley laughed.

"Mom didn't think that way when you two were married." The hairs stood on the back of Laz's neck when he recalled his parents' knockdown fights.

"Watch yourself." The serious timbre returned to Bradley's voice. "What happened between me and your mother is our business."

"It would have been if you didn't use me as bait, and we didn't have to hear the fights. But you didn't call me to rehash our past." Now that Laz's temperature rose to lava level, his skin dried enough for him to get dressed. "Besides, how can I compete with getting hot women when I'm with the original hunk of burning love?"

The compliment seemed to work. Laz heard his father laughing through the phone like he agreed with his son's assessment. Easing the tension between him and Bradley relaxed Laz's shoulders.

He slipped on a pair of boxers before throwing on his best suit pants. Laz would have to look amazing for the meeting with Section Eight, a hip-hop label known for the hardest rappers and artists who had become famous on social media first before signing their first deals.

The thought of it turned his stomach. Laz wanted to represent talent, not just flash. Immediately, he recalled that mystery singer's angelic voice. God, he hoped she still performed, and he could find her.

"Can I help it if I'm still hot?" Bradley laughed louder. "And is it wrong for me to want to spend time with my only son?"

With his father's wandering eye and his overly eager need to please, Laz wouldn't be surprised if he had a half brother or more out there somewhere.

"I thought you were seeing someone seriously now." Laz slipped on a button-down shirt and hung a gray-and-blue striped tie around the collar. "Lisa or Lorna."

"*Laura* was a very nice woman. We only had a few dates before I thought it was best that we keep it casual."

Laz understood Bradley's code of wanting to see other people. At least he hoped this woman got the courtesy of a warning before his father cheated on her.

"What about you? Please tell me you're not still seeing that one woman."

Laz heard Bradley make a noise that sounded almost like he wanted to vomit. He hated giving the old man news that would make him happy.

Laz sighed before he spoke. "Erin and I only dated a few times. Nothing serious."

The lie sounded better than admitting that Erin had hated the number of hours he devoted to his career than quality time with her. Laz would also keep hidden that his last serious relationship with Erin had occurred over two years ago.

"Whew. Good. Good," Bradley said. "You're young."

"Twenty-seven is not young. There's so much I wanted to have done by now." Laz would leave out the fact that despite having a bit of his father's charisma and a need to meet and date every gorgeous woman out there, Laz desired a steady relationship, which to him meant marriage and having a family. Unfortunately, the two didn't go together.

Unlike Bradley, Laz saw family as the structure that made him stronger. He wanted to impart that feeling to a wife and children they would raise together. Having a successful career would only help solidify a strong home structure. Too bad Erin didn't see it that way.

"Trust me. You have time." Bradley had a longing in his voice, almost like he regretted the choices he had made. Maybe he didn't want to have children at all. "Enjoy life. Experience as much as you can. And by experience, I mean—"

"I get it."

He knew his father wanted Laz to have as much sex with as many women as possible. Those actions didn't exactly fit Laz's character. He liked getting to know a woman. If in the course of their interaction it led to something more intimate, so be it.

Instead of getting in an argument with Bradley about his decisions, he continued with their previous conversation.

"Let's get back to talking about you. Marissa lives by you and she's single. Why don't you two hang?" Laz hated throwing his baby sister under the bus. He needed a break.

"She's busy. At least that's what she tells me when I ask her out to breakfast or lunch." Bradley sniffed. "And Josie is busy with her family. Again, that's what she tells me. Flora is too far."

"You're working part-time now. Go visit them and your grandkids." Laz finished getting dressed.

"And have them calling me *grandpa*? That's okay."

Laz shook his head as he reviewed his look before leaving his apartment for—what he hoped—would only be a few days at the most. "Pop, I got to go. When I get a moment, I'll give you another call."

"Sure. Be good, kid." Bradley ended the call before Laz could get to his phone.

Laz would load up his rental car just in case he would have to make a road trip, which he hoped he wouldn't. Not that he wanted to work for Section Eight Records in particular. He just wanted an opportunity.

He caught a cab to Manhattan. It still surprised him that a record label that named itself after a welfare program would have their headquarters in one of the richest locations in New York.

Laz approached the building surrounded by glass and chrome. At least the outside looked professional. He straightened his tie and smoothed his hand down the front before he buttoned one button on his jacket.

As soon as he walked inside, he got hit with a setup that looked like an airport TSA area. A metal detector met him first with armed guards standing on the other side.

"Put all metal objects in the dish and walk through." The mountain of a man that spoke didn't even seem human.

The impossibly tall white man wore a long, black T-shirt and black jeans along with black combat boots. The hanging badge around his thick neck had been the only clue Laz had about the legitimacy of this whole setup.

He placed his keys, watch, and change into a dinged-up plastic bowl before he walked through the detector. Laz kept his stare on the big man's eyes through the trip. He had a feeling that if the alarm had gone off, the guard would have tackled him to the ground. Laz wanted to be on the offensive instead of the defensive.

Once through the guard gate, he approached the reception desk. A beautiful young woman with stick-straight, black hair kept her face still even as Laz approached. She didn't even break a smile or introduce herself or the business.

Laz saw her as a challenge. For all of Bradley's faults, he had blessed Laz with his gift of charm.

"I'm here to see Miss Farook, but I was drawn to this spot because of your stunning beauty." Laz kept his stare on her with his mouth agape. When the woman gave him a suspicious stare, he continued. He scanned the bustling lobby area. "I don't know how these men"—Laz brought his gaze back to her—"and women haven't stopped what they're doing to just look at you all day. I would." He completed his compliment with a wink.

He thought he saw a small twitch at the side of her mouth like she wanted to crack her stony exterior and give him the smile he worked hard to get.

Laz straightened out his tie. "I'm Laz Kyson." He even extended his hand.

He assumed that in her position, most people didn't give her the respect she deserved. As a receptionist, people probably viewed her as a nuisance, someone to get over to get to the top. Laz would treat her like an important part of this process, get people to like him from the ground up.

The woman did a slow blink that somehow annoyed Laz before she gazed down at a tablet. "Have a seat."

"Thank you." He started to turn but stopped. "Hold on." He reached forward and with the tip of his middle finger, he managed to collect a small eyelash stuck on her cheek. "Got it. Nothing should take away from your flawless face." With his finger in front of her face, he leaned forward and smiled. "Eyelash. Make a wish and blow it away."

The receptionist wrinkled her brows as she regarded him.

"And don't waste your wish on something like wishing someone would appreciate you." He pointed to himself. "That's already happened."

At that line, she finally snickered.

Got her!

She puckered her rich, red, thin lips and blew the black, slender lash from his finger.

Laz chuckled. "Good things will come your way." He bowed his head and started to head toward the seating area.

"Um, would you like something to drink?"

Laz kept his back to her after he stopped in his trek. He had to get himself together before he addressed her again.

He turned around. "Thank you, but I don't want to trouble you for anything. I'm sure serving me was not the wish you just made."

Even without direction, Laz sat down in a white leather chair in a waiting area. He made sure to face the reception area so he could watch Stone Face make and receive calls.

To occupy his time, he checked his emails and messages on his phone. He only looked up when he noticed someone standing in front of him.

Stone Face now carried a slight smile on her face and a frosty bottle of water in her hand.

As Laz reached for it, she spoke. "Don't be so sure about me not wanting to serve you as my wish." She winked at him after he took the bottle from her.

"Thank you. I appreciate this." Now he had to reel back the charm. He knew well enough about leading women on and making them feel something that he didn't.

Laz had gotten there ten minutes earlier than his appointment time. An hour later, he finally met with Sanaa Farook, the head of Section Eight Records.

A guard escorted him in the elevator and took him up to the top floor. After the guard swiped his badge, punched in a code on a keypad, and pressed his thumb against a blank screen by the pad, the doors opened.

The guard ushered Laz into the bright room. Laz didn't want to glance around too much, but to him, it looked like Sanaa's office encompassed the entire top floor.

The woman, the boss and owner of Section Eight, strolled across the floor. The dark-skinned, heavyset woman carried a round face framed by long, chocolate brown feathered hair.

He didn't know if the woman had a positive attitude or if her face naturally carried a smile as her resting expression. Due to her smooth skin without one wrinkle, she looked like a teenager, not the head of one of the most successful record labels out there.

"Thank you." She addressed her guard and gave him a simple nod to the elevator to dismiss him. Then she looked at Laz. "Have a seat."

Her gold jewelry glowed against her onyx-colored skin. In her expensive, custom-tailored designer dress, she didn't appear to embody her Section Eight company name. Not her size, not her beauty, and particularly not her clothing.

Before sitting down as she had instructed, Laz extended his hand to her and shook hers. Her skin revealed how Sanaa ran a successful business. Hard, calloused spots covered parts of her palm.

"I appreciate your time, Miss Farook." Laz didn't expect for her to apologize for keeping him waiting or to pussyfoot around in this meeting.

For her, time equaled money.

"I've heard your name before." Sanaa's fingers moved deftly over her tablet screen where she kept her attention.

"I used to work at Universe in A&R." Laz sat up tall. "I want to not only acquire new talent, I want to manage them."

"And you couldn't do this for Zinner?" Sanaa glanced up from her screen long enough to study his face.

"He and I didn't share my vision." He smoothed his hand down his tie.

"Can you tell me about any talent you have found in the past? I'm interested in understanding what you find appealing as far as music."

Sanaa dropped her attention back to her tablet and continued typing like she had to relay nuclear codes to the president.

"I scouted and helped sign Ariah." When he noticed Sanaa's lack of response, he expounded on this talented singer. "She's an indy artist who's big in the alternative scene."

Sanaa's only sign of acknowledgment came with a single head nod. Laz would take it.

"I also helped sign Marcus Grace, Orli Skye, and the Butterfly Twins." When he didn't see a rise out of Sanaa, he decided to mention the names of artists with more of a hip-hop angle. "I was also the one who found the Sankofa Boyz."

At the mention of that group's name, Sanaa peered up.

Laz knew he would snag her full attention with this bit of news. "Before Chantel Evans, I mean Chantel Woodley, decided to branch out on her own, I was the one who went to bat for her to retain her at Universe."

"But that didn't work." Sanaa reclined in her leather swivel chair. "Your taste in music is eclectic." She nodded. "I do like that, although my company focuses on hip-hop and rap. We're going to dabble in R&B and maybe some pop. If you could get me someone like Shauna Stellar who is young and hungry, then we would have something."

Laz had to bite his cheek to keep himself from wincing when Sanaa referred to Chantel Woodley by her old stage name of Shauna Stellar. He didn't need to insult the person who could be employing him.

"If I were able to secure talent like that, would I have a place here at Section Eight, and would my job here be as a manager?"

"You don't mince words, do you?" She smiled. "I like that. Get talent like that, you would not only have a place here, you could talk about other development deals here with the company."

He exhaled. "Sounds promising. I am about to travel to some open mic places to do some scouting."

Sanaa raised her eyebrows. "On your own?" She nodded. "Great initiative."

The compliments got Laz to sit up taller. He felt like Sanaa Farook would be making him an offer soon.

"How is your relationship with Kat?"

The mention of the starlet's name sent an uncomfortable tickle up the back of his neck. "She's a Universe artist. She makes the company a lot of money, and she's extremely popular."

No way would he be caught saying anything bad about her. It still gave him a bad taste in his mouth to have been terminated because she came on to him.

"That was a diplomatic answer." Sanaa snickered. "If I hire you, are you able to keep it in your pants long enough to do your job."

Laz gritted his teeth before he spoke. "Miss Farook, I don't know what you've heard, but—"

"What I heard is that Universe just let someone go who dipped his pen in the company ink. Then all the sudden you're coming to me looking for work. Maybe you're looking to cast your net into a bigger pool." She sniffed and shook her head. "I understand how the industry works. You are hot as hell."

Laz gave her a polite smile. "I get it from my father."

Sanaa smirked. "Don't get cute. I appreciate your passion; however, I have no interest in bringing in drama."

Laz dropped his charming act and leaned in closer to her so that she could see the passion in his eyes. "I would say to not believe everything you hear. My only interest is in the music, always has been and always will be."

Sanaa rolled her eyes, and the expression made him realize that he lost her, both her interest and, possibly, her respect.

She stood. Damn. Laz felt she would be dismissing him soon. He would wait to stand until Sanaa said it officially.

"I have great A&R and enough managers. But I don't want it to be said that I'm not open or flexible, even though I'm not." She came around her large glass desk. "Since you're doing work on your own, you're more than welcome to contact me if you find that next big artist that's going to blow me away and bump up Section Eight's status." She extended her hand to him. "Until then, good luck."

Fuck!

Laz smiled as he stood. "Thanks for the opportunity. Hopefully, I'll be back to show you some great artists for your company. I'm hoping to meet up with an artist who fits that bill."

"I'll believe it when I see it, or I guess I should say, hear it." She sat back down and brought her attention to her tablet.

He took the elevator to the lobby. When he exited the elevator, he noticed the stares from the sour receptionist and the security guards. Damn, bad news traveled fast. He didn't know if the looks came because he had been dismissed or because of the stories about him and Kat...or both.

So much for the word not getting out. He didn't know if Zinner said something or Kat or both. Either way, Laz knew he wouldn't be able to redeem himself until he found the right talent.

He had to show people his professionalism. For now, he would have to go home, change, and hit the road. Something good would have to come to him soon.

Chapter 3

"Miss Shields!"

The raised voice got Avery's attention before the snickering around her from her classmates registered. "Yes. I'm listening."

First lie of the day. Forget burning a candle at both ends. Avery's candle had been thrown into a fire pit and melted all to hell. Going straight from cleaning toilets to a statistics class paled in comparison to being able to take a hot bath and then a long nap, one with the air-conditioning on while remaining bundled up under a cozy comforter.

Enough daydreaming. Avery blinked and even started bouncing her knees under her desk to look alert when she caught her professor's glare.

"What did I say?" He placed his fist on his hip.

Knowing Professor Klein, some sort of test or quiz would be on her horizon. She took a stab at the answer since she had almost zonked out a couple of minutes ago.

"Quiz on Friday." If she said it with confidence, maybe she would come off as attentive.

Her instructor regarded her for a moment before saying, "I sincerely hope you're ready for it."

Avery exhaled, but quickly realized she would be tested on subject matter she had no clue about. She needed to pay attention if she planned on graduating on time. For her final semester, she had to make this good.

At the end of the class, Avery gathered her belongings and started to go.

"Miss Shields, may I see you for a moment?" Klein waved his hand in the air to summon her to him.

Damn.

Avery slung her bag on her shoulder before she approached her teacher. Luckily, this class ended her day. She didn't have to rush off to another class or lab. Sleep sounded good, but she couldn't do that until she did some hard studying and finished a paper for another class. She hoped after all this hard work, it would be worth it in the end.

"Yes, sir." She stood next to the desk.

"There's a nice coffee shop downstairs." The older man slowly loaded books and papers into a vintage-looking briefcase.

Avery blinked at his statement.

"And at the convenience store across the street, I understand they sell those energy drinks that are supposed to make your heart race."

She started to understand her professor's agenda with this conversation.

"And if you walk early enough in the morning time before the sun comes out, it might get some blood flowing so that you feel revitalized." He pumped his fist covered in green and purple thick veins in the air.

"I understand." She started to walk away.

"No. I don't think you do." Professor Klein adjusted his horned-rimmed glasses on his thin nose before he approached her. "You're one of my better students in here." He cleared his throat. "When you're awake."

"I'm sorry for nodding off. It's hard juggling a couple of jobs, bills, and school." Avery looked back at the students milling out of the room. To her, they all looked like babies. "I'm not like the rest of these students. I have responsibilities."

"So do I." He clasped his hand in front of his body. "I need to make sure all of my students are grasping the work. That's my job." He pointed to her. "Your job is to show up. I don't mean just physically." He pointed to his temple. "You have to be here in your head, too. You have to work hard to get what you want because no one else is going to give you anything." He placed his hand on her arm. "If you need help or if you want to talk, my office door is always open."

The offer didn't come off as perverted or weird. Professor Klein regarded Avery like she would be conquering the world one day. Too bad she didn't feel that way.

"Thanks for the talk. I'll be more alert for the next class. I promise." She headed to the door.

"Chapters twelve and thirteen."

Avery turned back to her teacher.

"Read those chapters in preparation for the quiz on Friday." He met up with her at the doorway. "By the way, good guess on the quiz. I guess I'm a little too predictable."

Avery smiled. Yes, very good thing.

"See you in a couple days." He strolled down the hallway.

Avery took the stairs down to the bottom floor and rushed across campus to the library. She would need to find a quiet corner to hide herself for a couple of hours before heading to her quiet, lonely apartment.

She scaled the stairs up to the library's third floor, her usual sanctuary. She burst through the door and headed to the reference section. Thanks to Google, no one used that part of the library anymore. Therefore, it remained serene.

She got to the corner desk area where she normally sequestered herself, and had to stop in her tracks when she heard voices. Not voices really. Sounds. Moaning.

Avery stopped at the end of a wall of bookshelves and peered around the corner. She spotted a young couple kissing and groping each other in the place where Avery wanted to hide herself and study. Who knew that she had been using a spot that must have looked like the sexiest area in the library?

She watched the young man snake his hand up the woman's T-shirt. Avery could only see motions as his hand moved around under the thin fabric, but that didn't take away from the salacious nature of this impromptu show.

The woman let out a small cry at one point. Avery imagined that the guy must have squeezed her nipple. She couldn't see his other hand. Maybe he had moved it down her body to her backside.

Damn. Had it been that long since she had been in a relationship? Not even a relationship. Sex. Avery missed being intimate with a man. Touching him. Teasing him. Tasting him.

She had to get out of there. Forget studying. As much as she didn't want to because the place reminded her of her own loneliness, Avery would go to her apartment and attempt to study there.

After a hefty trek across the college campus, she got to her car and took her time getting home. When she got to her apartment building, she sat in her car for a while in silence.

Her mother hadn't called her yet, but she knew that would be coming soon. Her father should be sleeping. He had worked hard last night alongside her. Her friends all had serious day jobs where they couldn't call her like they used to when they worked at low-level retail or fast-food jobs.

Avery went into her lonely apartment. At least she cleaned it. If her mother stopped by, which she did sporadically without warning, she wouldn't have to hear her mother comment on the messy condition.

Avery started to head to the couch in the living room and stopped. If she sat on that thing, with its brown, suede-like material and overstuffed cushions, she would be out like a light in no time. Right now, she needed to be alert.

She set her items on the breakfast bar in her kitchen and sat on the stool next to it. Avery opened her book to the right chapter, took out her notes that she had managed to scribble during class, fired up her laptop, and stopped. Her thoughts kept tripping over the couple in the library.

Reckless behavior like that could only lead to trouble. Avery had been there before. She rested her hand on her midsection for a moment before she slid her hand down her thigh.

Come on. Get it together. Concentrate.

Avery read the first line of chapter twelve in her statistics book, and then reread it again and again and again. Every time she blinked, images of that couple entered her mind. If she didn't do something to purge the thoughts from her head, it would drive her insane.

A typical woman might have gone to her trusty battery-operated boyfriend. Avery pulled out a notepad she always carried with her and removed the purple pen she kept attached to the spiral ring. She opened it to a blank page and wrote *Secret Wish* across the top.

It took her no time to write a song based on lovers stealing away time to find each other. The more she thought about the song, the more she saw herself as the woman, hiding in a darkened corner with a sexy man. They would kiss and touch. As soon as it got too much for her to take, she would...run away.

Avery slammed her pen down. She had to stop letting her past rule her present, particularly when it came to her art. Songwriting and singing gave her the freedom to be herself.

She took a breath and leaned her head back for a moment before redirecting her attention back to her song. She ended the lyrics the way it should end. The woman in the song realized she could be stronger without him, and she got with the next man. Nothing lasts forever.

* * * *

"Come on, girl. You can make it." Avery's sputtering Ford rolled into the parking lot of Uncle Pig's Diner.

The slight sunlight in the early morning casted a faint glow over the restaurant. She exhaled as soon as she parked her old car by the back door. At least Avery made it to work on time.

Avery started to go around to the front door when the back door opened and Jessie emerged with a cigarette in between his fingers. As the dishwasher, he had direct access to the back door.

"Thanks, buddy." Avery patted the short man on his shoulder as she bolted through the open door.

"You know I'm here for you." Jessie laughed.

Avery deposited her personal items in a locker in the employees' break room before she rushed to the kitchen. She found two other waitresses and the cook milling around.

"Did you bring your books?" Bruno peered up at Avery as he checked out the flat-top cook top and grill.

Avery did all she could to not roll her eyes. "Did you and my parents get together and decide how to torture me or does it come naturally?" She picked up an order pad and pencil as she regarded the older man.

"I'm doing what I can to make sure you don't end up working here the rest of your life." He pointed to her with a silver spatula.

"You say that like it's a bad thing." Mona winked before she draped her arm around Avery's shoulder. "He is right, you know."

This time Avery did groan. "Not you, too. This diner is the only place I don't have to think. I just want to work, collect my shitty tips, and go home."

"We can dig that." Graciela strolled over to the group of them. "We also know that you have dreams. That's more than the rest of us have." She leaned in closer and lowered her voice. "You would get better tips if you wore the right uniform."

By *uniform*, Graciela referred to Uncle Pig's request that the waitresses outfit themselves with what Avery called bootie shorts, shorts so short and tight that a yeast infection would definitely follow. Besides that, Pig also wanted them to wear tight T-shirts. At least Uncle Pig provided the shirts.

"Respectable tips for respectable outfits." Besides, if Avery's parents showed up to the diner, which they have done in the past, she knew the lecture afterward would be legendary.

"Hey, I don't know what you're talking about. I look like fucking Queen Elizabeth in this getup." Mona nudged Graciela with her elbow. "Besides, my plan is to marry Mr. Wonderful."

"Good luck finding a guy like that at this shitty little diner." Graciela shook her head. "Oh, wait. You did find your Prince Charming. Or should I say Prince Pig?"

She reached back and pulled her hair into a high ponytail. In her assigned outfit, she showed off her womanly curves. That didn't mean that Avery would be going down that route. She liked her jeans and normal-fitting Uncle Pig T-shirt with its tasteless slogan, "Eat like a pig."

"Hey, hey, hey. Don't bad mouth the place that pays you." Uncle Pig walked into the kitchen area. "We're just about to open. You all ready?"

Mona and Graciela stood up straight and saluted their boss. "Yes, sir," they said in unison.

"Smart-asses." He shook his head. "Specials today are the pancake breakfast with a choice of eggs, hash browns or grits, and meat. We're also doing a breakfast burrito."

"You mean with all the stuff you couldn't sell yesterday?" Mona giggled.

"Again, smart-ass." Pig pointed to Mona.

"Good thing you love this ass." She turned her backside around to him.

For as imposing as Uncle Pig looked with his massive height, large belly, and big, bushy beard that made him look like Santa Claus's wayward brother, whenever he looked at Mona, his longtime, live-in girlfriend, he looked like he melted. Too bad to everyone else, he acted true to his namesake.

Mona reminded Avery of an older sister. The African-American woman's skin tone matched Avery's, but she kept her hair natural, large and fluffy.

"It'll be a good day today." Pig faced Avery. "Are you here all day or do you have classes?" He damn near rolled his eyes when he asked her about her classes.

"You've got me all day." She leaned against the large stainless steel sink. "I'll even stay after we close at three to help clean up."

"Or you can let her go so she can study." Mona nudged her man.

"Or, even better, Avery can come with us tonight to Songbirds and blow us away." Graciela nibbled on her lower lip as she stared at Avery with expectation.

"Did I hear a Songbirds trip tonight? I'm in for some karaoke." Jessie leaned his head back to corral his long, thick black hair before he covered it with a black-and-white scarf and tied it in the back of his head.

Graciela sidled up next to him. "Are you going to sing this time?"

He placed his hand over his heart. "I would, but I don't think you're ready to handle the Filipino version of Justin Timberlake." Then he proceeded to warble a few lines from one of the singer's popular songs.

Despite being a few inches shorter than Graciela, Jessie had more bravado than most men Avery knew. That also meant that he didn't keep a steady relationship.

"I would love to do karaoke tonight." Avery didn't have to think about it.

"I hear a *but*." Bruno shifted his weight to one side.

"I have a quiz tomorrow." With Avery's professor's warning, she didn't want to mess up her chances of doing well.

"So no staying late and definitely no club tonight." Bruno wagged his finger at her.

"And if you were my father, I would agree with you." Avery winked at the surly cook.

"Hell, even if Bruno was your daddy, you still wouldn't listen." Graciela bumped her hip against Avery's. "I can come pick you up since your piece-of-shit ride is on its last leg."

"All of you will be on your last legs and out of here if you don't get to work." Pig pointed to Mona. "Open the front door." Then he pointed to Avery. "I want you working the back tables."

Avery huffed and shook her head. Those tables equated to low if any tips. "Can I get the bar for part of the day at least?"

"Sorry. Mona's spot. Senior waitress gets first preference." Pig snorted.

Mona shrugged. "Sorry, dear." She pointed to herself. "Ten years over your year."

Avery couldn't wait to graduate and, hopefully, get a better job. "Fine. I'll smile my ass off." She started with one big enough that it hurt her cheeks.

"Good girl." Pig capped the statement with a pat on her backside.

Yep, he definitely earned his nickname.

"I told you about doing that." Avery faced the big man.

"Come on, honey." Graciela pulled Avery out to the dining room area. "You know he doesn't mean it."

"That doesn't make it okay. I'm not a piece of meat." She turned to Mona. "Or his woman."

Mona unlocked the door before she sashayed over to Avery. "Don't get sensitive about it. He does it to everyone."

"Yeah? Does he do the butt pat to Bruno and Jessie, too?" Avery crossed her arms. "You need to keep your man in check."

Mona's full lips pressed together so hard that it formed a thin line. "Don't get cute unless you want to have even more time on your hands to study."

Avery cocked her head and glared at the woman in front of her wearing an outfit suitable to work around a stripper pole. "Are you threatening me?"

Customers started filing into the restaurant just as Mona answered.

"Absolutely." She moved in closer to Avery. "Trust me. He doesn't want you. Be flattered and move on."

Avery shook her head. No way could this woman think Uncle Pig's behavior constituted as something normal or acceptable. Avery needed to get out of this hellhole, and soon. Until she could do that, she would have to put up with her boss's mess.

Graciela sauntered by Avery.

Avery captured her arm and pulled her back. "Pick me up at seven."

Graciela's eyes widened. "Drinks and singing?"

Avery nodded. "A whole lot of singing. Just don't say anything to anyone else. I know Jessie wants to go, but I don't need to hear a lecture from Bruno. I need to do this for me."

She did just that as soon as she got off work, took a couple of bites of leftover Chinese takeout she had in a carton in her refrigerator, and studied for an hour. Avery stopped thinking about school as soon as Graciela arrived.

Avery needed to release some pent-up energy. Nothing did that more than singing her heart out with an emotional song.

"You really shouldn't get so worked up by Pig." Graciela pulled into Songbirds' parking lot. "You know he doesn't mean anything by it."

"I don't care what he means. I know what it feels like to me and what it looks like to others." Avery shook her head. "It's disrespectful. If I didn't need the money, I would be gone."

"Don't let Uncle Pig hear that. He'll cut you quick." Graciela swiped her hand over her throat to illustrate her point.

"I'm sure I can get another waitressing job." A new job that would work with her schedule, especially mid-semester, would be challenging.

If pressed, Avery would go. Her dignity meant more. If her parents caught wind of her boss's impropriety, she would never hear the end of it.

Avery and Graciela strolled through the door of the bar/restaurant and got hit with a bad rendition of "Proud Mary." God bless the man who warbled the tune and included Tina Turner's hip shaking and frantic dance moves, but he definitely butchered the song. Good thing these places existed for people to have fun, not start a career.

"Hey, ladies." One of the regular waiters strolled over to Avery and her coworker. "Thank God you're here." He nodded toward Avery. "The talent is low tonight."

"Come on. The guy has a smile on his face. Must mean he's having fun." Avery went over to a table positioned to the side of the small stage area.

"At least he's having fun." The young man stood by Avery's table until Graciela sat down. "You are performing tonight, right? Don't tease me."

"Of course she is." Graciela winked.

"Damn. What are you, my manager?" Avery picked up the laminated menu that remained at the table.

Going from diner food to dive food didn't suit her, but she needed something to settle her stomach.

"Yeah. And if you don't start dating pretty soon, I'll be your pimp, too." Graciela laughed before she ordered her drink.

As usual, Avery stuck with water. "Loaded nachos for me."

"You got it." The waiter nodded.

"You think it'll get here before I go up?" Avery didn't need to look through the establishment's song book.

She knew which song she wanted to do. After the day she had, the song rolled around in her head all day.

"Oh, you are going to close this place down if I have anything to do with it. We definitely need someone strong to end the night." He gave her a wink.

Before Avery could argue that she needed to get home at a decent time, the waiter left to fill their orders.

"I can't stay late." Avery shook her head. "I have to go to class in the morning, and I have a quiz."

She had studied, but she could use a bit more time to go over the material before the morning.

"You will be fine." Graciela patted Avery's hand. "You're young, and things work out for you."

If only that had been true. Life had been a struggle for Avery, and getting harder daily.

"Don't forget. I have to go to work tonight, too. Since it's with my dad, I can't be late." It would be bad enough if she went to work smelling like cigarette smoke.

No one smoked inside Songbirds, but as soon as she hit the door to leave, all the smokers would be there, puffing their stench in her direction. At least she got to sing.

Two hours into their evening, Avery finally got her chance.

"Okay, folks. We have our resident star. Taking the mic is Avery who is going to be tearing it up with her rendition of the Donna Summer and Barbra Streisand hit, 'Enough is Enough.' Let's give her a hand." The DJ started the applause going and the modest crowd in the restaurant joined him.

As soon as Avery got up to the microphone on its stand and stood under a slightly brighter overhead light, some of the clapping became more enthusiastic. Apparently, Avery must have had some fans there who knew her talent.

The original song started off softly, but Avery wouldn't go that route. She had something to say, something to get off her chest. She belted the tune and kept it high octane throughout the song until the very end.

She didn't mind grabbing her audience by the throat and holding them hostage throughout her performance. At the high note at the end, she held it out as long as she could. Avery felt the muscles in her neck tightening each second of her closing note until she finally closed her mouth.

She felt purged. She certainly had had enough of everything. Drama, judgments, expectations, loneliness. Like the song said, no more tears.

The rousing applause from the diners lifted Avery's spirit. She did a slight bow as she smiled and went back to her table.

"You killed, lady." Graciela hugged Avery before she sat down. Then she pointed to the microphone. "That's where you really belong. Definitely not in school, and for sure not slinging hash at Uncle Pig's."

Avery chuckled. "As soon as DJ Khaled or some other record executive walks through that door and offers me a contract, you're going to continue seeing me hauling books and slinging hash."

When she pointed to the door, she froze when she saw a man come through who she hadn't seen at Songbirds before. In his suit, he looked out of place. Peanut and sunflower seed shells littered the hardwood floor, and the dim lighting, meant to make shy singers feel more comfortable, also managed to hide a multitude of sins in the audience.

He had his dirty blond hair parted to the side, which made him look ultra straightlaced. From where she sat and the darkness of the place, she couldn't tell his eye color. In her mind, she imagined him being a typical blond-haired, blue-eyed stunner. With fine guys like that, Avery needed to keep her distance. That didn't mean she couldn't fantasize.

She glanced down at her watch and cursed. "I'm going to be late for work."

"It's your dad." Graciela shrugged. "He'll forgive you."

"Doubtful." She finished off her water and stood. "I'll settle the bill. You get the car."

"Fine. See you out front." Graciela sauntered through the restaurant.

Avery couldn't help but notice her friend's double take when she walked by the man she had been staring at as soon as he walked into the restaurant. She also noticed that the guy didn't look at Graciela, a striking beauty herself.

Gay or married or both.

Or maybe he didn't get down with folks outside of his race. Graciela embraced her Latina look and heritage, which made her stunning. Avery kept her look low key and simple. So why, when he connected his gaze to hers, did he stop and stare for longer than normal?

Avery returned the stare, and felt her insides becoming hot. She chalked the feeling up to the spicy nachos she had eaten earlier and not the fact that this stranger, with his full lips and disarming good looks, just rendered her motionless.

If she had any hope of keeping her job, she would have to stop fantasizing and get going. After paying their bill, she cut her way through the crowd.

"Great song," one diner said to her as she passed a table.

Avery smiled and nodded, but kept it moving.

"Great voice." An older man patted Avery's hand.

"Thank you." She nodded to him.

"When will you be back?" a diner asked.

Avery glanced at the handsome man, who now made his way to the bar area. "I don't know. Hopefully soon."

"I would pay to hear you sing. You're incredible."

Nice to hear, but it wouldn't pay Avery's bills. Getting to work and finishing her degree would get her the life she wanted.

"Buddy, you just missed the best singer here."

Avery overheard their waiter making the comment as soon as she hit the front door. She turned in time to see that her waiter had spoken to Mr. Hotness.

As soon as he started to bring his attention to her, she bolted from the door. She had gotten enough admiration from people in the audience who she had seen there before. Questions from a stranger held no interest to her, and it would delay her from getting to work on time.

It did feel good to be complimented and admired like that. If she could bottle that feeling, she would take it with her everywhere. For now, she had coveralls to wear and toilets to clean.

Chapter 4

Laz started to chalk this trip up as a bust. He had been in Virginia for a solid week, torturing himself every day by listening to Destiny Starr's demo. Who was this woman and where could she have gone?

No. The real question had to be why the hell had it taken Laz this long to find her? In this age of digital media and the era of YouTube stars, Laz found it rare to still get audio recordings on CDs. In the intern area of Universe, Laz had seen a discarded box filled with discs with all kinds of covers. Some had groups on them. Some had risqué photos of men and women. Others had kept it simple with a landscape scene or something artistic.

As soon as he had spotted the disc in the clear jewel case, he decided to give it a listen. If nothing else, it would either give him a good laugh or a way to pass the time.

He still remembered the feeling he got when he heard her belting out that first note. His body went stock still as though preparing it for goose bumps to shoot all over him. Then from the top of his head down to his toes, he went from warm to molten hot. The singer had a way with controlling her voice and manipulating notes like an artist making a simple but artistically stunning stroke of paint over a canvas.

As soon as he finished listening to the demo, he should have reached out to her. Bad timing. He had been put on assignment to deal with the Shauna Stellar situation, as Zinner put it. Then the massive cleanup afterward took the rest of his time. He wouldn't have been focused on Destiny. He hoped beyond hope that someone else hadn't made time for her since he had missed out on his opportunity.

Each open mic and coffee shop and dive bar he went to offered him no inspiration. Singers came off as cutesy girls suited for Instagram, not an arena. Then again, his mind wrapped around the idea of finding this perfect singer who had invaded his life like a ghost.

At his lowest point, he decided to try a karaoke bar. He didn't like going to those places because people tended to copy what the original artist did when they recorded their songs. He wanted to hear originality and new voices. He had no interest in hearing someone copying Michael Jackson or Beyoncé.

It did make him curious about the act he had missed last night that the waiter told him about when he had arrived to a place called Songbirds. The other patrons in the place concurred with the waiter's assessment. When a snippet of this singer's karaoke song played back through the place, Laz had to sit down.

She sounded incredible and very close to Destiny Starr. Soulful yet gritty. Commanding, but still approachable. Just like everything else in his life, when he asked to meet her, the waiter said she had just paid her bill and left. Too little, too late.

Damn.

Laz also wanted to kick himself for not approaching that beauty he had seen across the room when he had gotten to the place. She looked stunning under the overhead light near the stage. He liked the way her dark brown hair framed her thin face. He also couldn't help noticing her full, rounded breasts under her tight T-shirt and the way her waist dipped in right above her hips.

If he had time and the inclination, he would have gone up to her and introduced himself. His personality would only get him so far. What woman would want a man without a job? At least he had prospects and ambition, which both had brought him down to Virginia.

Laz had gone to bat for Chantel Woodley a couple of years ago. He hoped that she remembered him enough to offer him a job at Charisma Music, since it seemed like Section Eight would only give him a chance if he brought someone good to the table. No guarantees of that during this trip. He didn't have any other prospects left after that place.

Laz outfitted himself with one of his best suits. He made sure his hair looked perfect. On top of that, he had demo CDs in his briefcase. He would come to this impromptu meeting with all guns blazing. He would have to, considering he hadn't made an appointment with anyone there.

The Charisma building looked nothing like Section Eight's huge skyscraper. The simple three-story building sat on the oceanfront side of the Virginia Beach strip. Laz had only met Fatima Evans, the founder of Charisma Music, once in his career.

The bubbly African-American woman had left an impression on him. He could see her laid-back nature setting up shop at a serene oceanfront location. Laz found it hard to believe that a huge star like Chantel Woodley, and her equally popular country-singing husband, Truman, would continue running the business Fatima had left her from this location.

Laz walked into the front door and couldn't believe he didn't get greeted by security guards that looked like bouncers. The two he saw in the lobby reminded him of men who would work for the Secret Service.

He strolled up to the receptionist desk. This woman actually made eye contact with him and smiled.

"Good afternoon. How can I help you?" She coupled her inquiry by leaning forward.

"Hi. I hope you can help me. My name is Laz Kyson. I was hoping to get a meeting with Chantel or Truman." He smiled as he stared at her.

The young woman glanced down at her computer screen first. "I'm sorry. I don't see an appointment for them for this afternoon."

"Probably not." He chuckled to lighten the mood. "I'm the one who called yesterday about meeting them for a potential job. I've worked A&R at Universe."

He wanted to bite his tongue as soon as he mentioned Chantel's former record label. The word must have gone out to all of her people about the place. As soon as he mentioned it, the receptionist leaned back in her chair and crossed her arms over her chest. She wouldn't be helping him today or any day.

"I no longer work there." Maybe mentioning that will melt away her frosty attitude. "I was hoping I could use my talents for Charisma. It would be great to discuss it with Chantel."

"Mrs. Woodley does not entertain unsolicited offers." The woman with a purple pixie cut hairdo and big green eyes shook her head as she leaned forward. "Please check our website for any open positions."

Laz looked around the nearly empty lobby area with the exception of two guards. "The type of position I'm looking for isn't usually posted. I want to go beyond A&R. I want to secure talent for this label and manage them. I'm looking for someone with your beauty and an incredible voice." He leaned forward and lowered his tone. "You wouldn't happen to be a singer, too, would you?"

The chubby woman with a pixie cut giggled while shaking her head. "No. Of course not."

Laz snapped his fingers in the air. "Just my luck. I can't seem to catch a break."

"Charisma isn't hiring managers. If you have a business card, I would be happy to pass it along to Mr. and Mrs. Woodley. If not, I can get your information." She pulled out a pad and pen like she knew he wouldn't have his contact information readily available. "You can give me your number, um, if you want to give it to me. Your number, I mean. Give that to me and nothing else."

Laz spotted her talking under her breath to herself.

"Stop talking. You sound crazy." Then she smiled, baring all of her small, white teeth.

"I would love to give you anything and everything you want." He smiled harder. "What I really need, though, is that meeting. I would like to wait if that's okay." Laz looked to the side and spotted a black-and-white striped couch along with a couple of chairs in a waiting area.

"You would be wasting your time." She shook her head. "I don't think they're coming in for the rest of the day. But I don't know that for sure. They sometimes pop in."

"Then let's hope today is one of those days. Besides, I'll get to sit here and stare at you the whole time." Laz continued to smile so that he didn't show this young woman his frustration. "I know that with the recent birth of their twins, both Chantel and Truman have been staying close to home." He adjusted his cuffs underneath his jacket. "I also know that both are still conducting business. Chantel just signed a new country singer a month ago, and Truman has been tapped to be a judge on a singing competition show that will film here in Virginia. Sounds like they're working pretty hard to me."

"I never said—"

Laz continued speaking. "Hard-working people like them will normally check in. When they do, I'll be here waiting." He reached into his pocket and pulled out a new business card that he had created after he left Universe. He placed it on the receptionist's desk and slid it to her. "Here's my contact information. It would be great if you could reach out to Chantel Woodley. She and I have history."

He had gone to bat for the talented singer when she got out of Peaceful Acres. He would leave out the fact that he also saw her the time she fainted off the stage on the day of her mother Fatima's funeral.

"If you're that close to Mrs. Woodley, why don't you—" The sassy woman stopped her query, and then firmed up a smile on her face.

Laz cocked his head while giving her a smile that Bradley Kyson would endorse. "I like an inquisitive woman with impeccable manners like yourself. Makes doing business a pleasure."

The receptionist did smile, and even looked like she took a much-needed deep breath before she continued talking. "Thank you for your information. I wish I could do more for you. Again, it won't help you to wait here."

"It also won't hurt unless you look away from me." He winked at her and sauntered to the couch where he sat right in the middle.

This receptionist didn't understand Laz's dilemma. He had no options. No job. No backup plan. He needed this to work. He needed a break.

An hour-long wait turned to two, then three, and before Laz knew it, the receptionist, who had gone to lunch and received packages from couriers throughout the day, now packed up her belongings. She would be kicking him out soon. Damn if she thought he would give up so easily.

It looked like she started to address him when another delivery man came through the front door. At that moment, Laz went to the men's room. He could wait it out in there, or at least stay there until he came up with a game plan.

The standard bathroom facility had an "L" shape, which he took advantage of while he thought about his next steps. He walked over to the other side away from the door and paced.

"Come on, man. Think." He muttered to himself without caring if anyone else had been in the place. "Being Mr. Nice Guy will only get you so far."

No one stood in front of the urinals, and although he didn't look under each and every stall door, he didn't notice any closed doors.

"If I stay here until they close, it's not like Chantel or Truman will show up." His pacing slowed the more he talked to himself. "I can't give up."

He leaned against the wall covered in white tile. He closed his eyes and thought about his choices. A fleeting thought crossed his mind that he shouldn't have quit his job at Universe. A glorified babysitter had to be better than being broke.

Laz shook his head. No way could he do that and be able to look at himself in the mirror.

He heard the main bathroom door open. His heart pounded as he slipped in the last stall and eased the door closed.

"I'll check in here," Laz heard a voice say from the door.

Apparently, the guards had the task of sweeping the office at the end of the day. Laz braced to be caught when he heard the opening of a popular rap song coming through a cell phone.

"Hey, babe." The gruff voice softened a bit. "Yeah, I'm on my way home now."

Laz heard the door opening again before silence filled the spacious bathroom. He exhaled but didn't bother leaving the sanctuary of the stall just yet. If nothing else, maybe he could leave a handwritten note for Chantel and Truman.

A note? No, he had to do more than that. He had to find talent. He wouldn't be able to do that from the bathroom, even one at Charisma Music.

Still in the bathroom stall, Laz pressed his back against the tile wall again and leaned his head back. "Come on. You've been in tighter spots than this before. You can turn this around."

Laz's phone buzzed in his pocket. He retrieved it and started to ignore the call when he noticed his sister's name across the screen.

"Hey, Stinky." Laz smirked.

"You know I hate it when you call me that."

He could almost see his baby sister with her septum piercing and lip ring sneering. "Why do you think I do it?" He kept his voice low while he spoke to Marissa.

"Okay. Either you're in a meeting or you're with a bad date and trying to get out of it." Marissa chuckled. "Why are you whispering?"

"It's a little of both of what you said. I'm somewhere where I'm trying to get a meeting, but it's turning out like a bad date." Laz had to face facts. He would need to leave soon and try to get through to Chantel the proper way.

"Speaking of bad dates, hold on."

"Wait. You're not on one right now, are you?"

"It's cool. It's a first date. We just met and she's really ditzy." Marissa laughed. "I wouldn't be surprised if she had one of those fidget things spinning around on her finger when I get back out there."

"Only the best and the brightest for you, right?" Laz chuckled, but tried keeping his voice down.

"Of course. Now, back on you. Did I hear that you're coming down the east coast?"

Laz never suspected that Marissa would have talked to their father. "For work."

"Coming to D.C.? I would love to see you. Plus you're chick bait." This time Marissa laughed.

"You are definitely Dad's kid." He shook his head.

"Ooh, low blow."

"Truth hurts." He loosened his necktie. No use looking neat and presentable when he had no one to appreciate it. "I'm actually in Virginia."

"Northern Virginia?"

Laz hesitated before he answered. "Virginia Beach." Before she could complain, because he had already heard her huffing, Laz explained himself just like he had to with their father. "I'm looking for a singer or group or, hell, both."

"Have you tried looking in a mirror?" Marissa asked.

"Now you really sound like Dad." Laz rubbed his hand across the back of his neck.

"And now I think I really hate you."

Before Laz could make a witty response, she placed him on hold. One thing he and his sister had in common had to be their love of music. While she had him on hold, a cool jazzy song played through his earpiece. He could listen to this for a while.

When it seemed like he had heard the full song and another one, he realized that his sister might have forgotten about him.

"Look at who needs the fidget spinner." He snickered and disconnected the call, at least, he thought he did.

Laz continued hearing music and singing. He looked at his phone's screen to make sure he had properly disconnected the call. When he found it blank, he pressed the phone against his ear again.

When he heard an echo, he realized that the beautiful music came from inside the bathroom, but it didn't sound like it had been pumped through a sound system. No, someone with an amazing voice sang, and damn if it didn't sound like Destiny Starr.

He stepped closer to the corner to get a better listen. The person, who he hoped had been female, sang an old-school Gladys Knight song like she had written it herself. He crept closer to the sound but made sure to keep his identity hidden.

As he listened to how she caressed and massaged each lyric, each note, Laz got swept away. The singer managed to make each note an actual being with limbs, eyes, a soul. He felt surrounded, but he enjoyed the sensation. He liked being captured this way.

The magnetism he felt from listening to Destiny Starr sing came through like a lover in person. At one point, he even closed his eyes and leaned his head back to take in the melodic sounds.

Talent like this, a voice like hers, needed to be heard by more than just him in a men's room. Wait. What would a woman be doing in the men's bathroom?

When that thought hit him, Laz needed to find out the reason. Even if the voice belonged to a man, it still sounded wonderful.

As he rounded the corner, he got face-to-face with a woman. Even in her gray, oversized coveralls, she looked amazing...and familiar. Her almond-shaped brown eyes sucked him in, and her plump bottom lip had him imagining things he shouldn't have with a stranger.

It hit him right away why she seemed familiar. He stared into those same eyes last night when he went into that karaoke dive bar. Laz spotted this beauty across the room. As soon as their gazes connected, he couldn't stop staring. He had that same feeling now.

After a beat, she screamed, which snapped him out of his fantasy.

Laz held up his hand to calm her down. He didn't need someone else claiming he did something inappropriate. "Easy. I was just using the bathroom."

"The guards said no one was in here." She clutched the handle of the mop she carried in both hands like she would use it as a weapon if needed.

"I didn't mean to scare you." He took a step forward, which made her take three steps back. "Was that you singing just a second ago?"

She dropped her gaze to the floor and shook her head. "Nope. I was playing music on my phone." She pulled a phone from her pocket to show him. "Sorry for the noise."

"I don't believe that. There were changes to the song that really showed some great artistry. That definitely wasn't a song recording. That was you." He pointed to her. "Are you Destiny Starr?"

When he asked the question, her eyes widened and she made a hasty retreat. "I'll come back here later."

No way could Laz let this woman go. "Wait." He went after her, but made sure not to touch her. "You are her, right? You sent a demo to Universe."

"I don't know what you're talking—"

Laz managed to block her from leaving. "I heard it. I've been listening to it every day since I was able to get my hands on it. You have an incredible voice."

"Please step aside." She wrung her hands around the handle.

Laz placed his hand to his chest. "My name is Laz. Laz Kyson." He extended his hand to her. When she didn't move but kept her stare on his eyes, he lowered it and continued. "I'm in the music business, and I'm looking for artists to represent. I would love to talk to you about representing you and where you see yourself in the music industry." He patted his pocket. "I have a business card."

The woman laughed. "I've heard that line before. Usually, though, the guy wants to take me back to his place to *talk*." She shook her head. "No thank you. Now if you'll move out of—"

"I'm not like those guys. I'm only interested in representing artists who—"

"I'm at work." She held her hand up. "I clean toilets and scrub floors."

Laz peered down to the floor but stopped when he noticed an open textbook on the counter. Between the multiple lines of text, he noticed the graphs and mathematical equations. He hadn't been so far removed from his college experience to forget about this course.

"And you're in college." He plucked his finger against the pages. "Statistics, right?"

She said nothing.

"I did really well in that class." He nodded. "If you want, I can—"

"I don't need to—"

This time he stopped her. "Dream? You don't think you deserve to dream?"

That same bottom lip he admired before now trembled like she wanted to say something, maybe agree with him.

"What's your name?" He wanted to know so much about this mysterious woman. "Please tell me it's not really Destiny Starr."

What did she look like under that bulky garment?

Damn, he couldn't think about things like that. For one, it would show on his face. He didn't want this woman thinking he wanted her for something lascivious. Laz had to show her he could be a professional, even in the middle of the men's room.

"Avery, are you done in there already?" The men's bathroom door swung open and an older African-American man stepped inside.

He did a stutter step when he spotted Laz with the woman he now knew to be Avery. Good name. Better than Destiny.

The man glared at Laz before looking at Avery and standing in front of her like a protective bulldog. "Who are you?"

"I was in a stall down there when I heard the most beautiful—"

"I forgot to make sure no one was in here first before I started." Avery took the man's hand and dragged him to the door. "We'll get out of your way."

"And I'll take care of cleaning this room." The older gentleman shrugged out of Avery's grasp and kept his glare on Laz before turning to Avery. "You can go down to the offices on the other end of the floor. I'll get up with you later."

"Yes, sir." Avery didn't even look at Laz as she started to leave the bathroom.

"Wait." Laz closed her hefty book and picked it up. "You forgot this." He held it up to her, but the man standing in between the two of them snatched it from Laz's hand.

Instead of handing Avery the book, he clasped it close to his barrel-size chest. "I'll make sure she gets this."

Avery scurried out of the bathroom.

The man, who had stood protectively in front of her, continued studying Laz even as he backed out of the room. "I'll stand outside and wait until you leave before I come back in here."

This other janitor made it obvious that he wouldn't be leaving Laz alone with Avery. Laz released a long sigh. He had finally encountered a beautiful, magical voice, but he couldn't get near the woman to ask her anything, and she seemed too scared to even acknowledge her magnificent gift.

"Don't bother. I'm just finishing up." Laz washed his hands, but kept his stare on the gentleman behind him.

After Laz dried his hands, he walked out of the bathroom and headed toward the front doors. He didn't even know the janitor had followed him until he turned around to see if he could spot the young woman again.

"You have a good evening." The man pulled the door closed and made sure it had been locked in every way possible.

Then he turned and went back to work.

"Damn." Laz could wait in his rental car all night until the woman came out to go home.

His luck, the other janitor would be there with her. He would keep her away from him. Plus he didn't want to come off as creepy or worse, a stalker. Searching for talent had been his primary focus.

Sleep. He needed rest to recharge his mind. He would go back to the hotel and get something to eat. Then he would start fresh again in the morning. This woman could be his ticket to getting back in the music business. If Chantel wouldn't take a meeting with him, Laz could always take her to Section Eight.

Now he had to meet Miss Avery and figure out how to get her alone… for work, of course.

Chapter 5

Avery didn't need to wait very long before the lecture came. At least Clinton hadn't heard the stranger call her by another name, one she hadn't used in a couple years. Here she thought no one at Universe had even listened to her demo. This guy admitted to mainlining her songs for a while. The idea of him loving her music shot a tingling sensation through her body.

"You have to be careful, especially around here." Clinton spoke to Avery while she dumped someone else's garbage.

"I know." She put a new, clear bag in the trash receptacle and placed it under the desk. "I asked the guard before I went inside."

"You always call from the door. Sometimes guards get lazy. You don't need to be that way." He wagged his finger at her.

Avery didn't need to vacuum the carpet, but she welcomed the noise to get her father to stop talking to her like a child. "It was all a big misunderstanding."

"Did he also misunderstand that you would want to be a singer?" Clinton planted his meaty fist on his hip.

Avery had hoped her father hadn't heard Laz asking about her singing voice. Seeing the man in the first place surprised her. When she realized that he had been the same man from Songbirds, her heart had pounded hard enough that it had shook her body.

He looked even better up close. Just as she imagined, as she had fantasized, he had sparkling blue eyes. His sleek nose pointed down to a full set of extremely kissable lips. When he picked up her textbook to hand it to her, Avery couldn't help but notice his large hand. To top it all off, he had stubble across his face that made him look even sexier, and he wore the hell out of a suit. In a fleeting moment, right when she first spotted him in the bathroom, she wondered what he looked like under his clothes.

Avery also pondered the idea that he could be serious about being in the music industry. Back when she actively tried to get into the music business, most of the men she had encountered seemed interested in her until discussions turned to business. As long as they could ogle her and try to put their hands on her, they seemed interested.

The man tonight, Laz Kyson, he hadn't touched her. He seemed to go out of his way not to put a finger on her although it did frighten her when he blocked her path to leave the bathroom. Had her father not come into the bathroom when he did, Avery would have either told Laz her name and her dreams, or kicked him squarely between his legs to escape.

"Avery, I'm talking to you. Did he ask you about—"

To avoid the discussion right now, Avery started the vacuum and slowly cleaned the office floor. If she couldn't admit to a stranger what she really wanted in life, how could she tell her father?

"You think you're cute." Clinton spoke loud enough for that to be heard over the vacuum cleaner's whirring sounds.

Avery tapped her ear. "Can't hear you!"

Clinton shook his head and moved on to another task. Good. She needed the break. Morning couldn't come fast enough.

At the end of their shift, Avery stretched her arms over her head. She so wanted to go to her apartment and take a nap. Too bad she had another job to go to right after she put all the cleaning supplies away. With classes every Monday, Wednesday, and Friday, working overnight during the weekdays cleaning office buildings with her father, and work at Uncle Pig's almost every day, it left little time for Avery to rest or even think sometimes. The busy schedule also kept her out of trouble. Left to her own devices, she could get into some things that would make her parents sigh heavily.

"I hope you don't think we're done with our conversation." Clinton pushed his cart into the closet on the first floor, then did the same with Avery's.

"Conversation? Doesn't that involve two or more people *talking*?" Without sleep, Avery could be very snarky.

"Fine. Just listen. I don't want you coming here to clean with me anymore." He shook his head. "It's too dangerous."

Avery crossed her arms over her chest. "It isn't. Nothing happened. I walked into the bathroom. I didn't hear him in there. He apologized for scaring me, and you came in on the rest." She would leave out his proposition and the fact that her heart had pounded so hard she thought it would come crashing through her rib cage.

"I'm not talking about him. I know you can handle yourself." Clinton put his hand on Avery's shoulder. "I'm talking about getting your hopes up that you can be a part of all this. You can't. You know that, right?"

Avery tried smiling for her father to give him some assurance that his warnings had gotten through to her. Like Laz had said, she wanted to dream about the possibilities, both as a singer and as someone who could be on that man's arm.

"Dad, I'm fine." She patted his hand. "I'm down to my last few weeks of school before I graduate. I'm paying my bills on time. I'm not on drugs. And on a good day, I remember to floss my teeth."

Clinton chuckled.

At least she had gotten her father to loosen up a bit. "I didn't pay attention to anything that man said, and you shouldn't either."

She unzipped her coveralls and stepped out of them. Her clothing underneath didn't smell like chemicals. Avery would be fine going straight to the diner. She could do her four-hour shift and then zonk out at home.

"And I'm not going to let you do this building alone. For one, it's not safe for *you*." Avery pointed to her father. "And second, I need the money."

"I'll still pay you."

Avery shook her head. "You'll pay me when I earn it. I don't want money for work I'm not doing." She held her father's hand. "Trust me when I say that I'll be fine." She glanced at her watch. "I have to go to the diner."

"You work too hard. You should slow down." Clinton walked with Avery to the back door.

"Work hard, play hard, right?" She smiled.

"No playing until you have that degree and better-paying job." He kissed her cheek. "Coming over for dinner tonight before we have to work?"

Avery did miss seeing her mother, and she longed for a great home-cooked meal. She had to remember her studies and other obligations. She barely squeaked by on that pop quiz.

"Probably not. Maybe Sunday night." She threw her coveralls in the backseat of her car before she pulled off and headed to job number two.

By the time she arrived at Uncle Pig's Diner, the place had already opened and customers filled the dining room. That meant Pig would be squealing mad that she arrived a hair late.

Avery darted through the front door to the back area where she locked up her purse and grabbed her apron.

"You're late." Pig stood in the doorway leading to the dining room.

"No I'm not. I'm really early for my next shift." Levity would have to help her in this situation.

Avery approached him so that she could get to work. "I'm sorry, but I am here." She wanted to couple that statement with the fact that she could barely stand and needed ten years of sleep.

Pig took a step to the side, which, for a normal-sized man, would have allowed her to get by without any problems. With him, she still had to brush against his protruding belly.

"Hurry up. We're drowning," Mona said to Avery when she passed her. Avery grabbed her pad and pen before going out to the dining room area. Graciela snagged Avery first. "You get the back area."

Avery rolled her eyes. "Not again." She shifted back and forth in her spot and almost felt like a moody child. "I don't mind taking that if I can also get the bar."

"No can do." Mona shook her head. "That's my spot."

"Hey, this is what happens when you roll in late." Graciela shrugged. "You lose the best tables, although..." She looked secretive as she leaned in close to Avery. "You have a special surprise in your area. It almost made me change my mind about giving it up to you."

"What? Lottery winner sitting in that section or something?" Avery laughed.

"Oh, this guy definitely won the good-looks lottery." Graciela fanned her face. "I don't know if you noticed this hot guy at Songbirds that night we were there. He's here." She nodded over to the section that Avery would be serving.

Avery gasped as soon as she saw Laz Kyson sitting at a small two-seater table near the back corner of the restaurant. He kept his head down like the weight of the world hung on his shoulders. Even distressed, he looked good.

"I tried hard to get him to sit in my section, but he said he needed coffee and quiet." Graciela sighed. "At least *you* can look at him."

Avery kept her stare on him. No way could she run from him now.

* * * *

Laz couldn't believe his dumb luck. He had driven from New York down to Virginia, making sure to hit as many clubs and bars that he could to find some talent. Who knew he would find the one person he wanted to get in the men's room at Charisma Music. Then he messed it up. He came on too strong with Avery.

Avery. What a sexy beast, even in her janitorial attire and without a stitch of makeup. He could only imagine what she would look like if given over to a stylist team. Hair, makeup, wardrobe. She would go from sexy to stunning.

Her looks didn't top the thing that made her incredible. Laz could still hear her melodic voice in his head. The first time in a long time, he thought about the possibilities with her, beyond work. Would she date him?

Laz shook his head. He didn't do this trip to find someone. He had a job to do, and a job to capture.

"Welcome to Uncle Pig's."

Laz heard the woman's voice but continued keeping his head down.

"The specials today are strawberry pancakes combo, and a chorizo-and-egg burrito meal."

He didn't respond. Neither sounded good to him, but he had lost his appetite the day Kat accused him of sexually assaulting her. Losing Destiny Starr really wrenched his desire for food. He couldn't stomach much more.

He only decided to come to this nearby diner to keep from holing himself up in his hotel room. Maybe he should go visit his father and sister on his way back home. He hated retreating, especially before meeting with Chantel and Truman, but he would have to this time.

"Something to drink? Coffee? Tea?"

This one wouldn't let up.

"Coffee. Black." He rubbed his forehead.

"Coming right up. I'll give you time to look over the menu."

She left before Laz could tell her that he didn't need anything to eat. After downing what he suspected would be substandard coffee, probably lukewarm to boot, he would head back to Charisma.

Part of him still wanted to meet with Chantel and Truman. If he could get to that powerful duo, he could show them his passion. Another part of himself longed to see Avery again. Who knew a janitor would get him thinking about romance?

Laz heard the mug hit the table before the soothing coffee aroma wafted up to his nose. He finally sat up to acknowledge the patient waitress.

"Thank you for..." He stopped when he saw who had been serving him. "Avery?"

She blinked. "You remembered my name, or..." She peered down at the plastic nametag in the shape of a pig bending over that she had pinned to her apron.

Laz shook his head. "No. I remember you." He looked around the place. "I swear to you. I didn't know you worked here. I'm not stalking you." He held his hand up to her like a shield or barrier.

He didn't need this woman accusing him of wrongdoing.

She nodded. "I know. I guessed." A small smile tugged at the corner of her mouth. "This is the first time you've looked up since I've been in here today. Rough night?"

"Probably easier than yours." He lied to her. Laz had spent the night alone in his hotel room thinking about the voice that had him spellbound and the woman who had him mesmerized. "I got to get some sleep." She didn't need to know he only managed to get an hour of sleep at the most. "Did you work all night and come straight here?"

"Yeah." She shrugged. She peered off to the side, and then quickly brought her attention back to Laz.

Laz looked in the same direction she had. He spotted a big, burly man who looked like a bouncer the way he sneered at Avery.

"You still look as beautiful now as you did last night." He topped his sincere compliment with a wink.

Avery studied him for a while. "Does that normally work?" She waved her pencil at him.

"What?"

"The fake come-on line."

Laz blinked. "You don't think I meant it?"

She snickered. "Last night I was in old coveralls. Today I'm wearing the outfit that the coveralls hid and no makeup."

He smiled. "And yet, I can't stop staring at you."

That confession got her to stare at him for a long time while her cheeks filled with a soft rose color. She had a fresh, easy beauty about her. Soft curls surrounded her face with delicate features and the most expressive eyes he had ever seen.

"Did you mean all that stuff you said last night about being in the music industry?" Avery stepped closer to him.

Laz's heart started pounding the closer she got to him. "Yes. I'm looking for the next big thing in music. I think—no, I know— you are that person if that was you singing in the bathroom. Was it? And are you Destiny Starr?"

Avery waited a beat before she finally answered. "Yeah, but everyone sounds great in a bathroom." She chuckled. "It's the acoustics."

Laz shook his head. "No, they don't. Trust me." He turned his full body to her. "What about my other question?"

She shrugged. "What about it?"

"Are you Destiny Starr?"

Avery chewed on her lower lip before glancing to the left and right. "I hadn't heard that name in a couple years." She glared at him. "You're a little late, aren't you?"

Story of Laz's life. "I got caught up in a lot of different things. I found your disc in a box with other discs. Even without a flashy cover, I chose yours to listen to. Believe me. I listened." He tapped his ear. "You have a gift. Have you ever thought about singing as a career, not just a way to pass the time?"

Avery smiled. As she opened her mouth to speak, the wannabe bodyguard waddled over to her. "Lots of other tables in here. Get his order and let's go."

Oh, so Avery's boss. He definitely fit the name of Uncle Pig. Before leaving her, he gave her a hard smack on her backside. It sounded like a wooden paddle slapping a slab of raw meat.

Laz thought maybe Avery and this guy must have been an item, until he noticed the disgusted look on her face.

Before he could stop himself, Laz bolted to his feet and grabbed the large man's shoulder to turn him around. "You owe her an apology."

"What?" The big man scrunched up his face, making his nostrils look like a pig snout.

"You touched her inappropriately."

"I touched her what?" He sniffed and it sounded like a snort.

Laz got in the cretin's face and gritted his teeth. "You smacked her ass. Apologize or—"

The piggy idiot stepped up closer to Laz. "Or what?"

Faster than Laz could stop himself, he spun the asshole around, grabbed one of his arms, and turned it up behind his back as he pressed him against the wall. It amazed him how fast his wrestling training from high school and college came back to him. He kept his feet planted in a wide stance to give him more leverage.

"I was going to give you the easy-way-or-hard-way speech, but you gave me no choice." Laz wrenched the guy's meaty arm up higher, making the pig dance on his tiptoes.

"Are you insane? Let me go!" Pig man whipped his head back and forth to try and get a good look at Laz.

Just like a pig, he couldn't twist his head far enough or lift it up high enough to see Laz's face. Because of the layer of sweat covering him, Laz wouldn't be able to hold on to him much longer.

Laz felt a hand on his arm. He turned to see Avery, looking concerned.

"Let Uncle Pig go. It's okay." She tugged on Laz's arm.

Laz shook his head. "I don't really know you, but even I could tell you didn't like him putting his hand on you." For good measure, he pulled up Uncle Pig's arm, making him cry out.

"Shit. I'm sorry. I'm sorry. Okay?"

Laz let his arm go and took a couple of steps back, keeping his stare on him in case he tried anything. In that moment, he realized that the inside of the place had gone deathly silent. He heard the sizzle coming from the grill in the open kitchen and smelled bacon on the verge of burning in the air.

He didn't dare turn around to look at the diners' reactions, but he could feel their stares on the back of his head.

Uncle Pig waved his arm around as he rubbed his shoulder. "You're crazy. I ought to call the police on you."

Laz nodded. "You do that. I'll tell them that you touched your employee in a manner that made her feel uncomfortable, and then threatened a paying customer."

Too bad he didn't have his cell phone out to record this moment.

"*Former* employee." Uncle Pig glared at Avery. "Get your shit and get out of here." He pointed to the door, but winced when he raised his arm in the air. Then he glared at Laz. "And I have a sign on the door that says I reserve the right to refuse service to anyone. You can carry your ass out of here, too."

Laz snickered. "Yeah, like I would stay."

"Wait. I don't know this guy. I didn't tell him to do that to you." Avery tried making her appeal.

The way Uncle Pig walked by her, he made it obvious he didn't want to hear anything she had to say. "I'll mail your final paycheck. Get the hell out of here. Now."

Avery stared at her now former boss as he sauntered away before she turned back to Laz. She growled at him as she removed her apron and threw it in his face.

After disappearing through a set of double doors, the waitress who had seated him when he came in the diner approached him. "She's getting her stuff, and I'm pretty sure she'll leave out the back door." She smiled a little. "Her car is crappy so I don't think she'll go very far very fast."

Laz went through the front door and headed around the back of the diner. Just as the waitress had predicted, Avery stormed over to an older model Ford. Once at the car, she kicked the tire before unlocking the door and going inside.

She managed to slam the door closed before Laz could get to her.

He tapped on the window. "Come on. Roll the window down or come out."

"Go away." Avery turned the key in the ignition. "Bad stuff happens whenever you're around."

The car sounded like it wanted to start, but didn't. It didn't even sputter. It gave her false hope that eventually it would turn over and allow her to leave. If Laz had to block her path to keep her from escaping, he would.

Laz put his hand to his chest. "Did I do something wrong?"

The question got a hard glare from her. She jumped out of the car. "I don't know who you are."

"Laz Kyson." He extended his hand to shake hers.

Avery ignored the gesture and instead put her fists to her hips. "And I don't care who you are."

He lowered his hand but remained in his spot, studying her.

"Yes, that was a crappy job, and, yes, I hated that jerk putting his hand on my ass. And, sure, I dreamed about quitting this dive someday. But it paid me. I got tips. Now I have nothing." She put her hand to her forehead. "No, I have rent and bills and school expenses." She cursed again under her breath.

"You have your dignity. I think that's worth a lot." He moved in closer to her.

"My dignity won't put a roof over my head, and I am not moving back in with my parents." She shook her head.

He lowered his tone. "You can make a hell of a lot more money with your voice. Let me help you."

Avery's bottom lip moved like she wanted to say something but she didn't. Barely a squeak came out of her mouth.

Laz could tell she wouldn't be an easy sell. "I can also help you with statistics."

She blinked. "Who said I needed help with that?"

"No one. Just offering."

"You want to help? Get me my job back and then leave me alone." She turned to go back in her car.

Laz held the door open, preventing her from closing it. "How about I find you a better job and become your manager?" He put his hands in prayer form. "Trust me. I believe in you. Please believe in me."

"I don't know you to believe anything." Avery looked at him for a while. "No." She snickered. "Dad warned me about guys like you in the music industry."

She tried starting her car again. This time it made a sad clicking noise before it eventually stopped making any sounds.

"Damn it!" Avery pounded her fists on the steering wheel. "The last thing I needed." She peered up at the back of the restaurant. "I can't leave this here. Pig will tow it or burn it. Or burn it *and* tow it. I can't afford to get it repaired. If I call my parents, they'll give me the I-told-you-so speech and will want me to come back home." She shook her head before resting it on the steering wheel. "I don't need this. I really don't."

"I'll make you a deal." Laz took out his phone. "I'll pay for the tow if you give me five minutes of your time."

She shook her head. "I don't want to owe you anything."

Laz held up both hands. "I promise you. No strings attached on the tow. You have my word."

"I don't know you to trust your word. I don't know you to trust that you are who you say you are. You're just some guy that literally fell from the sky into my world to, apparently, wreak havoc. My life was going fine until you stepped into it. Now I can't think straight." She took out her phone. "I'll just call my parents. No use escaping the inevitable."

"Okay. I'm sure they'll help you, especially when you tell them that you lost your job." Laz didn't want to hit her below the belt, but he didn't have a lot of time to be sensitive.

Avery hovered her thumb over the Send button. "Damn." She peered at Laz. "Did it ever occur to you that I might not be the one you're looking for?"

Laz cocked a smile at the corner of his mouth. "Did you ever think that I might be the one you need?"

Avery sat still for a moment like she had to process his words. "Five minutes."

Laz made an X symbol over his thudding heart. "Promise. We can go wherever you want to talk."

"There's a park near where I live."

Laz nodded. "I'll get a tow truck here in no time."

Then he would be that much closer to getting his dream.

Chapter 6

Avery must have lost her mind. In a blink of an eye, she managed to lose a job and, somehow, gain a potential music manager.

She sat on a bench in a park across the street from her apartment building. Avery kept her stare on her dead vehicle that the tow truck driver had left in front of her door. She wanted to go inside and sleep for a while. With her guest beside her, she couldn't leave. Not just yet. Not until she found out his end game.

"So, Avery…" Laz waved his hand in the air to encourage her to say more, give more.

"Is Laz your real name?" Avery wouldn't be putting herself out there first.

While keeping his steely gaze on her, he stood and removed a black leather billfold from his back pocket. After opening it, he removed a card and handed it to her.

Avery waited a beat before accepting it. She stared at his New York state driver's license. In her mind, she took mental pictures of everything on the card. The card stated he stood six-feet-two inches. That got her licking her lips. She didn't need to review the license to know he had blond hair and blue eyes.

She tried memorizing his address. She reviewed his full name last, the first thing she should have been observing.

"Lazarus Maurice Kyson." She peered up at him. "Yeah, I would have gone with *Laz*, too." She handed the card back to him.

When their fingers brushed against each other, she shook. Avery never expected to feel sparks like that from a stranger.

"Yeah, well, it's a great conversation starter." He returned the license to his wallet and put it back in his jeans before taking a seat. "Couldn't have been an accountant with a name like that."

"Music is all you ever wanted to do?" She never met someone who seemed to be into the industry like her.

He nodded and held his hand up about three feet off the ground. "Since I was about one. My parents tell me that I used to bang pots and pans before I could talk. Then when I did say something, I wouldn't just say it. I would sing it."

Avery laughed. "No, you didn't."

Laz surprised her by singing, "Mom, may I have some cereal?"

What he sang didn't surprise her. The beautiful tone caught her attention first. This man could sing. The idea of that had her sitting up straighter. She briefly wondered if she smelled like fried food or industrial cleaner instead of something pleasant. Damn, she needed to shower, change, and start this conversation all over again.

She also needed her bed, but not in that way. Avery glanced at her apartment again. She imagined her nice, comfortable mattress with her fluffy pillows, and suddenly, she started blinking a little slower than before.

"So, Avery...?" Again, he waved his hand in the air to her.

"Shields." Her voice lowered to a whisper.

"Like Brooke."

"Like guarded." She shook her head. "I don't let a whole lot of people in."

"Speaking of which, are we really going to conduct business out here?" He glanced at her apartment building. "You don't want to go in and—"

"No." She crossed her arms over her chest. "You said five minutes." To illustrate her point, she glanced down at her watch. "You have three left."

"Okay. Where did Destiny Starr come from?"

Avery hadn't prepared herself for that question. "I don't know if I want to talk about that yet." She scooted back as far as she could on the bench they shared.

"Why not? Looks like you have her buried. No social media, a post office box for an address, a disconnected phone number, and no singing gigs. You were literally a needle in a haystack." Laz beamed. "But I got poked by the needle, and I didn't mind it. So tell me about it."

Laz sounded sincere this time, more than he did in the restaurant earlier when he tried running that tired line on her. That didn't mean she wanted to bare her soul to him.

"I get it." He held his hand up. "Baby steps. Where did the name come from? My guess is you liked the group Destiny's Child."

Avery shook her head. "One of my aunts. She was my favorite. Her name was Destiny. She passed away a few years ago. Stroke." She stared down at the lush green grass under her feet to keep herself from bursting into tears.

Her Aunt Destiny had been the only one who wanted Avery to spread her wings and fly.

"Oh, wow. Sorry for the loss."

Avery didn't look up, but that didn't stop Laz from placing his hand on top of hers to show her a bit of comfort. With Uncle Pig, she hated being in his air space, let alone his touch. Avery didn't want Laz to break this connection. The warmth of his hand both relaxed her and revved up her heart...and libido. Her pulse raced. She didn't want to move her hand in fear he would pull his away.

Then he did. He slid his hand off hers when he pulled back from her. "And the Starr part? Was that a wish fulfillment thing?"

Avery smiled and shook her head. "No. Not really. It was from Brenda K. Starr." She glanced up at Laz when he didn't speak. "She was a singer popular back in the eighties."

He nodded. "I know."

Then he shocked Avery by singing a few lines from Brenda's hit song "I Still Believe."

Avery had to cross her legs this time when her clitoris throbbed. She never imagined a man singing that song, and she didn't expect a man to sing it that well.

To keep on track with their conversation, Avery continued. "I liked knowing that she helped both Mariah Carey and Jennifer Lopez early on in their careers. Plus I loved her voice and that song."

"It is a great song, but you have way more talent than to reduce yourself to a cheesy name like Destiny Starr. I don't see anything wrong with Avery Shields, or just Avery."

Suddenly, Avery felt a wave of cold hit her, like someone doused her with ice water. Cheesy name?

"Easy for you. You don't have push back from your family. You can go out there with your real name and full identity." She crossed her arms.

Laz nodded. "Now I get it. Your parents aren't on board with you singing. You came up with the name to hide your identity, right?"

She relaxed her arms. "I thought that if I created this new identity and put myself out there on YouTube and stuff, I would get noticed by the right people and unrecognizable to others. Then some kid of someone who goes to the same church as my family saw one of my videos and told my parents. Before they could even find it, I took all the videos down and deleted all accounts." As she thought about that day, she realized something else. "That was the moment I gave up on the idea of becoming a singer. If I couldn't be honest with my family, what made me think I could sing in front of a group of people I didn't know?"

"At some point, your parents are going to have to let you live your life and realize your dream. You can't keep—"

"Your turn. Tell me about you." Avery had no interest in hearing the same argument she had been telling herself for years.

Laz sat up taller. "Okay. I've been in the music industry for about ten years."

"How old are you now? You look close to my age." Avery stared at him as he answered.

"Twenty-seven."

His admission made Avery blink. Then again, everything made her close her eyes a bit more and more. Her sleepy nature had nothing to do with the distracting man in front of her.

Laz continued giving her his résumé. "I graduated high school early. I went to college in New York on a math scholarship, but I put my full concentration on music. I did several internships, starting my sophomore year, at a few labels. I was offered a job before I graduated. With diploma in hand, I hit the ground running."

"And your running got you all the way down here to Virginia?" She rubbed her eyes and hoped that would be enough to wake her up.

"Your voice got me down here." He pointed to her. "Besides, I like discovering talent in out of the way places." He chuckled. "When you hit it big, what a great story to tell that I heard you in a men's bathroom."

Avery didn't share in his humor. She stood, too exhausted to fake interest anymore. "Thank you for the tow. I appreciate it." She started walking toward her building. "And thank you for telling me all about yourself and your goals."

"You didn't tell me your goals." Laz stood and glanced at his watch before addressing her. "And I believe I have at least another minute with you."

Avery shook her head. "It won't help you. You come at me like the greatest thing since sliced bread, but the fact of the matter is, I'm a poor woman who is struggling to make it, but I do have a goal."

"Isn't it better to have a dream?" Laz moved in closer to her.

"No. Goals are obtainable. If I finish college, which I'll do in a few weeks, I can go for better jobs. Dreams derail you from goals and can get you in trouble."

Laz crossed his arms over his chest. "That sounds like something a parent would say."

"Sometimes parents are right. I'm twenty-two. If I was going to hit out there in the music world, I would have done it by now." She held up her hand and started ticking off points. "I don't do open mics."

"Karaoke." Laz cocked his head at her.

"That's not original music. I'm not sitting at a piano or on a barstool trying to live out a dream." She continued back toward her apartment. "I don't have a YouTube channel anymore."

"Those are overrated in my opinion. I know a lot of mainstream artists have been discovered that way." He shrugged. "Doesn't mean it's right. I prefer the old-school route to get you discovered. You send in a demo and you snag someone's attention." He held his hands up. "I'm here."

Avery put her hand to her forehead. "I'm not looking to get out there. All I wanted was to do my job, do well in school, and go home. I'm not even on any kind of social media. Let's face it. You have the wrong girl." She walked toward her apartment while her insides crumbled.

Even before Laz had said it, she heard her father's words the more she talked about abandoning her dream. If she followed Laz, she knew her parents would be disappointed in her again. It killed Avery to experience her mother's glare the last time she had let the family down. She couldn't destroy their trust in her now that she finally had gotten them to start believing in her again.

"One night."

Avery stopped in her tracks and spun around fast enough that her head felt like she had it on a spin cycle. "Excuse me?" She stomped back to him. "Because I won't sing for you, you think it's okay to hit on me? You think I'm going to have sex with you instead like some disgusting barter? I'm not that girl." She almost said "anymore" but caught herself in time.

She had half expected Laz to be either cocky or embarrassed to be called out on his sloppy pickup line. She didn't know Laz from any other stranger on the street, despite studying his license, but she didn't picture him as the love-em-and-leave-em type. From his clenched jaw and steadily narrowing eyes, she gathered that she assessed his character incorrectly.

Laz took a few steps back and put his hand to his chest. "I wasn't asking to take you to bed. I'm a professional. I've come at you like a professional. If anything I've said or done made you think otherwise, please call me on it."

Avery studied him for a moment before she spoke. "What did you mean by 'one night' then?"

Laz exhaled, evident by the way his shoulders relaxed. "Let me take you to an open mic. I want to see how you are performing in front of an audience, since I missed you at Songbirds."

"And I would like to see a contract. I don't believe a word you say until I can see something in writing." Avery waved her hand in the air as she backed away. "You know what? Contract or not, I've entertained this conversation way too long. You're putting thoughts in my head that I could be someone other than a student who works as a cleaning lady and a waitress. Or rather, *used* to work as a waitress."

"No. The important question is who put the thought in your head that you couldn't be more than a cleaning lady or waitress?"

Avery blinked at the question. Her parents only wanted the best for her. Steering her clear of fool's gold for a guaranteed future seemed like the right thing to do, the right path to put her on to a brighter future.

"Again, thank you for the tow. But I'll pass on all of it. I can't go chasing a fantasy." She put her hand out to shake his.

Even if she wouldn't be helping him with building a stable of singers, she could at least be cordial. Laz accepted her hand and shook it, but seemed like he didn't want to let her go. He kept his gaze down and appeared pensive, like he plotted his next steps in his head.

"It's the weekend." He gazed up slowly until he made eye contact with her. "No classes."

Avery tugged her hand gently at first. He still held on to her.

"Nope." She smiled, but inside her heart started beating hard.

"I'm assuming you have to work tonight, cleaning and stuff." He stared at her like some sort of truth-detecting machine, gauging her response.

"Dad contracts office buildings that usually don't open on the weekends, so no weekend work."

Laz's eyes widened. "So that guy in the bathroom with us was your dad? No wonder. Explains a lot."

Avery managed to get out of Laz's grasp. She wrapped her arms around her body. "I have to—"

"And you don't work at the diner anymore." Laz rubbed his hands together. "Thanks to you."

He held his hand up to her as though trying to defuse a potentially volatile exchange. "I'm sorry you lost your job. I'm not sorry for standing up for you. I'd do it again, for you or any other woman."

Avery should have been pissed at his response. So why did her stomach quiver? She hadn't felt that way in a very long time.

Laz peered over Avery's shoulder before reconnecting his gaze to hers. "And your car is out of commission."

"Are you gunning for the role of Captain Obvious, or do you like spreading sadness and disgust wherever you go?" She snickered. "I know my life sucks right now. I don't need you doing a play-by-play of it."

"I was assessing the recent events affecting you, because it looks like you could use a friend right now." He stood next to her but kept his stare ahead.

Avery redirected her attention to what had caught his interest.

"You go inside and get some sleep." He held his hand up. "Give me the keys to your car, and I'll see if I can fix it."

* * * *

It had been a few years since Laz tinkered in the engine of a car, but he had no other cards to play when it came to convincing this woman that she had an enormous talent that she wasted on singing in bathrooms.

"Are you serious?"

Avery's light voice reminded Laz why he bothered to bend over backward for her. "You are going to need transportation by Monday, I'm guessing."

Avery didn't confirm, but the way she shifted uncomfortably in her spot answered for her.

Laz continued. "I'll see if I can get your car up and running by Monday if you consider singing at one open mic."

"How much would I have to pay you?" She clutched her purse.

"Sing for me, and that'll be my payment. What do you say?" He put out his hand. When she slowed to accept it, he continued his sales pitch. "I asked you for five minutes of your time if I towed your vehicle home, and I did it. I'll work on your car, if you agree to sing." He held up one finger. "One place. One song. What do you say? If it doesn't work out, it doesn't work out. What do you have to lose?"

She mumbled something that sounded like she said, "My family," but Laz couldn't hear her.

"What was that?"

Avery shook her head. "Nothing." Then she exhaled. "Fine. One song. But that's it. That doesn't mean I'll sign with you or even go on tour or anything. I just want to show you how incredibly average I am."

"Sure. But when you do show me and, eventually, the rest of the world how amazing you are, you have to promise to sign with me and let me take you to the next level, which means a music deal." Laz could see so much for her. He wished she had the same belief, the same feeling.

Avery strolled to her apartment building. Laz couldn't help but follow her, not because he had promised to look at her car. Now he didn't even know if he did it for his career or hers. Her magnetic pull kept him in her orbit. Fate brought them together for a reason. He wanted to be near this woman.

When Avery arrived at her door, she unlocked it and turned to Laz. For a split second, he wondered if she would ask him to come inside for coffee and conversation. Despite their rocky first couple of meetings, he found an ease in talking to her more than he had with any woman he had been with recently. In the back of his head, he had to keep reminding himself that he had a job to do, not a relationship to start.

"Besides my dad, no man has ever gone out of his way to please me like you have." A small smile threatened to peek through her hard, outer layer. Avery managed to keep it in check. "You get my car towed here."

"Not as big of a deal as you think." He didn't have to admit to her that he had paid for it out of his own pocket. Laz considered anything he did for Avery as an investment into both of their futures.

"Now you're offering to fix my car." She nodded toward the faded blue vehicle.

"No guarantees that I'll be able to get it running, but I'll try."

"The point is that you're doing an awful lot for a woman you just met." She lowered her gaze before she made her next statement. "Won't your wife or girlfriend get upset at all the attention you're paying to another woman?"

Laz should have been pissed at her question. After making it clear that he would treat her like a client, she dared to ask about his personal life? Instead the subtle inquiry gave him hope and a way to ask her the same thing.

"No attachments right now. Even if I was married or had a steady girlfriend, I would hope she would understand that sometimes I have to do things for my clients that may not be orthodox." He held out his hand. "Keys, please? Or will your boyfriend or husband be upset that another man is under your hood?"

This time Avery did smile, a broad one that nearly split her head in two. She held her keys over his hand. "Knock on the door when you're done. Or, better yet." She held out her hand. "Give me your phone."

Laz didn't hesitate. He pulled his phone from his pocket and unlocked the screen before handing it to Avery. When she accepted it, she smiled a little before glancing up at him.

"Nice background."

Laz nodded. "Nina Simone was a great singer."

Avery typed something on his phone before handing it back to him. As soon as he had it in hand, he engaged the camera and held it up. The motion caused her to raise her hand and block her face.

"I've been working all night and I'm exhausted. You are not going to take my picture right now." She shook her head.

"Fine. Let me do this then." He found the saved number and dialed it.

Laz didn't get pleasantly surprised often. As soon as he heard the rhythmic drumming from the opening of Nina Simone's "Blackbird" as Avery's ringtone, his heart stopped before it drummed out of control. Who the hell was Avery and how did he get lucky to encounter her in his life?

Instead of acknowledging what Laz had been thinking and feeling, Avery removed her phone from her purse and answered the call in front of him. She stared in his eyes as he brought his phone to his ear.

"If I don't hear you knocking, give me a call. I'll be in bed." A sly smile slithered up at the corners of her mouth. "Sleeping."

"And your husband or boyfriend doesn't mind another man having your number and calling you while you're in bed?" Laz didn't mean for it to sound that salacious, but he kind of liked this subtle seductive play between the two of them.

Avery disconnected the call. "Good luck with the car."

Cute. Playing coy. Laz liked that.

She ducked into her apartment and closed the door. After Laz heard her lock it behind her, he started his work. Shedding his shirt and leaving his sleeveless T-shirt on would help him keep cool while he worked. At least he hoped it would.

Laz got into Avery's car and learned a lot more about the woman. He saw she still had a tape deck along with a six-disc CD changer. Beyond his control, he looked through her console and found CD cases for the albums she must have had loaded in her player. Looked like she listened to everything from Heart to Nine Inch Nails. How eclectic.

A music library like that would work well for him as a manager. He could pitch her different music genres and songs to see where she found her niche.

Laz opened her visor and saw a picture of Chantel Woodley clipped on the inside. His body tingled all over as soon as he realized that Avery must also get inspiration from her. Or maybe she had a crush on the woman. The idea of that had other thoughts running through his mind, fantasies that he needed to push aside so he could get back to work.

After a couple of trips to an auto parts store and several tries, Laz had gotten close to fixing Avery's problem, but he hadn't accomplished his goal. Until a bright light illuminated inside the engine, he didn't realize that he had been working on the vehicle all day into the night.

Laz peered next to him and saw Avery holding a flashlight and pointing it at the engine. Now rested, showered, and changed, she looked renewed and refreshed. She had her hair styled straight with a slight wave to it. Her skintight jeans and off-the-shoulder top gave her a sexy but relaxed feel. With only lipstick on her lips that he could notice, she still looked like an amazing, natural beauty.

"I can't believe you're still out here." She smiled.

That alone gave him all the thanks he could need, not that he did it for her appreciation.

"I'm a man of my word, although it's not looking good." He made one final adjustment and crossed his fingers before occupying the driver's seat and trying her car again. This time, beyond his wildest dreams, the engine turned over and the car started.

"Oh my God. You did it." Avery covered her mouth as she came around to the driver's side. "I can't thank you enough."

"I told you I used to work on cars. It was a long, long time ago, but it looks like I still have it." Laz turned it off and got out of the car.

She started to raise her arms to hug him, but he recoiled.

"Um, I'm dirty." He knew his thoughts had been. To illustrate his point, he lifted his hands and showed off the oil and grease covering them, his arms, and his T-shirt. "It looks like you showered and changed. You look very nice." He nodded and dropped his gaze to the ground.

Wow. She even had on strappy high-heel shoes.

"I have." She looked back at her front door. "Did you want to come in and shower?" She must have thought about how seductive the question sounded the way she squeezed her eyes shut. "I mean, if you don't want to go to your hotel smelling like a garage, you can use my shower."

Laz started to say that he had a hotel room, but he didn't. He had checked out of it that morning with the plan to go back home. Since he made that decision, he realized that it meant he had his clothes with him.

"Actually, I would like to take you up on the offer. I gave up my hotel room. I need to go back and rebook it. Before that, though, I can get cleaned up and we can go to an open mic from here. What do you say?" That plan would keep them on track.

"Sounds good. You go get your stuff." She held her hand out to get her keys.

Laz handed them to her, then ran to his rental vehicle and got his suitcase. He followed her into her home. He didn't expect that as soon as he went through the door that he would be met by a set of stairs that went up to her apartment.

When he got to the main apartment area, he did the same there that he did in her car. He scanned the place to get a good feeling about her. What made this woman tick?

The simple apartment furnishings matched the woman in front of him. The living room held one tan couch and a matching chair along with a coffee table, end table, and a lamp. She had one small picture on the end table. If given some alone time, he wanted to inspect it.

From where he stood, he got a view of a small, galley-style kitchen with a door that must have gone to a balcony. Across from him sat two doors. The bathroom sat directly in front of him, which meant the other door had to be her bedroom. Thinking of that had blood pumping to the wrong areas of his body.

He turned to her. "Tell me where you want me."

"You really want to know?"

Chapter 7

Avery had to stop pushing the boundary with this man. She couldn't deny that when Laz offered to fix her car, she started to feel that juvenile, giddy feeling. Then she got up to her apartment and watched him from her bedroom window working hard on her sad baby. When he took off his shirt, she had to take a cool shower.

She imagined running her hands down his long, muscled arms, and across his wide back. From her window, she couldn't tell if he had hair on his chest. It didn't matter. The large planes of it appealed to her so much that she remembered drooling at one point. Thankfully, he didn't catch her watching him.

He also never used the set of keys she entrusted him with to come into her apartment to give her a surprise visit, not that she thought he would. Laz practically bit her head off when she had accused him of propositioning her.

So now why did she like the idea of having this man in other ways than just a manager?

Come on, Avery. That's the old you. The wild you. Stay focused.

"The bathroom is right there." She turned on the light in the bathroom. "Fresh towels are in the cabinet under the sink."

Laz nodded. "Thanks. I won't be too long."

As soon as the door closed, it felt like he had been in there for hours. Avery paced in her small apartment. When she heard the shower start, she did a quick assessment of her space. It had been a while since she had anyone other than family or very close friends in her place.

Avery hid loose papers and bills in drawers, and then fluffed out pillows on her couch. She rushed to her galley-style kitchen and shoved her dirty dishes into her dishwasher without caring where items landed. Once she got Laz out of her bathroom and her home, she would put things back to their natural, messy position.

"Whew. Clean. Good." Avery nodded at her accomplishments and even plopped down in the center of her couch to admire her work.

She didn't have to worry about her bedroom because she wouldn't be inviting him back there. Avery had enough sense not to mix business with pleasure.

At the thought of pleasure, she sat up straight and cursed. She knew exactly what hid in one of the drawers in her bathroom. Avery hadn't thought about that little assistant until she encountered Laz and his incredible eyes and those large hands and his mouth. To top all of those attributes, he had also been kind, protective, and goal-oriented. No wonder Avery wanted to touch herself and think about him.

She didn't want to think about the fact that he could be delving in her bathroom drawers, looking for something innocent and stumble upon her personal stash. She also had no idea she would invite this man, this stranger, into her home. Bottom line, he had been a stranger, despite her studying his driver's license.

She saw him at the karaoke place briefly. She encountered him in the men's bathroom at work. Then he managed to get her fired from her diner job. That alone should have gotten him a one-way ticket to exile.

He had recognized something about her situation in a matter of seconds that people who claim to love and care for her either hadn't acknowledged or didn't want to respond to in over a year. Even her former boss's steady girlfriend had said nothing.

Avery's phone rang, and she quickly picked it up from the coffee table. Seeing Graciela's name across the screen brought a smile to her face. "Hey."

"How are you doing?" Remorse filled Graciela's voice.

"I'm okay. I knew I wouldn't be working there for long. I just thought I would be leaving on my own head of steam." Avery crossed her legs.

"Customers are still talking about it. Well, the customers who have chosen to come back. As soon as they heard the reason that guy pressed Pig up against the wall was because he put his hand on your ass, they wanted to kick Pig's ass themselves." Graciela laughed. "Uncle Pig has kept himself pretty much hidden in his office now. Mona can't even lure him out during the day."

Avery wanted to smile at that news. It sucked that the man had to be physically threatened in order to do the right thing.

"Since he doesn't come out that much anymore, maybe you can come on back." Graciela had a lilt in her voice full of hope.

Avery shook her head even though her friend wouldn't be able to see her. "No. I'm still a bit raw from the whole thing."

"But you're going to need money. And who was that guy who helped you? Did you know him?"

Avery stared at the closed bathroom door. Since seeing him, she had imagined things about him. She had certainly fantasized about him. She couldn't say she knew him.

"No. I don't know him." She cleared her throat.

"Hey, I'm free this evening. I can come by with a bottle of wine and we can watch bad TV."

"No. I have plans this evening." Avery squeezed her legs together when she felt that familiar throbbing again.

Easy, girl.

"You do? What's that? Are you going to Songbirds? I know how much you love singing. Right about now, you need to do things that make you happy."

Graciela had that right.

The shower turned off, and Avery's heart accelerated. She closed her eyes and imagined Laz exiting the cream-colored bathtub to dry off that body. Whoa. That body.

"Look. I have to go. I'll tell you about it later." She sat at the edge of the couch.

"No way. Why are you being so secretive? Tell me."

She could practically see Graciela grabbing her keys to head over to Avery's place.

"Later." Avery disconnected the call. She thought about the soaking-wet man coming out of her shower.

Avery fanned her face. If she couldn't deal with the fantasy of the man, how would she deal with him as a manager? Did she even want him to manage her? It all sounded wonderful and romantic and everything she had ever wanted. If this all came true, if she landed a recording deal, how would she explain it to her parents? She could almost see the disappointment covering their faces.

No, Avery needed to politely tell Laz that she couldn't go through with his plan. No open mic. No music career. No more seeing him on a consistent basis. Losing the last two hurt more than she thought it would.

Avery stood when she heard the doorknob to the bathroom jiggle.

"Stay firm. No means no." Avery repeated the positive mantras until the door opened and Laz put his hand out and only his hand.

"I just want you to know that I'm not fully dressed for a reason." He only left his arm exposed as he spoke to her from inside the bathroom.

"Holy hell," Avery said under her breath.

"I need something and it was easier to come out this way." Laz walked out of the bathroom.

His definition of not being fully dressed differed from hers. She had expected him to only have a towel around his waist. She imagined standing in front of him and pulling it down. That would be one way to convince him not to go to this open mic.

Laz came out of the bathroom wearing a dark pair of jeans and black leather shoes that looked too stylish to even touch her floor. He didn't have on a shirt, but he carried a garment in his hand. He thought being shirtless meant he hadn't been fully dressed.

He approached her but stopped at a comfortable distance away. "I spilled a little bit of toothpaste on my shirt. You wouldn't happen to have one of those laundry sticks or wipes, would you?"

Avery stared at the cobalt blue shirt with a telltale white stain on it before bringing her attention to his bare chest. Her curiosity had been satisfied. No hair on his muscular yet lean chest. She ached to touch his dark pink nipples that seemed to get harder the longer she stared at them. To top that all off, he had chiseled abs that she wanted to lick.

God, had it been that long since she had been in the room with a man? Did she want someone or did she really want Laz? She licked her lips.

"Avery?"

When he called her name, she snapped out of her haze. "What? Shirt. Yes. Um, no. I mean, no laundry thingy." She approached him. "Can it be rinsed out?"

She touched the garment and brushed her hand over his. The connection forced her to bring her gaze up to his. The energy that flowed back and forth between them electrically charged the air until Avery imagined hearing the distinct popping sound. Did she imagine it or did Laz's breathing increase?

His wet blond hair now looked darker. Yet, he had it styled already with a side part. Avery wanted so much to rustle her fingers through his damp tresses, and then grip it with both hands while she kissed him.

"I'll find something else to wear." He smiled and backed away from her, almost like he didn't want to stop looking at her.

She didn't speak as he ducked into the bathroom again where he had his suitcase. At that point, Avery exhaled. The man had her wrapped around every fiber of his being in a matter of seconds. How could he not have anyone in his life?

When she thought about that, she figured something had to be wrong with him. Terrible tipper, horrible to his mother, small penis. The last item had her giggling.

"It's funny what you discover about people when you're in their home." Laz continued speaking to her from the bathroom.

"Yeah? What's that?" Avery resumed her seated position on the couch while she waited for him.

"You don't have a boyfriend or husband."

She sat up straight. If she hadn't put her hand to her chest, she knew her heart would have pounded out of it at any moment. Laz had found her pink vibrator that she hadn't used in months.

Besides feeling the embarrassed heat in her cheeks, she gritted her teeth. She could have spit fire right now. How dare he violate her personal space.

Laz came out of the bathroom fully dressed while carrying his suitcase. He smiled as he approached her, but he wouldn't be pretty soon.

"How dare you." Avery planted her fists on her hips. As soon as Laz stopped smiling, she continued in on him. "I let you use my bathroom, and you use that time to spy on me and look through my things?"

"Excuse me?" Laz's eyebrows furrowed.

"Okay, yes. I have a vibrator." Just saying it enflamed her face even more. "Lots of women have them, including married ones. It's a toy, an enhancement. Some people call it a marital aid." Now she felt like she talked way too much. She needed to end this conversation quickly. "What I have in my bathroom is my personal business."

Laz waited a beat before he responded to her tirade. "I didn't go through your drawers or medicine cabinet. That bothers me when people come to my apartment and do that, so I don't do it to them."

"Oh. So why did you think I was single?" She lowered her arms, now feeling embarrassed for a different reason.

"Your bathroom is spotless. If a man lived here, there would be way more junk on the sink, plus a magazine rack." He smiled, almost like he wanted to defuse a situation.

"Oh." She put her hand to her forehead. "Oh, God. I'm so sorry. I—"

Laz held his hand up. "No need to apologize. We have some time before we need to go. You want to get some studying in?" He pulled out a chair at her breakfast bar.

"You were serious about that?" Avery approached him cautiously, still wary from her recent false assumption.

"I don't kid about education." He pulled out the other barstool for her. "And I did promise." Then he patted the seat. "Where are your books?"

Avery nodded back to her living room. "On the couch."

Laz glanced at it and then her. "Bring them over so that we can get started."

Maybe he felt the same tension between them that she felt. Instead of acknowledging it, she grabbed her books and notebook, and met him over at the breakfast bar.

"Since you offered, I am having problems with something we're going over right now." Avery sat down. "As a matter of fact, we had a quiz on this yesterday, and I don't think I passed it." She shook her head.

"That's not good. What is it?" He leaned forward and gave her his full attention.

That both excited her and made her nervous. "Bayes' Theorem." She jumped up from her seat. "You want something to drink? I'm getting some water."

"I'm fine."

Yes, Lord.

Avery pulled out a bottle of water from her refrigerator, and immediately placed the frosty bottle at her neck and chest, out of Laz's view, before turning around to her guest and possible business partner. She sat down next to him and opened her book to the section giving her the hardest time.

"Bayes' Theorem is a conditional hypothesis." Laz looked at her while he spoke, which gave him an air of authority over the topic.

"Yes." Avery took a sip of the cool liquid and nodded. "I can't believe you remember this stuff."

"To be honest, I can't believe I remember this particular theory. But it's all about comparing the real with the probable, like what's the likelihood that you'll win the lottery, or—"

"Make it in the music industry." If she had to calculate that, she didn't expect to get the result she wanted.

"Not really a good example." He shook his head. "Most of those who make it do it because they were at the right place at the right time. This is your time. I can feel it."

She wanted to feel the same thing, but Avery had been through this before. She had to admit that Laz had gotten closer to her than most in the industry.

An hour into studying and Avery started to like what Laz taught her. His patience had her thinking about his performance in the bedroom. Would he be a slow and easy lover?

She had to get her mind off his body of work. "You fix cars. You know statistics. You're in the music business. You're like Prince Charming and

I'm Cinderella." She laughed. "A modern-day one, that is. I feel like at some point my foot is not going to fit into that glass slipper."

Laz studied her for a moment. "It will. I feel it. Good things happen to talented, beautiful people."

"Now you sound like one of my former coworkers. Good things will happen when I graduate."

"If I can help you get to that point, I'll do that, too. I'm here for you."

Avery connected her gaze to his and couldn't break from the stare. If she didn't know any better, it felt like her face moved toward his. She moistened her lips in anticipation of a kiss. What the hell was she doing? She couldn't kiss this man. She shouldn't want him. Damn if he didn't move his face down close to hers, too, until he stopped.

Laz cleared his throat before standing. "I think that might be enough studying for right now." He slid his hands down his shirt and jeans to straighten them out. "If you're ready to go, I am. I'll drive."

Before she could say anything else that would incriminate herself and her actions, he walked down the steps to the front door and walked out.

When he disappeared, Avery paced and shook out her hands, which now tingled. "He thinks I'm an idiot. No, worse. He thinks I'm a horny idiot." She leaned her head back and growled. "Why can't you learn to shut up?"

Instead of beating herself up even more, she grabbed her purse and keys. This would be an awkward ride and a long night.

* * * *

During the entire car ride to the bar, Laz's mind filled with images of Avery pleasuring herself with a vibrator that he didn't even know existed anywhere in the bathroom. Now he imagined the shape and size of the faux phallus and how she had used it in the past, since, by her response, she had used it before.

He also thought about the fact that if he hadn't stopped himself, he would have kissed her. Helping her with her homework reminded him of being a student in college and doing the same with his college sweetheart, only those situations ended up with hot, sweaty sex. Laz couldn't and wouldn't have that with Avery.

Laz had to keep himself and Avery distracted. She remained quiet during the ride as well, probably questioning whether or not to even trust or believe him.

"So singing. Tell me about it." Laz drummed his thumbs on the steering wheel.

"What do you mean?" Avery crossed her legs, which matched the crossed arms over her chest.

She had officially shut down. He had to make her open up again.

"When did you start? When did you know you could sing really well? Why didn't you pursue it as a career?" Those questions should keep her busy and keep his mind occupied.

"Wow. You really want to know it all, don't you?" She chuckled. "Okay. If you ask my mother, I didn't start talking first. I sang. As I got older I would put on little shows for family and friends. If you came over to the Shields house, expect a performance complete with intermission." Avery smiled.

Laz liked this side of Avery. He split his attention between her and the road.

"I knew I had some singing ability when I got to sing more solos in church. And I always landed in first chair when I was in chorus all through school. I went to college directly after high school."

"Really? Which one?"

"University of Pennsylvania."

"Wow. Nice." He nodded.

"Yes, it was. It was close enough for me to drive home if I needed to, but far enough away from my parents...."

Laz caught something in her response. Sounded like she didn't have a great relationship with her parents. Then again, he couldn't wait to get out of D.C.

"So final question." Laz pulled up to a stoplight. "Why haven't you pursued a career in music before now?"

"What makes you think I haven't?" She sank her arms in a little deeper.

Oh, no. Laz felt her pulling away from him again. "It just surprises me that someone as talented as yourself hasn't been snatched up before now."

She let out a long sigh. "I had made some headway into the industry. I sang the national anthem at a few Norfolk Tides games. I did so well at that, I got to do it at a Washington Nationals game." She paused.

"Then something happened, right?"

The light changed and Laz pulled off slowly.

"You could say that." Avery cleared her throat. "I made some mistakes. My parents were not happy with me. To be honest, I wasn't pleased with myself. After my sophomore year, I left college and came back home."

"But you went back. You're in school now." He had to build her back up.

"Yeah. After knocking around for a year, I eventually went back to college, taking classes here and there. I got in on an academic scholarship, believe it or not. After that first year, the rest of my tuition, books, and other expenses would be on me and my parents. I decided to finish school at home. I'm on my last semester." She pumped her fist in the air. Instead of returning her arms back into the crossed position over her chest, she rested her hands on her lap. "The week after next is spring break. And then a few weeks after that, I'll graduate, hopefully. My parents should be proud of that."

"I'm sure they're proud of you now. And, hey, we all make mistakes. It's how we respond to them that makes a difference." He wanted to pat her leg, touch her somewhere.

That would have been too much. He shouldn't have come out of the bathroom without a shirt. He didn't think it would be a problem until he caught Avery staring at his chest. He wanted her to do more than stare. Had she reached out and touched him, they would have never made it out of her apartment.

"So why don't you have a girlfriend?" Avery smiled. "I can't be the only one revealing myself here."

"Fine. I did for a while. She said I was too involved with my work." He turned to Avery. "For you, that's a good thing. I'm dedicated to my job and, apparently, nothing else." He brought his stare back to the road in front of him. He turned to her. "Why don't you have someone in your life?"

Avery hesitated before she answered. "Like you, too involved. With me, it's school. I work different jobs like I'm Ryan Seacrest. I don't have the time or the energy."

"Maybe you haven't met the right man yet."

"Or maybe the right man needs to be patient and let me live my life first. I will be a much better person and partner once I get my life together." She uncrossed her legs and sat up taller. "So where are we going? It's not me to blindly get in a car with a stranger."

"Have you heard of or ever been to a place called Honey's in Virginia Beach?" Laz kept his stare on the road until he realized Avery hadn't answered.

When he turned to her, she finally spoke. "I've heard of it. Kind of like an artsy coffee shop, right?"

Laz nodded. "At least that's what the website described it as being. I thought I would see if you sing there first."

"First?" She snickered. "Why do you think there will be other chances?"

Laz's audible turn-by-turn navigator on his phone directed him to turn into the parking lot of Honey's. He parked his rental and turned it off before he spoke to her. When he did, he turned his body toward her.

"I can tell you really want this. If you do, I can help you. I really do want to help you." Laz had to grip the stirring wheel with one hand and sat on his other hand to keep from reaching out and touching her.

Avery's skin looked like chocolate velvet, both smooth and delicious.

"What if you're wasting your time on me?" Avery shrugged.

"You let me decide how I spend my time." Laz got out and crossed in front of the vehicle to the passenger side.

Avery already had the door open, but he held it open while she exited. When she got out, he walked next to her up to the building, again, doing everything in his power to keep from touching her, but yet he couldn't help but place his hand at the small of her back.

He opened the heavy wooden door for her. It creaked as she stepped inside the dimly lit place that smelled of coffee and specialty teas. The spicy aroma stung his nose as he navigated their way to a table.

"You sit here. Order whatever you like. I'm going to find the manager or whoever it is that organizes the talent." He pointed to the stage where a young woman sat on a barstool with an acoustic guitar and sang an emotional song.

Laz walked over to a bar area and got the female bartender's attention. The hard part of getting Avery to this place had been overcome. Now he would need to get her on the stage.

"Hey, I want a singer to do the open mic tonight. Who do I need to talk to in order to make that happen?" The bartender looked disinterested, but entertained him anyway.

"Open mics are on Sunday nights. Tonight is her gig." She pointed to the singer.

He didn't even look at the singer on stage. He had no obligation to her. "That's not what the website says."

"Needs to be updated. Check our Facebook page. That's always updated." She started to move away to take care of other customers.

"Wait. I'm sure she needs a break, right? Can I get my singer on the stage for one song when she stops performing?" He wouldn't leave with his tail tucked between his legs.

Avery already seemed tentative. He had to seal this deal.

"She's not going to let you use her guitar unless your singer plans on going a cappella." The bartender pointed off stage to a large object under a black tablecloth. "You can use the piano if you or her know how to play it."

Laz stared at the object like it would grow legs and long, sharp, pointy teeth, and bite his head clean off his shoulders. He would have much rather have that scenario happen than to be on stage with her playing the piano.

People would stare at him, judge him, laugh at him. Twenty-seven years old and the thought of that still had him worried.

"I don't think she'll need it. But good to know that it's there." He hated not to use all the tools available to him due to his crippling fear. With everything he had riding on this and not a lot of time left, he should have taken his own needs out of the equation and put himself out there for Avery.

"Dude, whatever. Sure. She has another five or ten minutes left on this set. Then she takes a fifteen-minute break. If you use the piano, you'll have to set that up, do your song, and break down the set in fifteen minutes."

Laz nodded. "Understood."

He pushed himself away from the bar and went back to Avery, who wrung her hands over and over again.

"No one's really paying attention to her, and her voice is really beautiful." Avery stared at the singer.

"It's Saturday. Date night. Maybe people are paying attention to their dates than her." He would make sure to keep Avery in a positive headspace.

"She's really good. I mean *really* good." Avery shook her head. "I'm sure she's tried getting into the music business, too. What makes me any different?"

"You have me. I'll fight for you." He nodded. When he noticed more of her doubt creeping in her head, he continued. "Do you know what song you want to sing?"

Avery looked pensive. "I hadn't thought about it because after I made a fool of myself back at my apartment, I was going to back out."

"You didn't do anything to be embarrassed about. I've already forgotten it."

"Liar." She laughed.

"Anyway, your song. It has to fit your audience and complement your voice. I was thinking maybe some Mary J. Blige or Aretha."

Avery looked at him and blinked. "I don't think this audience would appreciate that type of music."

"What? Good music? I didn't ask you to do Nine Inch Nails."

She blinked. "So you don't go through my bathroom drawers, but you have no problem going through my car console."

Shit. He didn't mean to reveal that.

"Never mind that. Your song. It needs to be something that people will remember and that will showcase you and your talent."

Avery dropped her gaze. A smile crept up on her face as soon as the audience gave a modest applause to the singer on stage.

"Thank you. I'm going to take a quick break." The singer stood from the stool while holding the neck of her guitar. "You folks enjoy your tasty beverages. Don't forget to tip your waiters and waitresses. I'll be right back."

Laz stood. "Okay, let's go."

"Wait. Now?" Avery's eyebrows pinched together in confusion. "I just ordered my drink."

"It'll be here when you get back."

He put his hand on the small of her back again to guide her to the stage area. The possessive touch felt natural. Having her so close to his body would definitely do him in if he didn't separate from her.

"This isn't an open mic night, is it?" Avery had her back to the audience as soon as Laz got her to the stage area.

"No. But we have fifteen minutes to make this work."

Avery shook her head. "Don't bother." She started to leave the stage area. "Amateur hour."

Laz netted her around her waist with his arm. "Hey, I made something happen here out of nothing. No, this wasn't ideal. But we have something. You have an opportunity to sing. Don't get caught up in details. And don't get scared."

Her panting breath did scare him.

"Breathe. Calm down. You're an incredible talent. You're going to kill it." He peered over at the bar area. "You can only do one song." Then he looked down at his watch. "And we don't have a lot of time. What song are you going to do?"

Avery looked deep in thought before she acknowledged him. "Stand aside. I got this."

"Wait. Let me first introduce you." Laz approached the microphone. "Ladies and gentlemen, the staff here at Honey's has graciously allowed my friend here a unique opportunity to sing a song for you before the show resumes."

No one in the audience looked up or even paid him any attention.

"Okay, so without further ado, here's Avery, um, Avery." One-named stars did well.

Avery had a unique enough name to carry it off. Laz just wished he knew her plan. He stepped back from the microphone to allow her to step forward.

Then he rushed to the side to get to the piano. His breathing came out as heavy pants as he braced his hands on top of the tablecloth covering the instrument. Before he could remove the tablecloth, he heard the most angelic sound ever. Without any instruments backing her, Avery started singing Bob Dylan's "To Make You Feel My Love."

He became mesmerized in the song and the simple and easy way she performed it. As he watched her, he realized he had a unique opportunity on his hands. Abandoning the piano, he got out his phone and started recording her.

Avery kept her eyes closed for most of the song. Rookie move. He would have to show her the video and discuss her stage persona, like a wrestling coach talking to one of his students.

The more Avery sang, the more Laz felt every hair on his body stand up. He looked out in the audience. The people who hadn't paid him any attention before, now couldn't take their stares off Avery. Everyone stopped talking. No one drank. Even the bartender stopped serving customers while Avery sang.

Laz smiled and had to keep from giggling like some schoolgirl when he saw what he had recognized from the very beginning. Avery had a gift. She had magic in her pipes. It would be a shame for her not to use it. No way would he get anyone else to represent her.

At the end of her song, the audience roared its approval by giving her a standing ovation. Avery opened her eyes and looked shocked by the reaction. She laughed but had tears running down her cheeks.

Laz stopped recording and stood next to her on the stage. In her ear, he whispered, "You did it. You were incredible."

Out of nowhere, he planted an innocent kiss on her temple before ushering her off stage. When he did, he noticed a few female patrons who also dabbed away tears.

By the time he got her back to the table, her drink sat waiting for her.

"That was insane." Avery covered her mouth. "I've had people react that way at karaoke, but nothing like this. I felt free."

"Did you feel like you belonged up there?"

That would be the crucial question.

Before she could answer, the bartender put her hand on Laz's shoulder to get his attention.

"You didn't tell me you were bringing in a lethal weapon." She smiled. Then she put her hand out to Avery. "Dot."

"Avery. Thanks for letting me sing."

"Anytime. That's why I came over here. Our regular open mic is on Sunday nights. You're more than welcome to come back then, too. And if you want a regular spot, let me know. Pay is based on draw and drinks sold. Do well, bring in a lot of customers, you could do okay." She pulled out a business card and started to hand it to Avery when Laz snagged it out of her hand.

"Thanks. I'm Laz Kyson, her manager. I'll let you know." He nodded.

As soon as the bartender walked away, Avery snatched the card from Laz's hand. "Until I sign anything with you, I'll handle my own business."

Damn. He had arranged this whole impromptu performance. Didn't she see that he had her best interest at heart? The fact that she didn't allow him to take over so easily actually intrigued him. Laz had been used to people, especially women, doing what he wanted.

"So if I bring you a contract, you'll give me back that card and let me make decisions for you?" He stared at her to gauge her reaction.

Avery looked a little pensive before she answered. "It depends."

Laz sighed. "I've been in this business for a long time. I know how to navigate through the industry a little better than you. You're going to have to trust me."

"And you're going to have to listen to me and understand my needs."

If Laz could do that, he would have had a girlfriend and, maybe, his job at Universe.

After slipping the card into her purse, Avery fidgeted in her chair and spun her coffee mug around so much that the contents splashed on to the table.

"That was fun. I want to do that again." Avery stood.

Laz laughed as he held her hand and guided her back down to her seat. "Not our night. Not really. We'll have other moments. But this one was huge." He nodded. "Drink your coffee and enjoy the night."

He had to make big plans for Avery. If he plotted this right, she could hit from this one performance and have companies lining up to sign her. That would be the dream.

After a couple of hours, Laz drove Avery back to her apartment. From the way she smiled the entire trip back, a welcome change from how they started the evening, he could tell she still felt pumped about her performance.

"You did a fine job on stage. Did I tell you that?" Laz pulled into her apartment complex.

Avery nodded. "You did. But it's awesome to hear. They wanted to book me. Me!" She put her hand to her chest. "That's insane."

He pulled up to her apartment building. "Like me, they recognize talent." He got out of the car.

Like before, he went around to her side to open her door. This time, she let him. He walked her up to the door.

"Thank you for getting me to do this and for pushing me. I was ready to hightail it out there, but luckily, you wouldn't let me." She smiled.

"I recognize not only your incredible voice, but your drive. You want this. I can tell."

Avery unlocked her door and opened it. "I want a lot of things." She peered up at him. "Thank you." She wrapped her arms around his neck and pulled him in for a hug.

Laz held her. He liked feeling the softness of her body. He had to stop himself from sliding his hands down to her ample backside. Gentleman. Professional. He had to remember those two things.

"I can come in and finish helping you with your schoolwork." He rubbed his hands up and down her back.

In response, she massaged his shoulders. Immediately, in his mind, he thought about having sex with this incredible woman and feeling her holding on to his shoulders while positioned between her thighs. If he thought about this now, he knew he would need to go soon.

When Avery pulled back from him, she stopped when she got face-to-face with him. She inched her face forward. Laz should have recoiled back like he did earlier that night, kept up that professionalism. In response, he eased his head down. As soon as her lips brushed his, he released a long, low moan.

What the hell was he doing? He just posed the argument in his head to be professional, to not cross the line. With Avery, it didn't feel like this kiss didn't make sense.

He pressed his lips against hers and cradled the back of her head with his hand. Damn, she felt good.

Laz felt bold enough to slide his tongue into her mouth. He braced for her to push him away. Avery sucked on it and pulled on his shoulders as she stumbled back into her apartment. He didn't stop kissing her when her back hit a wall.

His whole body throbbed, but mainly below his belt. To keep from going too far, he gripped her waist, but he still pulled her forward, brushing his crotch against her stomach. When she moaned, his pulse quickened.

She broke from the kiss first. "If you want to stay here, you can." She tried catching her breath as she spoke to him. "There's a couch."

Laz had a feeling that after that kiss, he wouldn't be staying on the couch. Every part of his body wanted her and wanted to take her to bed. He had already crossed the line by kissing her. He didn't need to further ruin the start of a potentially great working relationship.

"I have a lot of work to do and I don't want to keep you awake…by working." Laz backed up and suddenly felt so cold. "You have my number. Call me tomorrow or I can just come over." When she didn't say anything, he filled in the blanks. "I'll come over." He held on to the doorknob as he closed the door. "Good night."

Damn.

Chapter 8

Stupid, stupid, stupid! Avery shouldn't have kissed Laz, apparent from the way he bolted from her. She, for sure, shouldn't have asked him to spend the night. Her old impulsive self returned in a blink of an eye. Yet with Laz, it felt different.

Yes, kissing him had been hasty. Her feelings, though, stemmed from a deeper connection. They spoke the same language when they talked music. As she imagined, his lips felt amazing on hers.

If only she didn't feel the intense bond to him, especially after she sang. If only she didn't feel the need to express her gratitude physically.

No, the reason for the kiss came from more than a simple thank you. She wanted this man. Even with the brief but intense kiss, she could tell Laz would be a passionate lover. As soon as he slid his tongue in her mouth and tightened his hold on her waist, she wanted more. Her heart pounded recalling the moment.

His cooler head prevailed when he didn't take her up on the offer to stay in her apartment last night. That didn't stop her imagination—and her vibrator—from running wild last night.

Maybe with her fantasies and body now satisfied, she can get down to business. That meant focusing on school. She chalked up her impulsive kiss to the excitement of performing. Nothing else. If only Avery could convince her jittery belly of that.

It didn't help that Laz had sent her a text message with a copy of her performance after leaving her last night. Avery must have watched it a hundred times before finally falling asleep. Hearing herself sing didn't excite her. The enthusiastic response from the crowd curled her toes. She could hear that applause for the rest of her life and be happy.

A knock sounded at her door. Avery glanced at the clock on the wall. She could always count on her parents' Sunday morning arrival. Convincing her to go to church had become more of a sport to them than a sincere goal.

Still in her sleeping shorts and loose T-shirt, she bounded down the stairs. She knew as soon as they saw her in her pajamas with her hair piled on top of her head in a messy bun that they would get the message, again, give her a lecture, and leave her alone. That didn't mean she didn't enjoy their weekly visits.

Avery unlocked and opened her door. "Good morning."

Seeing Laz on the other side had her wanting to slam the door in his face. She had forgotten that he mentioned he would come by to see her. For that reason alone, she should have showered, shaved her legs and more, and worn something a little better than an old Bart Simpson shirt and baggy shorts.

"Good morning to you, too." Laz looked so good in his jeans and white T-shirt that showed off his tanned skin. "May I come in for a moment?" He stayed planted in front of her door until she spoke.

"Um, yeah. Sure." She took a step to the side to allow him to come into her apartment again. "Excuse my appearance. I just woke up." A lie but it would have to do under the circumstances.

"I would have called you first, but I assumed you would be awake." He followed her up the steps.

She realized very quickly that he could probably see up the legs of her shorts and had a bird's-eye view of her panties. Could this day get any worse?

"Would you like something to drink? Coffee? Tea?" She winced when she realized she sounded just like she used to when she waited tables.

"No. I'm fine." He glanced at her couch. "May I sit?"

"Of course." Avery waited until Laz sat down before she found a spot at the other end of the couch from him.

"Before we talk about anything else, I need to say something." Laz sat up taller and made sure to make eye contact with her.

The blue eyes reduced her to a pool of jelly, but she stiffened up her back to show confidence.

"You are a very talented woman, and I'm not talking about your kissing skills, which…" Laz trailed off like he had to corral himself.

Avery smiled. No matter how long she lived, she would never get tired of hearing that, especially coming from Laz, which seemed strange. She shouldn't want praise from a stranger. The warmth in his eyes and his strong convictions that kind of matched her father's, Avery started to not see Laz as a stranger. Unfortunately, she didn't see him as a manager either. She pictured him in another crucial role, which might not help her singing career.

Laz took a deep breath before he continued. "But I can't represent you." He quickly stood up. "I'm sorry."

Before he turned, Avery, still stunned from his quick declaration, grabbed his arm and pulled him back. "Wait. What did you say?"

"You were right the entire time. I'm not the right person to represent you and I'm sorry for wasting your time." He wouldn't even look her in the eyes.

Laz kept his gaze either above her head or aimed down to the floor.

She shook her head. "No. I'm not accepting that. For days, you've been on me about my talent. Now all the sudden, I'm not good enough for you anymore?"

"I never said that." He finally connected his gaze to hers. "You're an exceptional singer. With some work, you'll be an even better performer." He put his hand to his chest. "I'm not the one who should be getting you to that next level."

When he started to leave again, Avery did like he had done when he first saw her in the men's bathroom, and she blocked his path. "I have never thought about myself seriously as making it in the business until you came along. I never thought I was talented enough or had enough drive or even pretty enough."

At her last statement, Laz looked like he wanted to reach out and touch her. He restrained the desire and kept his arm down to his side.

"You made me think of myself differently. Fine. So I'm drinking the Kool-Aid now. I'm buying what you're selling. Now you want to up and go? Why?" Her breathing came out hard.

If this man didn't tell her what she needed to know soon, she would faint from lack of oxygen.

"What happened between us last night when we got back to your place should have never occurred." His face became somber. "You're new to the business. I don't want you thinking that everyone you deal with is out to sleep with you." He gritted his teeth for a moment before he continued. "*I* did not pursue you because I wanted something physical. I don't involve myself in relationships with people I work with, particularly clients. I'm sorry if I've made you feel uncomfortable. That wasn't my intention."

Avery's heartbeat slowed down. She kind of hoped he enjoyed the kiss, the connection. She felt it. Didn't he?

"That was very nice to say. I appreciate your honesty." She nodded.

"Good." He wiped imaginary sweat from his brow and laughed. "I didn't think you would understand. I thought this would be awkward."

"It probably still will be." She made sure he reconnected his gaze to hers before she spoke. "I liked the kiss. Even though it's not what I should want, especially with what I have going on right now, if it happens again, I wouldn't stop it."

"You wouldn't have to. I would, that's if I stayed. But I'm not." To punctuate his point, he shook his head and even crossed his arms like he needed the barrier.

Damn if he didn't appear sexy saying the most honorable and unsexy thing in the world.

"So you didn't like kissing me?" Avery crowded his space by moving in closer to him.

"I didn't say that." Laz shook his head.

"There's a lot you're not saying for a man who hasn't stopped trying to sell me on this idea since meeting me. So if given the chance, you would kiss me again?" She raised her eyebrows.

"I didn't say that either."

She got close enough to him to feel the heat coming from his body. "And if I kissed you, would you push me away?"

Laz exhaled through his nose and dropped his gaze. "A physical relationship is not what you should want out of your manager."

Avery nodded. "You're right." She stared at him. "Out of the right *man*, it's exactly what I want."

He looked a bit stunned and speechless. His mouth hung open as he stared at hers. Without thinking, she licked her lips. She didn't realize the effect she had until he growled.

"I came here to finally give you what you've been wanting." When Avery's eyes widened, he continued with his statement. "Your freedom. You said so yourself. Ever since I came into your life, bad things have happened." He waved his hand in between their bodies. "Us working together would be a bad thing. You deserve way better."

"I don't accept that." She held on to his thick forearm and pulled him back into her living room. "For the first time in years, I saw myself doing more than scrubbing floors, taking orders, or singing in karaoke bars. You did all that in a few days."

Laz's face relaxed a little, but he continued to leave his arms folded.

So Avery continued, hoping to soften his stance. "You're getting me to dream, Mr. Lazarus Maurice Kyson."

Using his full name made him smile.

"If you leave, it'll turn into a nightmare."

His smile melted.

Avery looked behind herself. "And I believe you mentioned helping me with homework. I'm starting to get that Bayes' Theorem, and that's all because of you."

Laz laughed, then became serious. "If I stay, it's strictly business." He scanned her place. "I've stayed a lot longer in your place than I should have. From now on, we'll do proper meetings in public places. I'll find studio space for you to cut some demos. We'll meet with execs. Everything will be across the board right and fair. And"—he reached in his back pocket and pulled out his phone—"I make it a habit of recording most sessions. Keeps me honest. I respect you. I want you to know that upfront."

Damn. There he went being honorable again. Avery really needed a shower, and not because she had a guest in her house.

"Thank you." She pulled him back to the couch. "Will you please have a seat now so that we can talk?"

Laz glanced at his watch.

"Are you late for something?"

What did this man need to do at ten in the morning?

"No. Like I said, I hadn't intended on staying this long." He jutted his thumb over his shoulder. "I can go wait in the car."

Avery snickered. "Now you're acting crazy. We can be adult about this."

She sat down first to make him more comfortable about staying.

Laz remained standing. "I do want to work with you. What I saw last night showed me that you're someone special."

"Ow. My neck is killing me having to look up at you to have this conversation." She crossed her legs and patted the couch cushion next to her.

Laz exhaled. "Fine." He sat down, but so far away that he practically sat on the arm of the couch.

"Better." She smiled, hoping to relax him a little. "We can talk music and you can help me with statistics."

"At a library or Starbuck's. Not here." He shook his head.

"You're really serious about this, huh?"

The men Avery had encountered in the past would say anything to get in her pants. This man made sure to say everything he needed to stay out of hers.

"I saw a couple making out at the library. Might not be a great place for us to go." She leaned forward. "Might give me ideas."

"There's no denying that you're beautiful and sexy and talented. I definitely got carried away by your voice and that song." He clasped his hands together, and it looked like he wanted to drop to his knees and pray. "Make no mistake, I have never done something like this before."

"Wish I could say that." Avery settled back into the couch. "My parents were super strict with me while I was growing up. I was determined to do the opposite of what they wanted. I saw it as being rebellious. Really, it was me being young and reckless."

Then Laz started to relax into the couch. "We were all reckless as teenagers." He laughed to himself like he had told himself a private joke. "I remember when I was sixteen, I had just gotten my license. A few friends and I had driven down to the beach."

Avery blinked. "That doesn't sound so bad. What? Was it on a school night or something?"

"No. I grew up in Maryland, close to D.C. We drove down to Florida. This was back in the days of flip phones, and our parents were calling us like crazy. None of us answered." He shook his head. "I would kill my kid if they did that to me. But we thought we were grown back then."

Avery laughed. "Wow. I bet you put a lot of gray hairs on your parents' heads."

"When I got back home, the car was taken away from me. As a matter of fact, I was homeschooled for the rest of the school year, and I could only go outside to mow the lawn and wash the family cars. I didn't see my friends until the following school year. But, man, the experience made it worth it." He tapped Avery on the back of her hand. "So what was your rebellious moment?"

She shook her head. "Nothing like yours. Forget it."

"No. I want to hear about you. I want to know more about you and what you went through. So tell me."

Avery took a deep breath. She hadn't told this story to anyone, and hadn't planned on sharing it for the rest of her life. Deep down, she knew this would explain her need to do the right thing, be the perfect daughter. Even after the kiss, though, Avery didn't feel the need to reopen that wound.

"What I did was worse." She shook her head. "Yeah. You think being stuck in your house was bad? I got that plus I had to work in the church every day with the preacher reporting my every action to my parents. I didn't get a car until my freshman year of college." She laughed and leaned her head back. "I was fine my first year of school. My second year, I was a little wild. I knew what to expect and I had made some friends. One night, I hung out with some friends and met this guy. He seemed really nice. We got to talking and right when we were about to kiss, cops rolled up on us and arrested him and took me in with him. He had warrants stemming from drug sales. I got dragged in because of him. I called my parents because I was in jail and scared. They both drove for hours from Virginia to Pennsylvania to help me. Eventually, I was released when they realized I didn't know him. But I will never forget the look of disappointment on my parents' faces, especially my mother. She looked at me like she didn't know me anymore." She looked at Laz. "As you can see, I don't make the best decisions, especially when it comes to men."

Laz sat up with his shoulders back. "I'm here for work. Nothing else. I won't do anything to compromise you or betray your trust. Agreed?" He put his hand out to her.

Avery looked at his hand before returning her gaze to his. "Agreed." She shook his large hand.

Tingles went through her body and down to her toes, her naked toes. She really needed to take that shower.

He laid his arm across the back of the couch, but didn't touch her even though his fingers sat millimeters away from her shoulder.

"My past mistakes are the reasons I work so hard and am trying to get my degree. I have let down my parents so much. At one point, I lost their trust. I've slowly regained it by keeping to myself and not making waves. I haven't dated anyone since that guy."

Laz scratched his chin with his free hand. "So you're saying my kiss was your first kiss that you've had in years?"

Avery hadn't thought about it that way, but Laz had been right. "Yes. You broke my kissing slump."

He laughed. "I'll cherish that honor." He slapped his hands together and rubbed them back and forth. "Now, let's get to work. Did you look at that video I sent you last night?" He clipped something to his phone and looked around the room before he settled on a semi-blank wall with only a few pictures.

"I've watched it so many times I think I've burned the image into my brain permanently." She brought her attention to the wall and suddenly saw an image of her at the coffeehouse. "Oh."

"If you did sports when you were younger, I'm sure your coach took video of you playing so that you can get a critique of your performance. Same here." He started the video. "I have absolutely nothing to say about your voice. Flawless."

A tingle went through Avery's body, but she didn't turn around to acknowledge him. She feared she would have the same impulsive reaction to him again. "Thank you."

"With one exception."

Avery blinked. In her entire life, no one had critiqued her singing. She understood getting feedback on her performance since, besides the karaoke bar, she hadn't really performed in front of a different crowd.

"What's that?" She balled her toes into the rug under her feet while she awaited his answer.

"You need to control your breathing." He pointed to the image on the wall. "I noticed you losing your breath on the longer notes."

"I was nervous and excited." She felt that way now as she talked to him.

"I know. I can help you with that, too, with a few exercises." He put his hand to his stomach. "It's all about control."

"And what about my performance?"

"You keep your eyes closed when you perform." When Laz pointed to the image on the wall, Avery saw his hand in her peripheral vision. "You can't do that. You connect to people with the song and your voice, but it's not enough. When you look out into the audience, you have to make a connection with your eyes."

"It's difficult. Singing sometimes makes me feel like I'm exposing a part of myself. I can't look at someone and share my pain." She crossed her legs again and wrapped her arms around her knees.

"Don't you see? That's what audiences want. They want to feel like you know exactly what they're going through. Yeah." He moaned. "They want you to speak for them."

Avery stared at her image until it became uncomfortable at first to watch herself, then it became unsettling. "I have tried holding down the desire to want to do this, to want this life."

"Why is that? Fear?" Laz stopped the video.

Avery had to regard him this time. She turned to him while nodding. "I've been doing everything I can to not fail my parents again. They would hate knowing that I still want to make singing my career."

"How can they be upset with you after hearing you?" Laz sat his phone on the coffee table.

"Doesn't matter. They think I have a great voice. They just don't see a future in music. Not stable." Thinking about their opposition had her boiling mad. She felt stifled. Avery had no one to blame but herself. She had made crucial mistakes in her past that fractured the trust bond she'd had with her parents. "I've decided, though, that I need to take more control of my life." She beamed. "For that reason, I've uploaded my video on YouTube." She pulled her phone out. By the time she started to show Laz, she noticed his very serious expression.

"What video?" He looked at the wall. "That one? The one I sent you?"

She nodded. "Of course."

Laz's tanned face transformed to a deep shade of crimson. "Why would you do that?"

"Feedback. I wanted to see if other people liked my singing. Like you said, lots of popular singers now got their start this way." Avery would have thought Laz would have been proud of her.

Laz shook his head. "I wish you wouldn't have done that." He shoved his phone back in his pocket.

Avery snickered. "I so can't read you. First you're on me to work with you. Then you try to drop me before we really get started. And then when I get on board and I'm trying to be proactive with this new career, you don't like that. Why aren't you happy about me loading this video?"

He exhaled like he needed to collect himself before speaking. "Usually people who resort to gimmicks like this, and this is a gimmick, it's because they lack talent and need to do something sensational to get attention. You're good, damn good. You don't need to do this. I don't know what I need to do to make you trust me. You have to let me lead."

"Easier said than done." Avery stood. "I guess we're both a little stubborn and bullheaded." She peered behind herself. "I'm going to take a shower and change. Will you please wait in here? No need for you to sit out in your car."

Laz stood with her. "Sure. When you come back, you can delete the video."

"We can talk about that. I'm just wondering if you'll even listen to me." She smirked before disappearing into her bedroom to get an outfit to wear after her shower.

Avery decided to go simple. She would wear a great maxi dress that wouldn't show off her body but with skinny straps to keep her cool while talking to the very delectable Laz Kyson. She had to be thankful that the man had enough willpower to keep their arrangement professional.

Yes, this relationship with Laz, a working relationship, would be good for her. She just had to keep this from her parents. They wouldn't understand.

After her shower, she dressed, pulled her hair up into a curly bun, and even sprayed on a small amount of perfume on her neck and wrists. The man had sat with her before she had showered. He deserved a reward for that.

"Okay, I'm ready." Avery emerged from the bathroom and froze in her spot.

"Ready for what?" Clinton asked with his fists on his hips.

Oh, shit.

Chapter 9

Laz thought he had done a good thing answering Avery's door for her while she showered. When he saw the same man he had seen with Avery in the men's bathroom at Charisma, he knew he had allowed her father entry into Avery's home. The woman with him had to be Avery's mother.

He definitely saw where Avery got her beauty. Her mother carried the same walnut-color skin tone as Avery. Their almond-shaped eyes drew him in but in different ways. With Avery, he wanted to keep staring at her because whether she knew it or not, she seduced him with her stare. With her mother, he felt the disdain she had for him simply because he shared the same oxygen as Avery.

The scowls they carried made it obvious they didn't like him and they really didn't want him in Avery's home. Her father stood next to Avery near the bathroom. Her mother stood behind Laz. They had him surrounded.

Considering Laz had dealt with a music executive who used to place his 9mm gun on the table whenever he made a deal, this standoff shouldn't have made him nervous. With what Avery shared with him, he felt more anxious for her.

When she stood stock still, he knew he had her reaction pegged right. All the scene needed would be a tumbleweed to roll through and a bad spaghetti-western type theme song to play.

"Who is this?" Avery's mother pointed to Laz.

If Laz had a chance of making a good impression, he had to take control of this situation. "My name is Laz Kyson." He held his hand out to her, but she didn't accept it until Avery's father cleared his throat.

The older woman pursed her lips before only offering the tips of her fingers to Laz as her way of shaking his hand. Although she didn't stand as tall as her daughter, the woman still carried an imposing presence.

Laz would accept the standoffish greeting considering what he learned from Avery. By the time he turned back around to Avery and her father, he found Avery guiding her father back into the main living room.

"Mom, Dad, how are you?" Avery tried smiling but her lips twitched. She pointed to her mother while looking at Laz. "Laz, this is my mother, Hazel Shields." Then she turned to her father. "And you've met my father, Clinton, before."

"Oh, so you've met him?" Hazel glared at her husband. Before Clinton could respond, Hazel barreled through with her questions. "You didn't answer me. Who is this, and I don't mean his name. He gave me that already."

"Laz is, um, just a friend." Avery peered up like she wanted him to go along with her story.

Laz prided himself on being a straight shooter. "I work in music." He moved in closer to her parents. "I think your daughter has—"

"Um, I'm not going to church today." Avery tried hard to get her parents to leave short of pushing the duo down the stairs.

"What do you think my child has?" Hazel shrugged out of Avery's hands to get around her and confront Laz again.

"Nothing." Avery tried laughing.

"Is he going on about the music thing again?" Clinton turned to Laz. "Avery is going to school right now. That's her future. Like I've told her before, if she wants to sing, she should come to church." He stared at her.

Before Laz's eyes, he watched Avery shrinking before him. She kept her gaze aimed down to the floor, and had her shoulders slumped and rounded.

He couldn't watch her crumble. "She could sing in church, and should. I could never do that." Laz put his hand to his chest when he heard a collective gasp from her parents. "It's not that I don't go or anything." He glanced at Avery. "I have a problem singing in front of people."

Avery brought her face up to connect with him. He felt warmth and softness from her eyes, although the rest of her face showed that she didn't fully believe him.

"What's the old saying? Those who can, do. Those who can't, teach." He drew his shoulders back. "Avery has a real gift, something you don't run across often. She could be our generation's next Whitney Houston or Adele. She's special."

"We know she's special. She doesn't need the world to acknowledge that for her life to have value." Clinton took a step that placed him in between Laz and Avery. "Now if you'll excuse us—"

"No." Avery spoke up, and it surprised Laz. "Dad, you're not dismissing anyone in my home." She held Laz's hand.

That gesture resulted in a second audible gasp from Hazel.

"So you would rather let this stranger stay in your home than your parents after everything we've done for you?" Clinton directed his attention to Laz. "What are you preparing to offer Avery? Have you presented her a contract at least, or is this some sort of under-the-table kind of thing? You see this young woman and maybe saw an easy target."

Laz started to answer when Avery stepped in.

"Laz, will you wait for me in the living room while I escort my parents out?" She stood at the top of the stairs that led down to the front door. "I hate for you two to be late for church."

"Avery, do you understand what you're doing?" Hazel tried talking low but Laz could still hear her clearly. "You've made mistakes in the past and we can't keep bailing you—"

"Thank you, Mom. I'll be fine." She smiled, but it looked strained. "I won't be able to make it to dinner tonight." She turned to her father. "I'll see you at work tomorrow night, okay?"

Clinton held his daughter's shoulders and moved her aside. He directed his full attention to Laz, who had yet to sit back down and get comfortable. "Avery is our only child." He wagged his finger at her. "She may not have done everything perfectly in life, but we love her. We're not going to ask for forgiveness for being overprotective. And we've seen her make this mistake before. I'm sure it's not a coincidence that she came out of the shower when we got here."

"Dad!" Avery grabbed his arm. "That's enough. I'm sick and tired of being characterized as a problem child when all I've done in the last few years is work and go to school. I deserve some credit. And if you can't do that, I need you two to leave. Now."

She could barely look at her parents as she pointed to her front door. Hazel descended the stairs first, muttering something under her breath on her trek down. Clinton kissed Avery on her cheek, and then glared at Laz before joining his wife.

As soon as the front door closed behind Avery's most important relationship, Avery exhaled. Laz approached her. He didn't know what to do, but standing away from her didn't feel right.

When he opened his arms to embrace her, she held her hand out and tried getting around him.

"No. I'm okay. I'll be okay." Yet she wrapped her arms around her body like she needed to soothe herself.

"Then do it for me. Your parents are tough customers." He wrapped his arms around her and cradled her head against his chest.

Rocking her back and forth and humming came naturally. Laz didn't expect this tough cookie to crumble. When he heard her sniffing, he held her tighter. Her soft body molded against his so easily.

After the extended hug, Avery pulled away from him. "I'm okay." She rubbed her hand under her nose.

"I didn't mean to cause problems between you and your parents." Laz followed her back to the couch. "I heard the knocking and thought I was being helpful by answering."

"Tell me something." Avery sat on the couch facing him. "Did you really mean what you said about not being able to perform in public?"

Laz sighed as he sat down. "Didn't mean to blurt that out, but, yeah, it's true. Unlike you, I did not put on a show for friends and relatives at the Kyson household. But I loved music. I would sing in my bedroom and the shower. My mother heard me and tried getting me into chorus. I think she would have been happy if I started a band. I couldn't. I would get in front of a crowd, go to open my mouth, and freeze." He smiled at her. "You can sing in front of people. You're over half the battle. Now you just need to open your eyes." He tapped his hand against hers. "You have something else on me."

"Yeah? What's that?" She gave him a cutesy but suspicious sideways stare.

"You are a gifted songwriter." He glanced around the room until he spotted the purple spiral notebook. "I read some of your songs while you were taking a shower. They're great." He started to reach for the book when Avery darted to it and snatched it up.

"You had no right to read what's in here." She clutched her baby against her chest.

The way she looked, Laz suspected that Avery would have rather had him find her vibrator than read her lyrics. Being around musicians, he understood that some songs meant the world to them. They poured their lives out in meaningful lyrics. With Avery, she must have stripped herself down in each song.

"Hey, I didn't mean to pry." He made sure to look her in her eyes so that she saw his sincerity. "If I knew it would bother you, I wouldn't have snooped."

"It's more than just songs. It's…" Avery shook her head. "You don't go through a person's life like that. You don't—"

"I get it." He had to corral her back down before she spiraled out of control. "I'm sorry. I don't want to lose your trust before we even get started."

"I'll be back." Avery darted from the room.

Ten seconds later, she returned without her precious notebook and looking lighter and happier. Laz would have to break her out of her shell. Looking at her audience and sharing her art would make her a mega-selling artist.

Baby steps. She didn't kick him out after his unintended intrusion. He would have to tread lightly with her.

Avery smiled. "Are you ready to get to work?" She opened a textbook. "You help me with my breathing technique now, and then tonight, we go back to Honey's."

He smiled back at her. "Sounds like a good plan."

"But my dad made a great point. We do need to talk about that contract."

* * * *

As much as Avery didn't like her parents' intervention earlier, she had to admit that her father brought up a great point about a contract. If she considered being in the music industry as a serious goal, and she truly trusted this man, then she had to think about all aspects in a business-type way. She would no longer be singing for pleasure. Part of that kind of bothered her.

"Okay." He rubbed his hands together. "I need a small scrap of paper."

Avery felt her eyebrows rut together. "Anything?"

"Anything. An old coupon. A chewing gum wrapper. A piece from a notebook page. Doesn't have to be big." He scanned her room.

Avery went into her kitchen and opened up a drawer she used for menus and general items she didn't need visible like pens and chip clips. She pulled out an old menu for a place that no longer existed. Since she didn't know what size Laz needed, she handed him the entire menu.

"Do you still need this?" He held it up to her.

She shook her head. "Long gone. I should have thrown it away months ago."

He tore off a two inch by two inch piece. Then he looked around the room. "Come here." He pointed to a spot between the kitchen and her small dining room area.

Avery stood by him.

"No. This way." He turned her around so that she faced the wall.

Now she felt like a bad student.

"Get a little closer." Laz put his hand on her back and eased her closer to the wall so that she now stood six inches away. He held the paper up on the wall in front of her mouth. "Blow on this to hold it up on the wall. Keep it up there for as long as possible. My personal best is over a minute."

Avery flashed him a suspicious glare.

"This will help with breath control." He looked at the paper, and then back to her. "Ready?"

Avery took a deep breath, filling her lungs as much as possible before she concentrated a stream of her breath on that spot.

Laz let the paper go and stood off to the side. "Nice. Keep going."

She did, blowing on it and watching the scrap of paper waving back and forth as she attempted to keep it in the air. Her chest started to burn and squeeze in the longer she blew.

Laz rested his hand on the wall next to the paper. "Thirty seconds. That's impressive."

Avery didn't want to merely be impressive, not if Laz bragged about doing this for a minute. She continued, trying tactics to try and reserve some air for herself, while keeping that paper airborne. Then she felt his hand on her back.

All thought and reason went out her head. Her neck strained trying not to look at him. If she did, she would have broken her connection with the paper. When she felt his thumb caress her back, she stopped and backed up.

"You're still the winner." She smiled as she tried catching her breath.

Laz managed to catch the paper before it hit the ground. "You weren't competing with me." He held the paper up to her to take. "You need to compete with yourself. Keep trying to best yourself each time you do it. It'll open up your lung capacity and give you the endurance needed for those long notes."

Avery accepted the paper. "Thanks. I will."

Laz backed up to the stairs that went down to the front door. "You keep practicing and studying. I did manage to get a room back at my same hotel. I'll go back there, try to get some work done, and I'll come back later tonight."

Avery nodded. The extra time alone would give her the opportunity to study, practice her breathing exercises, or work on the song she would sing that night.

Laz took one step down with one foot up on the main floor as he held on to the rail. "It's an open mic, so just like last night, you're only going to get one song to knock out the audience. Think about what song you want it to be. I'll see you in a few hours."

Avery still remembered that megawatt smile Laz carried as he walked away. Despite their agreement to keep their relationship professional, she couldn't deny the physical pull she felt whenever she stood near him. She nearly melted when he touched her during the breathing exercise.

In the short time she'd known Laz, he had proven to be a different type of animal. He showed her respect, more than the previous boys and men she had been with in the past, starting from high school.

Laz's cool head also impressed Avery. He could have flown off the handle when Avery's parents went in on him like he could be anything like that idiot she thought had it all together.

Avery wished before her parents had rushed to judgment that they would have had a conversation with him and seen that he had more going on than most young men his age.

For that reason, when Avery got ready that night, she decided to go with something a little more seductive. She knew Laz wouldn't be broken again, but that didn't mean she couldn't have fun teasing him.

Since the weather forecast called for warmer-than-normal temperatures, Avery slipped into a flowered wrap dress that fell right at her knees. She released her shoulder-length hair and gave it soft waves throughout. She kept her makeup light, only applying a sheer lip tint, black eyeliner on her upper lids, and mascara.

With the last swipe of her mascara wand, a knock sounded on her front door. Avery sprayed some light, flowery perfume over her neck, wrists, and the backs of her knees. In her mind, Laz would be smelling that area.

Avery bounded down the stairs to the front door. She took a deep breath before opening it, afraid to find her parents on the other side.

She opened the door and had a huge smile that melted when she saw the person standing there.

"Why aren't you happy to see me?" Graciela scanned Avery up and down. "And why are you all dressed up? Do you have a date?"

Without an invitation, her friend sauntered into the apartment with a bottle of wine in her hand. Avery tried nabbing her before she could make it up the stairs.

"I have plans this evening." Avery followed her friend.

Graciela whipped around to her. "Two nights in a row. Did you meet Mr. Right or something?" Her eyes went wide. "It's that guy from the diner, isn't it? You're seeing him, you lucky devil." She gave Avery a playful slap on her arm.

"I'm not dating, and I'm not seeing that guy." Avery would have to clarify before Laz came over and made her out to be a liar. "Yes, I did talk to that man. His name is Laz."

"Laz? Sounds exotic." Graciela kicked her feet out of her heels and sat on the couch with her legs curled under her. "So are you seeing him tonight or do you have a different man on the hook?" She winked.

"Don't say it like that. Laz is in the music business. He's going to try and help me get into the business."

Graciela cocked her head. "Really? And you believed him?"

Avery rolled her eyes. "Now you sound like my parents. He's been great so far. He's shown me some good breathing techniques to improve my singing. He fixed my car. And you saw how protective he was at the diner."

Graciela sprang to her feet. "You've got that look in your eyes."

Avery snickered. "What look? What are you talking about?"

She shook her head. "Don't fall for it. Keep this at a business level. Good fortune like this only happens in sappy romantic comedies and romance novels. A great guy like that has to have some skeletons in his closet." Graciela held Avery's shoulders and stared into her eyes. "Don't get suckered in by his good looks."

"I'm not." Avery pulled Graciela's hands off her shoulders. "I wish you wouldn't worry so much."

"Maybe you need to worry a bit more. You know the saying. If it's too good to be true…"

A knock sounded on her door. Avery looked down the steps but felt frozen in her spot. She didn't even notice that Graciela had put her shoes back on her feet until her friend started to go down the steps.

"I'll get it." Graciela winked at Avery as she descended.

"Wait." She followed her until she got to the door.

Graciela opened it. "Well, hello." She smiled at Laz, who looked confused at seeing her.

"She was just leaving." Avery pushed Graciela out of the door. "I'll call you."

"I'm sure you will." Graciela looked at Laz. "Nice to see you again." She sauntered to her car.

With the distraction gone, Avery had a chance to really get a good look at Laz.

"Oh." Avery didn't mean for the declaration to come from her mouth, but she couldn't believe how good the man who stood on her front stoop looked.

Laz looked amazing in his jeans, crisp, white button-down shirt, and black jacket. Avery had to pat herself on the back for opting to wear a dress this time instead of jeans. She never thought Laz would outdo her. Here she thought she would be the one to seduce him.

"Something wrong?" Laz peered down at his outfit.

"Uh, no. You look really, *really* good for a coffee shop." She tucked her hair behind one ear.

He smiled. "I can say the same for you. Are you ready?"

"As ready as I'll ever be." She locked and closed the door behind herself.

When she walked with Laz to his car, he got to her door first and opened it. She waited until he got inside to question him.

"Mom or dad?"

Laz faced her and furrowed his eyebrows. "What do you mean?"

"Who taught you to open doors for women? Your mom or your dad?" She smiled as she awaited his answer.

"Believe it or not, it was dear ol' dad." Laz shook his head as he took off. "I wish I could say he did it for all the right reasons."

"What do you mean by that?" Avery placed her purse on her lap.

"Nothing. It's better that you don't know. I don't want you judging me harshly for his actions." He volleyed his attention between the road and Avery. "That woman who left your apartment, why does she look familiar?"

"She's a waitress from Uncle Pig's Diner. She was there that day you, um, straightened out Uncle Pig." Avery cocked her head at the statement.

"Oh, yeah. She was the one who told me where to find you."

So Graciela didn't mind Laz associating with Avery. When it came to business, her friend wanted Avery to have a careful eye on him.

Laz pulled out of the parking lot to head to their destination. "So what song are you doing tonight?"

"You don't want to be surprised?" She chewed on her lower lip.

Laz shook his head. "I don't do well with surprises. I'd rather know things upfront."

"Yep. Total control freak." She nodded. "You might be right about that seeing how I want you on stage with me."

He nearly slammed his foot on the brake. "What?"

"You don't have to sing. I need someone to play piano. I don't mind singing a cappella again. But it would be nice to have someone up there with me." She turned to the side to face him. "What do you say?"

She noticed right away how Laz's breathing increased. If he kept going, she had no doubt that he would hyperventilate. She wanted to push him as much as he had pushed her, but not at the expense of his sanity or health.

"You know what? That's okay. I know you have to record me singing anyway, right?" Letting him off the hook seemed to calm him down.

Laz's breathing slowed down a bit until he finally took a deep breath at a stoplight. "I would ruin your moment on stage. I would freeze and make people pay attention to me instead of you. I don't want the focus to ever come off you."

That reasoning sounded good, but Avery knew the truth. She didn't know that he would have such a strong reaction to the idea of performing in public.

"May I do something?" Avery sat up taller.

"Depends." He glanced at her.

"May I hold your hand for a while? I'm a little nervous. I feel like a lot is riding on this one performance. The vibe tonight is different than last night." Avery wrung her hands together while she awaited Laz's answer.

What he didn't say verbally, he made up for with his actions. He held his hand up for her and waited for her to grasp it. When she did with both hands, she rested them on her thigh.

"I don't get it. What's different now?" Avery rubbed one hand over the back of his.

"You want it this time so it's important to you." He squeezed her hand. "All of those other times, you were having fun. Now it's become a real goal. And you have someone who believes in you and is supporting you 100 percent." He smiled.

That smile calmed her racing heart. Too bad her stomach still churned.

"Speaking of goals, have you ever thought about which label you would want to sign with?" Laz rubbed his large thumb over her knuckles.

Damn if that didn't feel good.

"Absolutely. That's the one thing that's crystal clear in my head. Charisma." She nodded emphatically. "Shauna Stellar is such an inspiration for someone like me."

"Chantel Woodley," Laz said, quickly correcting her.

"I'm very old school. I was there for her first CD. I remember saving up my money and begging my parents to take me to the store to get it. I wore it out playing it so much that I've had to buy at least two back-up copies. I still listen to it to this day. Now her voice is flawless." Just talking about the Princess of Love Ballads had Avery's heart skipping its own beat.

She practically worshipped Shauna, or Chantel. Chantel started off dirt poor like Avery. From hard work, she made a great name for herself. Avery envisioned a career path like that. Of course, Avery made her musical start about ten years too late. By Avery's age now, Chantel had had her nervous breakdown along with diamond-selling hits.

"I felt the same way about her when I fought for her to remain at Universe." Laz shook his head. "My boss wouldn't listen to me or her. They let her go."

Avery let that story process in her head. When Chantel needed an advocate, Laz had been there for her, but it still didn't help. Would it be the same for Avery? When the going got tough, would he simply give up?

"That's the other label I would want to go to. Universe puts out a lot of great female singers. They were the first to sign Chantel. And they have Kat, who—"

"No." Laz shook his head. "That's not the right label for you. You can do better. Trust me."

"But they have star power and plenty of cash to—"

"No. You're not going to them. Over my dead body." He pulled his hand away from hers to put it on the steering wheel.

She took the move to mean he would pull his support for her if she pushed this. His reaction seemed deep rooted in something that went beyond how the company did business. From the way his jaw flexed, he hated the organization.

"What's wrong with Universe?" She had to know why her future manager limited her options.

Laz pulled into Honey's parking lot and parked at the back row. When he turned the car off, he turned his full body to her to answer the question. "Universe does have plenty of money. With that money, they'll use it to control you. They'll make you sing songs you may not like. You write your own songs."

Hesitant to speak, Avery nodded.

"Keep them to yourself. If the songs are good, they may want to let someone like Kat sing them, and they'll let you do covers." He reached his hand up and stroked his fingertips down the side of her face. "You're beautiful."

His touch raised the hairs on her body. She sighed and trembled at the same time.

"They would make you put on a pile of makeup and outfits that showed off your body. I have a feeling you wouldn't like that. I know your parents wouldn't like to see their baby girl in fishnets and bright red lipstick." Laz cradled her chin. "You're too good to sink down to their level. I have a better plan for you. Do you trust me?"

Staring into his eyes, even in the darkened parking lot, she saw Laz's soul. He meant every word he'd said. She nodded in agreement.

"Good." He unhooked his seatbelt. "Now, what song are you doing? You never told me."

Avery found she liked teasing Laz. "You'll see when we get inside."

She heard him growling as he opened her car door and escorted her up to the building. As soon as he opened the door, Avery wanted to run away. For one, the person singing on stage could not find the right pitch even if it landed on top of his head. Second, her fear and nervousness returned.

Like she had done it a million times before, she grabbed Laz's hand as she scanned the place, looking for an empty table. She spotted one in the back toward the center.

Laz must have seen it, too. He walked her to it and sat down.

"Avery and her manager." Dot bounded to the duo. She rested her fisted hands on the tabletop as she bounced her attention from one to the other. "I was really hoping you were going to come back."

"Wouldn't miss this for the world." Avery hoped no one heard her voice trembling. From the way Laz looked at her after she spoke and how Dot's smile started to fade, she had a feeling they had caught it.

"I'll send a waitress over so you can get something to eat or drink. If you knock it out of the park tonight like you did last night, your food and beverages will be on me." Dot's big smile returned.

"Speaking of waitress, are you looking for any?" Avery sat up taller.

"She's kidding." Laz laughed to support his claim.

"No, I'm not. I just lost my waitressing job." She would leave out the fact that Laz caused her to get fired. "I'm looking for other work."

"And by that, she means the steady gig you were talking about last night, not a waitressing spot." Laz grabbed Avery's hand and pressed it down on the table like he wanted to quiet her.

No. She still had a life and bills.

"I mean both. Until this singing thing takes off, I need to find a job. I go to school in the daytime, but my early evenings are free. I work as a janitor overnight."

The more she spoke, the more Laz squeezed her hand.

"As a matter of fact, I am shorthanded. After you do your song, come see me." Dot winked and walked over to the bar area.

"I wished you wouldn't have done that." Laz released her hand.

"Why? You know I need the work." She crossed her arms over her chest. "It's called paying your dues."

"You are too good to be waitressing again."

"But I'm okay cleaning toilets, right?" She cocked her head.

"No." He looked at her. "I'm saying you shouldn't be doing any of that anymore."

"So you want me to be a homeless singer?" She chuckled.

"No. I want you to realize your worth. You are exceptional." Laz stared at her.

Avery couldn't stop looking at him until she heard someone clearing their throat. The sound got her attention.

A waitress stood on the other side of the table from them. "Welcome to Honey's. Would you like something to drink or eat?" She pointed to menus at the center of the table.

"Chamomile tea." Laz rubbed his forehead.

"I'll have a caramel latte, please." Avery would need something to perk her up.

Right now Laz had her wound up in both a good way and scary way. He saw her like no one had ever envisioned her. With him, she felt perfect.

Like Graciela had said, he had to be too good to be true. She hadn't encountered a man like him before. At some point, the other shoe would have to drop. For her, it always did.

"Still not going to tell me your song?" Laz rested his hand on the back of her chair.

Avery felt the heat permeating from his skin. To experience more, she leaned against the back of the chair. "Will you be recording me?"

"Of course."

The waitress returned with their drinks. Avery pursed her lips and blew her breath over the steamy beverage before taking a needed sip.

"Good. If I see a kind face in the audience, it'll help me with keeping my eyes open." She set her drink down, but kept her hands wrapped around the mug.

"That's it?" He shrugged.

"I gave you a big hint about the song." She tried not smiling before taking a second sip, but she couldn't help herself.

"What did I tell you about surprises?" He raised his eyebrow. "By the way, I noticed you didn't take the video down like I had asked. I checked it out. It's gotten fifty thousand views so far."

Avery stared at him without speaking to get his impression for the response. She knew he didn't like her loading the video.

He shrugged. "For an unknown, that's excellent." Then he sipped his tea.

Avery's mouth hung open. "Are you serious? Fifty thousand people listened to me sing? That's amazing."

"That still doesn't mean that I approve of what you did."

"But it looks like it wasn't a bad thing either. This could work in our favor." She patted the back of his hand and hoped he would get on board with her.

"Aren't you afraid that your parents are going to see that video and call you on it?"

Avery had considered that situation. She smiled. "I doubt they'll see it. For one thing, my parents aren't big into YouTube unless they're searching for gospel videos. Also, I loaded the video under a different account."

"I did notice that. A Very Good Day. Clever." He snickered. "But I did notice one problem with your video."

Her eyebrows drew together. "What's that?"

"You cited me as your manager in the description." His lids appeared heavy.

In the dim light of the place, the expression made him look even sexier.

"Is there something wrong with that?" She sat up taller and leaned in closer to him.

"Until you sign the contract, I'm not really your manager yet, now am I?" He patted his jacket pocket. "I do have a copy of it."

"After this. My second performance might not excite you."

Laz rested his hand close to hers on the table. "I sincerely doubt that. Everything about you…" As soon as he looked into her eyes, he lost his thoughts.

Avery exhaled and slid her hand back away from his before picking up her mug. "Things are rolling along."

He held up his mug. "Let's hope for success."

She picked up her mug and clinked it against his. "Cheers."

When Avery's turn came up for her to sing, the wild birds of prey returned to her stomach. She leaned over to Laz. "Tell me something. Anything. I'm ready to run out the door right now."

Laz held her hand. "You can do this. You're talented. You're brave. I'm here for you. You keep your eyes on me."

She smiled when he said that. "I had planned on doing that." She winked and stood. "Record me, okay?"

Laz took out his phone. "On it."

Avery sauntered to the stage. When she got behind the microphone, she tapped it a couple of times to make sure it worked. When she heard the thumping sounds through the speakers, she nodded.

"Hi." Her voice squeaked. She cleared her throat and tried again. "Hi. My name is Avery Sh—"

From the back of the room, she heard Laz coughing loud enough that she got the hint.

"Avery." She took the queue to keep it simple. "Tonight I'm going to sing Roberta Flack's 'The First Time Ever I Saw Your Face.' That's been a favorite of mine for years."

Recorded music started behind her and it startled her. Avery jumped and missed her spot to start singing.

She waved her hand in the air. "Will you cut the music? I'll do it without." She didn't like the diva move, but she had practiced this at her apartment after Laz left. She knew exactly what to do.

Avery started singing and feeling each word. It didn't take her long to realize she had closed her eyes. So she quickly opened them. Through the dark, she found Laz. She spotted his hypnotic eyes. The strength in his stare forced her to keep her eyes open. She didn't want to miss a moment of having him hear every word.

The longer she sang, the more her knees knocked together. At one point, she thought she would forget the words, which for a singer, would have been death, especially a singer ballsy enough to sing without a musical accompaniment.

At the end of the song, Avery felt wrung out. Her auxiliary power came from the uproarious shouts and screams from the diners in the restaurant. A few people stood. Laz, who had been standing the entire time, beamed from ear to ear.

Avery leaned into the microphone. "Thank you."

She rushed back to the table where Laz embraced her so hard she felt breathless in the very best way. She wrapped her arms around his broad shoulders and held on to him for dear life.

"I'm so glad you left that as a surprise." Laz rubbed his hand up and down her back. "That was a hell of a song to sing." He kissed her forehead.

"And I sang it to you," she whispered in his ear.

"I heard every note. I couldn't stop looking in your eyes." His warm breath feathered over her face when he whispered in her ear.

At one point, it felt like his lips brushed the shell of her ear. Her insides already felt like lava while she sang the song to him. The longer he held her and the more she felt his heart beating against her chest, the more her resolve melted.

She didn't feel impulsive. Touching him, tasting him, having him felt natural, like the next logical step.

"I'm ready to go home now." Avery's heart drummed just as hard in her chest.

Laz set her down. "Are you okay? Do you need to sit down? You want some water?" He scanned around the place like he wanted to locate a waitress.

"I feel fine." She held Laz's hand. When he brought his attention back to her, she reiterated her statement. "I'm ready for *us* to go."

Laz didn't question her. She didn't even bother to stop to talk to Dot about the job or potential singing gigs. Avery wanted to get back to her apartment. Now.

Laz placed money on the table and held Avery's hand as they marched out of the place. As soon as they got in the car, they raced home in silence.

Avery felt both euphoric and still a bit scared. She glanced over at Laz, who kept his stare on the road until he reached Avery's apartment complex. Instead of putting the car in park and walking her to her door, he parked it and turned off the car. Then he opened her car door and escorted her to her apartment.

Even their trek to her door remained quiet. As soon as she unlocked her door, she finally heard Laz.

"You drive me crazy with your voice." He chuckled until he made eye contact. "And you looked beautiful up there." He leaned forward and nuzzled his nose against her neck. "And you smell delicious."

Avery closed her eyes and enjoyed his touch. She stroked the back of his head before he pulled back from her.

"I should go back to my hotel room." He had his hands braced on the doorframe. "I should tell you good night and go. I shouldn't be thinking what I'm thinking about right now." He stared at her. "Tell me good night. Tell me to go."

Avery peered up at him. "I can't. I want you." She licked her lips before finally shaking her head. "I want you to stay."

Chapter 10

Laz released the doorframe, backed up for a second before charging toward Avery. "Shit."

He pressed his lips against hers so hard she now needed him for air. He broke from the kiss long enough to close and lock the door behind him.

When Avery started to walk up the stairs, he stopped her and scooped his hands under her backside so that she had to wrap her legs around him. He carried her up the stairs so fast that she didn't recall the trek.

At the top landing, Laz pressed Avery against a wall. Even as he smothered her in kisses, she worked on taking off his jacket. Then she worked on his shirt. She had to restrain herself from pulling it open and making his buttons fly all over the place.

"Bedroom." Avery nibbled on Laz's ear.

Although she wanted him right there and then, the protection she needed for them both awaited her in that room.

As soon as she gained footing, Avery held Laz's hand and walked toward the place where she would experience feeling free again, free of responsibilities, free of judgment, free to be herself. She stopped when she felt a tug on her hand. When she looked back, she found Laz looking conflicted.

The bulge in his pants showed he wanted her, but his stare down to the floor let her know his head remained in business. For that reason, she desired him even more.

"I know." She moved in closer to him and put her hand to the side of his face.

"I don't do—"

"I know." She nodded.

"I pride myself on being—"

"Professional." She kissed his cheek. "Tonight, let's forget about the manager and the singer." She pulled back and didn't speak until she gained eye contact with him again. "It's Avery and Lazarus, okay? It's just us." She waved her hand between their bodies. "I want you." She finished undoing the buttons on his shirt.

"Protection." Laz nearly growled the word.

Avery smiled. "Bedroom. Now."

While she walked backward toward her room, he followed her as he undid the buttons on his cuffs. He removed his shirt, revealing the chest she had admired before. Avery couldn't help but reach out and touch him, run her fingertips over his taut flesh. While she circled one of his pebbled nipples with her fingers, she latched on to his other with her mouth. Her tongue circled it. She liked feeling it get a bit harder the more she manipulated him.

He reacted the way she thought he would, the way she wanted him to respond. He growled first before pulling back from her and smothering her in a soul-releasing kiss. When he cradled the back of her head, she felt protected, wanted, needed. Plus, she liked that this man saw her as a sexy woman, not a conquest or an experience. She, for damn sure, viewed Laz as a man. Could he be her man, though?

Avery felt Laz moving from side to side. When she stopped teasing him for a moment to look down, she noticed that he had toed off his shoes. Not content to let him undress himself, she put herself to work undoing his jeans.

That action prompted him to pull the tie on her dress. As soon as she undid the button fly and pulled down the zipper, she let him go long enough so he could remove her dress completely.

Laz scanned her body. "Beautiful." He nodded before reaching behind her with one hand and undoing the clasp of her bra.

The man had skills. Avery curved her shoulders forward to slip the undergarment down. Then she waited a beat before making eye contact with Laz again. She had to blink when she caught him staring back at her and not keeping his full attention on her naked breasts.

For that, she wrapped her arms around his shoulders and pressed her nipples against his chest as she kissed him. He slipped his hands down her back to her ass. Then he eased both hands down her panties to grip her cheeks.

This time Avery had to moan. Laz had her in the palms of his hands, and she liked it.

"Condoms. Where are they?" He kissed the side of her face and moved down to her shoulder to nip it.

Before answering, Avery pushed his jeans down his legs. She had to see him, all of him. She dropped her gaze long enough to be impressed by the sight. His jutting penis looked long and thick. She wrapped her hand around it, which made him grab her wrist.

"Condoms." The desperation in his eyes couldn't be denied.

She let him go. "Sit."

Laz removed his jeans completely and sat on the edge of her bed looking like *The Thinker* statue except he kept fully engaged with her.

Avery removed an unopened box of condoms from her nightstand. As casually as she could, she scanned the expiration date at the bottom of the box. She'd purchased them as soon as she moved into her apartment, thinking that she would live freely now that she didn't have to be under her parents' thumbs. She chose to stay away from men…until now.

After verifying that she still had another year before she would have to replace her stash, she tore open the box and pulled out a string of condoms. When she felt Laz palming her ass again and massaging it, her hands shook, not out of nervousness. She wanted this man so badly.

"You want me to do that?" He pointed to her hands.

She shook her head. "I got you."

Avery dropped down to her knees in between his legs. Staring at the length of him with a nest of light brown hair at the base and a bead of pre-cum at his tip, her mouth watered. She could only imagine pleasuring this man in every way possible. She would get what she could for now.

After opening the package, she rolled the thin plastic over the length of him. The farther down she went, the straighter his posture became. It took her no time to climb onto his lap, straddling him as she gripped his shoulders.

While keeping his stare on her, Laz skillfully aimed himself at her core. She impaled herself on him and didn't exhale until fully seated.

Like she needed the assistance, Laz swept her legs around his waist and cradled her backside in his hands. Avery's body took over and she started to undulate her hips, but stopped suddenly.

"Wait." She coiled her legs around his waist. "Wait." She shook her head. "Never happens. Not like this. Not this fast." She gripped his shoulders as her stomach tightened into a ball.

Avery didn't mean to curse, but since everything else in her body had gone out of control, she shouldn't have been surprised that some profanity made its way out of her.

"Let it go." Laz kissed her shoulder. He thrust his hips ever so slowly. "It's okay." He dragged his lips to her neck. When he reached her ear, he whispered, "Come."

As though he commanded it, Avery's body trembled. Her intimate inner walls constricted around his shaft, and she released a long, low moan. Until she relaxed her hands when her body came down from its high did she realize that she had embedded her fingernails into Laz's shoulders.

"I'm sorry. I'm sorry. I'm sorry." She rested her head on his shoulder and licked the spots where she had left her mark.

"Why are you apologizing?" Laz eased her back, and then framed her face so that she could make eye contact with him, which she reluctantly did.

"I didn't mean to hurt you." She coasted her thumbs over the indented spots on his shoulders.

He shook his head. "You didn't."

"And I didn't want to be the first." She hoped he understood what she didn't say out loud.

Laz smiled. "For you, it's way better than coming last." Then he winked. "Don't ever apologize for feeling how you feel."

Avery leaned her head back. "Oh, God, you have no idea how good looking you are."

The statement got him to laugh.

His laughter pushed her to move faster. She ground herself down on him harder and gyrated her hips faster.

"You have me all night." He kissed her. "I'm here for you."

Even hearing that didn't stop Avery. She hadn't touched a man like this in a long time. She wouldn't waste the opportunity.

Avery hovered over the crest of another climax. This man had no idea of the power he possessed. Not only could he jumpstart her fantasy career, but he did a hell of a job reminding Avery that the fire inside of her hadn't been doused yet.

After her second and most explosive orgasm, Laz didn't give her a chance to catch her breath before he stood with her still on him and placed her on her back on the bed.

"Let me drive." He smiled as he gave her long, easy strokes that made her feel both relaxed and wound up at the same time.

She coiled her legs around his legs and curved her hips up to meet each one of his strokes. Laz moaned after she repositioned herself. She felt her body vibrate when he made the sound.

Just like she had done on stage, Avery stared at Laz in his eyes. She stroked his hair, damp with sweat, but still felt so good under her fingers.

"You are so big." Avery wanted to put her hand over her mouth over that admission, but she couldn't help what came out of her head.

Laz didn't smile, didn't laugh, didn't even smirk. He kept his stare on her and kept his thrusts even, hard, and deep.

"This isn't real." Avery shook her head. "I'm going to wake up and you won't be here. I'll still be working at Uncle Pig's and struggling in school."

Instead of verbally answering her, Laz leaned down and brushed his lips over hers. Then he swept his tongue over her lips, the top one first before swiping her lower lip. With his tongue still out, he plunged it into her mouth.

Laz didn't taste like bitter tea like she thought he would. He had a minty flavor to him like he must have popped a mint in his mouth before getting her back to her apartment.

He pulled back from the kiss. "Touch me." He nodded. "Put your hands on my chest like this." To illustrate, he cupped her breast and massaged it.

Avery put her hand to his chest and swept her fingers down to his nipple. As though mimicking her movements, Laz circled his large thumb around her nipple. The feeling had her arching her back and wishing the moment would never end.

Now feeling emboldened, she coasted her hands down to his ass. As she suspected, his firm cheeks barely moved when she squeezed them.

"I'm real. This is real." He nodded. "I want you. Damn, I need you."

Relief swept over Avery and she smiled when he made his statement. Then a small voice of doubt crept in her head. What if the sex had everything to do with getting her as a client rather than starting a real relationship with her? What if she put too much stock into this act than she should have? Maybe she should look at this moment as just that, a moment, an experience. Laz Kyson could probably get any woman he wanted. Why would he bother with a broke student?

Laz kissed her hard as though he wanted to banish the thoughts in her head that, this time, she hadn't made audible. Then he slipped out of her and moved behind her. After easing his arm under her and sweeping her leg over his, he reentered her again from behind.

When he groaned, she gasped and reached back to grab a fistful of his hair. He held her shoulder while kissing the back of her neck and cheek. He used his other hand to hold her hip steady.

When he must have realized that she wouldn't be going anywhere, especially after she pushed her ass back against him, he reached around and slid her clitoris between his index and middle fingers.

"Oh my God." Avery gripped his hand that held her breast. Before she could stop herself, she came again. "You are incredible."

"You're not so bad yourself." Laz breathed heavily in her ear.

The man didn't stop. Laz kept up his thrusting for what seemed like an eternity, and Avery didn't mind. If he wanted to keep having sex with her and treat it like a job, she would let him. He felt incredible inside of her, and he made her feel like he couldn't do without her.

Sweat coated both of their bodies. Even with the air conditioner on, Avery could have used some more cool air. Maybe Laz could take her from behind in front of an open freezer door.

"Close."

Avery barely heard the word Laz growled in her ear, but she felt his leg shaking. Then he cursed in her ear. Before she knew it, he pulled out of her long enough to roll her back on her back and ease in between her thighs.

While keeping his stare on her eyes, Laz pumped harder and faster. From the way he gazed at her, Avery thought he wanted to say something. In her head, she imagined he wanted to bare more of his soul.

She held on to his arms and remained open to him. Just doing that tipped him over the edge. Laz came hard, grunting and pushing himself inside her until it felt like he had fused himself into her body.

When he collapsed on top of her, she held him tight. She didn't care that the heft of his body limited her air supply. She needed this man. She didn't realize how much she needed this experience until she looked into the man's eyes across a crowded room and experienced a connection she had never felt before. Now she wondered if this would last. What will happen now?

Chapter 11

Laz had made a colossal mistake, and this time it had nothing to do with business. His old self crept into his head, the side of himself that his father had influenced. He could hear Bradley telling him to get his clothes on, get his stuff together, and go, leave this woman and to never look back. Clean break. Laz couldn't do that.

Despite holding this gorgeous woman in his arms after such a wonderful evening, it couldn't eliminate the guilt Laz still felt. When Avery sang that incredible song, seemingly right to him, emotions stirred inside him that he hadn't experienced in a long time.

The song combined with the woman herself had Laz weakening his resolve. Even though he fought against having a physical relationship with a person who could be his first client, Laz could no longer deny the feelings he had since first seeing her.

Leaving her wouldn't happen, shouldn't happen. That wouldn't take away the fact that Avery would have some expectations after this.

Avery stirred a little in his arms, but remained sleeping. Good. Laz still needed to process what all had happened and his next steps. When her ass brushed against his dormant penis, the motion ignited some lustful feelings again.

He looked over her body to the other side of the bed and spotted the box of condoms. He could slip out of bed and get them, but he didn't want to jostle her. He did want to do something he didn't get to do last night. If Avery woke up and decided that what she had done with him had been a huge mistake, he wanted to make sure to do everything he wanted to do before getting kicked out of her home.

Laz slid his arm from under her body first. Again, Avery stirred and moaned a little, but remained sleeping. He positioned himself on top of her body, and kept his upper body propped up over hers.

"Hey." He kissed her forehead and the tip of her nose.

Avery moaned again and moved her head back and forth. He admired her body, something he couldn't do last night. Her round breasts sat up high with chocolate-chip tips topping them.

He kissed her shoulders, going from one side to the other, eliciting another round of moans and writhing from Avery. He moved his mouth down between her breasts. No way could he skip these succulent mounds.

Laz massaged one breast. "Good morning."

Avery took in a deep breath and exhaled through her nose, but didn't speak, didn't open her eyes.

He latched his mouth on to her other breast and circled his tongue around her nipple, making it hard. It reminded Laz when Avery pressed her breasts against him. She still smelled of a flowery soap aroma even though they had done a whole lot of sweating.

Thinking about Avery's enthusiasm had him getting hard again. If she wanted to go another round, he would be up for a quickie session.

Laz moved over to her other breast and sucked and licked it while he massaged the one he had just laved.

"Mmm, Laz." Avery smiled, but still kept her eyes closed.

Good to know that she thought of him when she dreamed of something sexy.

"Are you going to wake up?" Laz licked her soft skin down her midsection to her stomach.

He kissed across her lower abdomen, right above her cleanly shaven vagina. Laz pushed her legs apart, but he wouldn't go any further until Avery acknowledged him.

"Avery." He massaged her inner thighs. "Come on." He kissed the soft flesh. "Open your eyes."

When he nibbled her skin, Avery finally moaned and opened her eyes. She peered down and smiled. "Not a dream."

Laz shook his head and parted her labia. When Avery spread her legs wider, he took that to mean he could keep going. He took one long, slow swipe from the base of her pussy to her clit.

"Oh, God." Avery arched her back and drew her feet back. "So good."

Laz used the tip of his tongue to circle her hardened nub, now getting hard the more he teased her. She tasted exactly like he imagined, like salted honey. He could drown in her essence and die a happy man.

When he felt her legs crowding around his head, he knew she liked his technique. When she gripped his hair, he knew she wanted more. He continued licking her and diving his tongue inside her as far as he could.

"Laz. Laz. Laz." Her body trembled. "Yes. Yes!" She bolted straight up while holding the back of his head.

He didn't need the encouragement to stay. He wanted to get her off in as many ways as possible before the glow of the euphoria wore off and sobered them both to their situations.

As soon as she settled against the bed, she blurted, "Inside. I need you inside me now."

Laz didn't need to hear anything else. He sat up on his knees and reached over to the nightstand for the condoms. As soon as he sheathed himself, Avery got on her knees and grabbed his shoulders.

"On your back." She nudged him back.

"Yes, ma'am." He smiled as he got on his back.

Avery straddled him while holding the base of his shaft. When she eased him inside of her tight channel, Laz gripped her hips.

"That's it." Laz nodded.

She rested her hands on his chest. "What a way to wake up." Avery smiled. "I could get used to this."

So could Laz. While he had his cock inside her, he had to think about the implications of trying to work with her and start a relationship, because at this point, he couldn't turn back.

Avery leaned forward and planted a kiss on him. He wrapped his arms around her and held her against his body. This feeling, this life, he wanted all of it to last.

Laz met her gyrations with his thrusts until they both came.

"Oh." Avery kissed him and smiled. "Perfect." Then she glanced to the side and her eyes went wide. "Oh, shit!" She hopped out of bed.

For a brief moment, Laz suspected that Avery came to the conclusion that she had made a mistake sleeping with him.

"I'm late for class." Avery's completely nude body captured his full attention.

He sighed in relief. "I haven't heard that line after sex since college." He slid to the edge of the bed. "I meant what I said."

Avery stopped at the bedroom door and looked back at him. "Which part? You've said a lot since I've met you." She winked before ducking into the bathroom.

Laz snatched up his underwear from the floor and stepped into them as he headed to the bathroom. As much as he wanted to join Avery in the shower, he would refrain. Besides, he liked smelling her essence on him. He could wait to go back to his hotel room to shower and change.

He got to the bathroom door by the time Avery hopped into the shower and pulled the curtain covered in musical notes closed. He still saw her amazing body through the clear plastic.

"I don't sleep with people I work with." He leaned against the doorframe. "For that reason—"

"You don't want to represent me anymore?" She stared at him as she bent over to turn on the water. She waited until he answered.

"Of course I still want to represent you. I believe in your talent." He exhaled when he saw her smile and finally turn on the water. In order to speak to her seriously, though, he had to stop watching her running her hands up and down her naked form.

Damn, he had a point to make.

"So what's the problem?" She raised her voice over the rushing water to speak to him.

"If you want me to manage you, we need to not have sex again. I'm going to do everything I can to get you into the music industry. The next thing we need to talk about is a contract." He ran his hand over his hair and felt the messiness of it.

"You said you had a copy with you." She slathered soap over her arms, chest, stomach, and down her legs.

"In the car. So you're serious about moving on to the next step?" He had to make sure he didn't waste his time or hers.

"Yes." She rinsed off her body.

"Even if your parents don't approve?" He could tell from Avery's reaction when her parents showed up at her apartment that she couldn't tell them about her dreams.

He didn't want that to hold her back. She would be out in the public eye. If she needed their support, she had to get that now.

"I'm an adult." Avery turned her back on the streaming water. "They'll have to accept my decision."

"And you understand that our physical relationship would have to stop?"

Avery glanced at him. Through the wavy plastic curtain, it looked like she nodded her head.

Laz accepted her answer and wouldn't push it. As long as she had the passion, he could take over the world with her. Right now, Avery put on an unexpected sexy show. Her foamy, soap-covered hand slid down to her pussy and slid over her nether lips.

Every cell in Laz's body wanted to join her in the shower and have her, taste her, again. As he took a step toward her, he heard his phone ringing from the bedroom. He darted from the doorway and scrambled to find his discarded jeans. Once he did, he fished his phone from the pocket.

Ordinarily, he didn't answer calls from an unknown caller. He had a good feeling about this.

"Hello." He sat on the bed.

"Uh, yeah. Mr. Kyson, we need to talk."

A shiver went up the back of Laz's neck. As a result of recognizing the voice on the other line, he sat up taller. "Ms. Farook. Good to hear from you again."

She sounded as distracted as when he had met her in person. "Come to my office today."

Like she could see him, Laz stood. Now that he had a company on the hook, he still had to come off like he had control. "Tomorrow. My agenda is pretty full today."

Sanaa didn't have to know that he had to pack up his belongings at the hotel and hightail it back to New York.

"Already keeping me waiting." Her clipped tone let Laz know she had zero interest in dealing with him. "Not a good look for you."

He also figured out that word must have gotten out about Avery. He would have to play this cool.

"You know how the business works. Things move fast when you're talking about a hot commodity." Laz started pacing.

He figured Avery's video would cause some buzz. Not exactly the way he wanted her career to start, but if it got one of the biggest fish in the music ocean to bite so soon, he wouldn't fault the method.

This untimely call also gave him an easy way out of this situation to give him some time to think. He still wanted to represent Avery. Sex complicated everything. Always did.

He glanced up and looked at the wall that separated the bedroom and the bathroom where Avery showered. Her singing voice got his attention in a matter of seconds. Avery could snag the world's attention.

"Be in my office first thing in the morning. We have some things to discuss." Sanaa disconnected the call before Laz could agree or disagree.

Even though he wanted to pace this meeting his way, he couldn't assert himself but so much. Sanaa had the power. He held the key to the talent.

Laz heard the shower stop. To keep his mind off the vision of Avery drying her naked body, he got dressed. By the time he slipped his feet into his shoes, Avery appeared in the bedroom with a towel around her body.

"If you don't want to stay in your hotel room, you can stay here with me."

Laz could tell she tried playing this off like it didn't matter. She kept her back to him, but as she spoke, Avery stole little glances.

She dropped her towel long enough to slip on some underwear and a bra, then shimmy into a long maxi dress. "It's not a huge place, as you can see, but it's clean and quiet." Then she gave him a nonplussed shrug. "Plus you can be here to help me with my homework. I'm really struggling in my statistics class. And you can help me with my breathing technique. Did I do better with it last night?"

Shit. This wouldn't be easy. He ran his hand over his hair again before he approached her.

"I know I'm hitting you with a lot of stuff right now." She slid a headband on to control her wild curls. "Let's get back to you staying here. I'm not here during the day, so I wouldn't get in your way." Avery slid her feet into some well-worn, black and white flip flops.

"If you're not here, what's the use of me being here?" He smiled. Being charming would ease this blow. "I appreciate the offer. That's extremely kind of you. But I have to go."

The smile slipped down Avery's face. "Oh." She nodded. "I see."

Laz felt her pulling away. From the way her jaw flexed, he knew she didn't like his statement.

"Guess it was fun while it lasted." She kept her back to him while she hoisted her bag on her shoulder.

No way could he let her leave with the wrong assumption. Laz held on to Avery's shoulders and didn't speak until she made eye contact with him.

When she finally peered up, he spoke. "I have to go back home to New York for a meeting." Laz squeezed her shoulders.

Avery snickered. "A meeting. Is that what the kids are calling it now?"

Laz blinked at her statement. "I want you to come with me, but I know you have school and work this week."

She put her hand to his chest and pushed him back. "I get it. We both got caught up in a moment. It's okay. I'm learning to stop feeling so guilty for being selfish."

Before she could pull her hand away, Laz captured it and pressed it against his chest again over his heart. "Look at me."

He hoped she didn't take his statement this time as being something sexual. Laz wanted Avery to see him, see into his soul like the way she had when she sang last night.

Avery huffed and shuffled in her spot. "I have to go."

This time Laz framed her face in his hands and planted a soft kiss on her lips. When he pulled back, he stared into her eyes. "Me leaving is not the end of us, okay?"

She shook her head. "There is no—"

Laz wouldn't allow her to finish that statement. He barreled on in hopes that she would understand him and his actions. "This is your last week before spring break, right?"

After a beat, Avery nodded.

"I'll be back here Saturday morning to come get you." He thought about leaving money for her to get a plane ticket, but the gesture would look like he paid for sex. He wouldn't give her that impression. "I want you packed and ready to go with me for a few days. Will you do that?"

Avery held one of his hands he still had next to her face. "You don't have to lie to me. I told you. We got caught up in a moment and were very adult last night." She pulled away from him. "You don't have to say anything else. You are an exceptional lover."

"I'm an even better manager." He followed her in the cramped apartment. "I want you to forget about what we did last night, and I want you to remember what I really came here to do."

"Which is?" Avery completed the question with a hand on her hip.

"To make you a singing sensation."

She snickered. "I hate having to admit my father and friend were right in anything."

Laz caught up to her when she reached her front door. "Will you stop sounding so defeated, especially when there's no reason for it?" Before she could open the door, he spun her around and pressed her back against it. "I need to go back home to, hopefully, secure something for you." He pressed the tip of his finger against her chest. "Things are starting to happen, which is a good thing. Right now, I need to get to work, and you need to get to school." He wrapped his arm around her waist and pulled her forward, pressing her body against his. "I have your number. I'll call if there are any changes. You have my phone number. Call or text me anytime. The next time we see each other, we'll be mapping out your future, okay?"

Avery studied him for a while before she opened her door and held it open. "This was fun while it lasted, but I have real life to get back to, and you have some other starlet to meet." She shook her head. "I'm not the one."

No way. No way could Laz get this close to perfection and have her dismiss him. "Avery, we have to—"

"Just leave while I still have my dignity." She kept her stare down to the floor.

Laz wanted her to do more than just stare at his feet as he stood in front of her. "I'm not giving up on you. Don't turn your back on this opportunity."

At that statement, Avery looked up and finally smiled. She placed her hand to the side of his face. The softness of her skin had him thinking about their lusty night together and the way she touched him.

With a smile, she said, "I'm not giving up on this opportunity. I'm giving up on dreaming."

Avery's face became serious and she took a determined step back as she nodded out the door. It didn't help that she had her backpack on her shoulder and looked like she had become one of his old high-school sweethearts dumping him over something trivial.

Instead of retreating with his tail tucked between his legs, Laz leaned forward and kissed her, quick enough that she wouldn't have time to reject him, yet tender enough to make her regret this decision. Deep down, though, he knew sex and intimacy wouldn't keep her. He would have to show her results. Meeting with Sanaa Farook would have to go well.

"I'll be back for you." Laz walked out with a plan in his head and hope in his heart.

Chapter 12

Even after getting back to New York, it didn't relieve Laz of his anxiety. He wished he could have had a different outcome with his encounter with Avery. After all he had done and everything they had been through, she still didn't trust him. Then again, he hadn't given her a great reason to believe him, either.

She didn't believe him when he said he would work hard for her to get her in the business. Now he sat in the CEO's office of Section Eight Records, waiting to hear why she wanted to meet him so quickly.

Laz had a feeling he knew why. The video Avery had posted had gone viral. Comments ranged from wanting to know Avery's identity to calling her the next Whitney. He relaxed back in his seat as he thought about the positive reactions. Then his actions may have lost it all for him.

Not calling her as soon as he had gotten home didn't ease his guilt. The old Laz reared its ugly head. He also wanted Avery to reach out to him, to want him, to need him. Why hadn't *she* called *him*?

Like a whirlwind, Sanaa entered the room, this time with an entourage. The voluptuous woman wore all red, from her shoes to her knee-length dress, to the color painted on her full lips. As she had done before, she kept her attention on the tablet she had in her hands, even after she took her seat behind her desk.

The three people following her, a short, stocky man in a suit, a young, slender woman with heavy box braids, and a tall, imposing man in a track suit, all stood off to the side of her desk and remained quiet and obedient, probably like she had trained them.

"A very good day." Sanaa kept her attention on her device until an image appeared on a large-screen TV off to the side.

Laz had to bite the inside of his cheek to keep from smiling when he saw the video he had taken of Avery the first time she had sang at the coffee shop.

"Thank God this woman credited you in the description." Sanaa nodded her head toward the screen and set her tablet down to focus on him. "You work fast. Who is she?" Sanaa leaned back in her black leather swivel chair as she stared at him like she wanted to dissect him.

Laz shook his head. "So this meeting isn't about me getting a job here?"

He wouldn't be revealing anything until he got something concrete. With the traveling and other expenses, Laz's savings started to dwindle down faster than he had anticipated. He would need to find work soon or he would be living out on the streets.

Sanaa stared at Laz for a long, uncomfortable moment. Laz didn't blink or even swallow. He couldn't show fear or trepidation. He glared right back at her, expecting her to crumble soon. If she didn't, he would leave this meeting and head right back down to Virginia to Avery.

A smile curled at the corner of her mouth. "You're like a dog with a bone, aren't you?"

Laz exhaled while still maintaining his composure. "I'm more like a man with a plan. If you plan on getting anywhere with me as far as business, then I need to know where this is going." He glanced at her squad. "I don't remember these people from the last time we had spoken."

"That's because things have changed since that time." Sanaa gave the slightest of head nods, and the portly suited man rushed over to the corner of the room where behind a hidden wall panel sat a refrigerator. He pulled out a bottle of water, rushed it over to Sanaa, and poured it into a glass for her before assuming his original spot again. Yes, she had these people well trained.

"If all goes well with this meeting, Mr. Kyson, you will be a part of the Section Eight family, and so will that amazing talent you found."

Laz smiled and gripped the arms of his seat to stand when Sanaa took the wind out of his sails.

"But, before any of that, I want to meet her. I've been duped in this business before. Videos can be altered." She took a sip of her water. "So my team is here to look out for my best interest."

He regarded the group again, who now all stared at him.

"I will add you to my artist management team if you can secure that artist here with Section Eight."

On the outside, Laz kept calm. His face didn't even crack. On the inside, he fist pumped, did cartwheels, and could hear imaginary fireworks going off in his head all at the same time.

"You will get the job once you bring her here to my office and I hear her myself. If what I hear is real and I'm impressed, I'll sign her to a contract." Sanaa placed her hands on top of her desk, and drummed her fingernails of one hand on the top. "Sound like a deal?"

Again, Laz had to keep his cool. The only way he would be able to maintain control would be to act like he could do without this deal even though he knew he had to have it.

"I want to see this contract first." He uncrossed his legs and planted his feet on the floor.

"I figured you would say that. That's why my attorney is here." She pointed to the group.

Laz's attention automatically went to the short, overweight man. The track suit guy stepped up and handed Laz a leather-bound folder.

"I'm sure you'll find everything is in order and is fair." The man's deep voice rolled over Laz like a steamroller. "It's our standard boilerplate contract."

Laz accepted it and rested the folder on his lap.

Sanaa continued. "If you get the job, you'll meet with our human resources department about your contract terms."

Before Laz could peer over at the young African-American woman in the room, the short man ran over to Laz and dropped his folder first before picking it up and handing it over to Laz.

Laz's curiosity got the better of him. He directed his attention to the woman. "If he's her attorney and this guy works in H.R., what do you do?"

"Don't you worry about that." Sanaa wagged her finger at him. "Trust me when I say she's essential."

The woman simply smiled at Laz. Looked like he couldn't make assumptions about this company. Conversely, Sanaa or anyone at Section Eight shouldn't assume he would simply roll over or run simply because they dangled a carrot in his face. He had something to prove and Avery's interests to protect.

"So when can you get her here to me? My schedule is tight." Sanaa picked up her tablet again.

Laz took that opportunity to stand to excuse himself. "I'll have to get back to you on that. I need to coordinate with her schedule."

They didn't need to know he would also have to get her to talk to him again. If she would at least answer his call, he could share this great news.

"Will you have time next week in your schedule?" Knowing that Avery would be out of school next week would free up some time in her schedule, but he also realized she had an evening job and she had to trust him. The second obstacle would be massive to overcome.

"I'll check my schedule and have my people get back to you." Sanaa nodded toward the door.

Apparently, she wanted Laz to leave and take her subtle cue as his sign to go.

Laz smiled and extended his hand to her. "Very nice talking to you again. I look forward to working with you soon."

The sudden motion had the young woman standing off to the side making a few strides forward. Maybe this woman worked security for Sanaa.

Sanaa shook Laz's hand and, again, nodded to the door.

This time he took his signal to leave seriously. He strolled away until he got outside the building. Away from the prying eyes and ears, he finally pumped his fist.

He'd done it. Beyond all odds, he made his way back into the music industry and with an artist he believed in and could fully endorse. He saw a lot of great things happening for Avery.

Laz pulled out his phone and started to call her. That side of him that wanted to be wanted stopped him. Fear prevented him from hearing her rejection over the phone. He told her before he left that he would see her on Saturday. He would be a man of his word and do that instead. She couldn't turn down the surprise visit. At least, he hoped she wouldn't.

* * * *

Avery sat in the back of the class with her head down in the hope that Professor Klein would overlook her. She knew her teacher liked to push her, but right now she needed a break.

Trying to push Laz's hasty retreat from her apartment almost a week ago still plagued her thoughts. Boning up on her schoolwork should have cleared her mind of extracurricular activities. Focusing on her education highlighted the fact that she would have to stick to this path.

After Klein allowed other students to answer his questions, he must have decided within the final minutes of the class to direct his full attention on Avery.

"Miss Shields."

Her professor's raised voice got her attention. Then the stares from her fellow classmates snagged her notice. She had been daydreaming again about life outside of these school walls and Virginia. She couldn't keep it together for a few more minutes before Klein dismissed the class and she could do what she wanted for a week while on break.

"Yes, sir?" She sat up tall to feign interest.

"Bayes' Theorem."

Avery blinked. Like Pavlov's dog, the mention of that theory had her heart racing and her thoughts going directly to Laz and his naked body. "Yes, sir?"

"Will you remind the class of that first-level statistics theorem?" He stood in front of the class with his hands clasped behind his back, which made his rounded belly protrude even more.

"Yes, sir. I can." She cleared her throat in hopes to buy her some time so that she could recall that concept. "I could, but wouldn't it be better if we all read about that theory again on our own, like during the break? I know I would gain a better appreciation for it."

Klein regarded her for a long stretch before he glanced at his watch. His disappointment couldn't be hidden. Avery managed to do it again. She let down someone she respected.

"You all have your assignments for the spring break holiday." He gathered his belongings and started stuffing them in his briefcase. "Although at least one of you will have an additional project to do over the week-long break."

Hoping she hadn't been the intended target for this additional assignment, Avery grabbed her bag and tried making a speedy retreat to the door.

"I know you didn't think I wasn't talking about you, right?" Klein sighed.

The heavy exhale alone halted her in her spot and got her to walk back to him. "I was kind of hoping."

"Even after giving you sufficient warning, you still did not do well on your last quiz." He rested his hand on top of his case.

"I got a high C." She didn't mean to sound indignant, but she had to prove that she had paid some attention in class.

"You think corporations are interested in hiring C-level students? You have to do better. You know this." He picked up his case and stared at her. This time, disappointment didn't fill his eyes. He had a questioning expression. "What's going on with you?"

She blinked. "What are you talking about?"

"A couple of weeks ago, you could barely keep your eyes open in my class. Not very flattering to an instructor, but I get it." He put his hand to his chest. "I was a student once. But now, all this week you've been acting like your soul has been pulled from you. I feel like I'm only talking to the shell of you."

"I told you before. I'm tired." Avery hiked her backpack on her shoulder. "I have a lot going on in my personal life right now."

Avery would spare her favorite professor all her issues. Now that Laz had been eliminated, her problems lessened. She could get back to reality.

"Care to talk about it?" He gazed down at her and gave her that fatherly expression she sometimes hoped her father would give her.

"It's nothing. I'll get it together. I promise." She even held up her hand like a Boy Scout. "I've got free time on my hands now. I've cut out a couple of distractions, and I'm on the hunt for a new part-time job."

Klein tilted his head and exhaled. "Okay. If that's all that it is. And so that you keep that focus, I want you to do a paper on Bayes' Theorem, apply it to something going on right now, and have it to me by the first week of May before exams."

Avery's shoulders slumped, and she wanted to kick herself for her juvenile reaction. In real life, she would be hit with extra work and curveballs all the time. School should be no different.

"Yes, sir."

He gave her the details of her assignment before he patted her shoulder. "If I were you, I would get this assignment knocked out sooner rather than later. That way you can enjoy your break and not get overwhelmed with other work. You should take as much time as you can to recharge your batteries."

Avery smiled. Since Laz had given her that lame excuse and ran from her, she had made an effort to stay away from everything that reminded her of him, including the coffee shop where she sang a couple of songs. That meant the waitressing job she had talked to Dot about wouldn't be hers. How could Avery go back to that place, see the stage where she sang her heart out, and not think of Laz Kyson?

The extra time on her hands allowed her to concentrate on school. That didn't mean she didn't think about anything else. Thoughts of her life as a professional singer and songwriter, along with being a college graduate, and being with Laz interrupted her concentration and dreams on a minute-by-minute basis.

The lack of calls from Laz didn't help. He truly did hit it and quit it, or rather her. She wanted to at least hear his voice so that the tickling feeling in her belly that she liked would return. The man had no idea of the power he possessed.

After class, Avery went back to her apartment. She did what she had done each day since Laz exited. She pulled his phone number up on her phone. She hovered her thumb over the Send button, and then she stopped herself. Despite the openness she had felt to ask him anything, and his willingness to respond to all queries, she couldn't handle it if she asked him if he thought having sex with her had been a mistake. Deep down, she knew he would have said *yes*.

Laz had looked conflicted before they even started. He said over and over again that he didn't have intimate relationships with his clients. Why would she be any different? What made her think she would be special?

Avery went back to her contact list and called someone who she needed to call anyway.

"A little late, aren't you?" The sassy tone in Graciela's voice couldn't be hidden.

"At least I'm calling you." Avery sat on her couch and kicked off her shoes. "So how are you doing? How's everything at the diner?"

A pause lingered on the line before Graciela spoke. "Are you kidding me with this right now? You go out with Mr. Hotness and you want to talk about me and the diner? Oh, no."

Avery could almost imagine Graciela wagging her finger at her.

"You are going to spill it. I haven't seen or talked to you in a week after you forcefully pushed me out of your apartment."

"A gentle nudge was more like it." Avery chewed on her lower lip. "Besides, my life is boring. You're the one who's always going out and doing things. I work and go to school."

"And see Mr. Hotness. Where is he anyway? Is he sleeping, trying to get his electrolytes back that you depleted?" Graciela laughed.

"You are so inappropriate. No, he's in New York on business."

Another pause lingered on the phone.

"Did you two have sex?" Graciela's question came out of left field and made Avery wonder what she said that made her ask that.

Maybe it had to do with the tone in Avery's voice. Did she sound sad or too forlorn? She did miss Laz. Pride and fear kept her from dialing his number. What if she called him and he didn't answer? What if she called him and he did?

"That's not an appropriate question to ask." Avery smoothed her hand over the plush arm of the couch.

"You just said I'm inappropriate. And because you didn't answer, I'm taking that to mean you did." Graciela sighed. "I told you to watch out for him."

Avery squeezed her eyes closed. She had a feeling an I-told-you-so speech would be coming. It didn't hurt less hearing it from Graciela than her parents.

"Anything I did was what I wanted. I have no regrets." She sat up taller.

"And yet you sound like you've lost your best friend." Graciela tsked.

"I do not. I'm talking to you." What Avery wanted to say, she couldn't utter over the phone. Soul baring should be done face-to-face. "You want to do dinner tonight before I have to go to work?"

"I wish I could. Jessie and I are going to Songbirds." She gasped. "You should come with us. It'll get you out of the funk you're in and get your mind on something else. Besides, aren't you officially on spring break now?"

Avery nodded. "I am, but I'm not in the singing mood."

She definitely didn't want to go back to the place where she first saw Laz. What if she went there and saw him searching for other talent?

"And are you and Jessie dating?" Avery made a lewd cooing sound.

"Of course not." Graciela snickered. "I mean, sure, we're fuck buddies, but we're not dating."

That admission made Avery blink. "What?"

"I thought you knew. If I'm not seeing anyone and Jessie is available, we meet for a little something-something. It's not serious."

Before Avery could say something about Graciela's cavalier manner regarding sex and ask why she couldn't give Avery a break for sleeping with Laz, Graciela continued.

"We both know the deal with our relationship. We talked about it before anything went down so that there would be no hard feelings. That's how grownups do it."

Avery rubbed her eyes. "Sounds like that works for you." She looked at the clock in the room. "I'm going to get some sleep before I go to work tonight. Have fun at Songbirds. Tell Jessie I said hi."

"I will. If you change your mind about coming out—"

"I won't. But thanks for the offer." Avery disconnected the call.

Avery's mind raced with so many ideas. Maybe Graciela had been right. She should stop avoiding Laz's calls. She needed to put on her big-girl panties and talk to Laz. Whether he wanted to be with her or not, or whether he changed his mind about representing her, she had to get her feelings out. Keeping them bottled up affected her life.

After barely touching her dinner and trying to take a nap before work that night, Avery arrived at the Charisma Music building ready to do her job. Cleaning toilets held no glamour or prestige, but at least it paid the bills. Barely. She definitely needed that second job.

Since her father hadn't said anything to her about seeing Laz in her place, she chalked up her week at work as a success. The last thing she needed would be an argument with Clinton Shields over nothing. Avery wouldn't be leaving her current duties or career path to follow a crazy dream.

"I can do the bathrooms this time." Clinton pushed his cart toward the men's bathroom.

When Avery looked at the door, she flashed back to when she first met Laz. "You've let me do the bathrooms all week. Why change now?"

She dragged her cart over to the same location.

"I thought you might need a break. I'm a good boss." Clinton smiled before adjusting his glasses on his thick nose.

"And I'm an excellent employee who will not stand by and watch the man who not only pays me but the same one who gave me life scrub a toilet." She turned his cart around. "You do the offices like normal. I have this."

"Are you sure?"

Avery's gut twisted seeing the worry in her father's eyes. "I'm fine. I'll check the entire bathroom first, and I'll make sure to leave it all spotless." She reached into her back pocket and pulled out her phone. "If anything happens, I have my phone. I'll call you or the police."

At the word *police*, Clinton's eyes widened.

"But nothing will happen. It's an office building. It's quiet. I'm good." To assure him, she gave him a nod. "Now I'm going to get going so that we can leave here on time for once."

Avery ducked into the bathroom and used her cart to prop the door open. "Hello."

She waited a beat before moving. Instead of doing what she did the last time Laz surprised her in this same room, Avery ventured in deep, checking each stall until satisfied that she occupied the space alone. Only knowing that didn't please her.

Although she had been avoiding Laz, she wanted to see him again. He had given her something no one had in a long time, and it had nothing to do with the incredible sex. The man had given her hope. Now she had to get back to reality. These toilets wouldn't clean themselves.

By the time the sun rose the next morning, Avery and her father had finished their work.

"You might see me in church this Sunday." Avery didn't mean to sound so defeated, especially when talking about going to service. "No guarantees."

"Really?" Clinton lifted his ball cap and scratched the top of his head. "Isn't this your spring break week?"

She nodded. "I've caught up on my schoolwork." A lie, but she needed a break. "And it's not like I'm going to Fort Lauderdale or anything. Besides, I'll get to spend time with you all." She patted her father on his back. "That is if you don't mind me cramping your and Mom's style."

He chuckled. "You know it's never a problem with you coming over. I think it's a great idea, actually. Your mom was a little concerned about you after our last visit." He strolled out of the building toward his car. Clinton unlocked the door but spoke before getting inside. "What was up with that guy anyway?"

Avery wanted to blurt her true feelings, but instead held off to keep her father calm. "Just a guy. No big deal. We had a couple of dates, but that's all. He went his way. I'm still here." Where she would always be, she wanted to add. She kissed her father on his cheek. "I'll talk to you later."

On the drive home, Avery went past Uncle Pig's restaurant for old time's sake. She didn't stop, although she missed working with Graciela and the gang. If she could have bent Graciela's ear some more, she would have. As soon as Avery spotted her ogre of an ex-boss waddling out of a side door, she turned her head and sped down the road.

Thanks to Laz, she had to forget about that part of her life. Truly, she had to thank Laz for standing up for her when she knew she couldn't do it for herself. He had recognized Uncle Pig's jerk ways in the millisecond he encountered the man.

Without a job to go to now, Avery would have to go home and relax, a first in a long time. She pulled up to her apartment building and got out. The coveralls she still had on smelled of harsh chemicals. She couldn't wait to strip out of them and take a much-needed shower, maybe a relaxing bath instead.

Avery unlocked her front door but stopped when she heard her name being called.

"Avery."

She recognized the voice and so did her body. When she turned and saw Laz standing behind her, she nearly collapsed to her knees.

Laz approached her. "We need to talk."

Chapter 13

Waiting out in front of Avery's apartment for several hours would have disappointed Laz's player father. Laz knew what he wanted. He had to keep his focus on business. He had already slipped up once. Looking at her now, even with her getting off work and looking exhausted, he still found her incredibly sexy, and she hadn't said anything to him yet.

"Good. You're home." Laz clapped his hands and rubbed them together. "Time to get to work." He stood on the stoop in front of her door while Avery sought refuge in her apartment. "How are you?"

"Tired." To illustrate her statement, she leaned against the door that she steadily tried closing on him. "And uninterested in you interrupting my life again."

Smile. Keep being charming.

"You're going to like this disruption. I want you to come back with me to New York." He saw her blinking like she had gotten caught in a dust storm.

"Are you kidding?" She stepped out of her apartment to get in his face. "You get my hopes up. You push me outside of my comfort zone. You"—Avery paused and looked around before continuing her rant—"have sex with me. Then you leave."

Laz hated to admit it, but Avery had him pegged. She had gotten too close too fast. He had to control this and set the pace. "I was working for you."

Now he understood why she didn't answer his calls. No way would Laz text her his true feelings. Maybe he could have put off Sanaa Farook an extra day to make sure Avery understood his stance. Avery hadn't heard the phone call he'd had with Sanaa, since she had been in the shower at the time. He kept her in the dark and wanted her to trust him on blind faith and the basis of good—no—excellent sex. He owed her a lot more.

Like he hadn't said anything, she continued. "And now you want me to leave and go with you? For what? What's in New York for me?"

Laz smiled and leaned forward, getting his face inches away from hers. "I want you to meet with a record label." He saw her hardened demeanor soften a bit. While he had her on the hook, he kept on his sales pitch. "Can I talk to you about this inside?" He raised his hands in surrender. "I promise you. I only want to talk business. Nothing funny."

"There was nothing funny about the last time you were in my apartment." Avery looked him over for a moment. "You're full of it."

"If by *it* you mean hard work and determination, you're right." He tried to keep his breathing in check, since it now started to accelerate.

"You're not listening to me." She poked his chest with the tip of her finger. "I don't trust you. I don't believe you."

He snagged her finger and held it. "Ever since I met you, I have been nothing but honest." She didn't have to know he meant that in a business sense.

Avery laughed. She snatched her finger out of his grasp.

"I told you why I was in town. I towed your car. I fixed your car. I got you singing in front of an audience. And I showed you my license. You know more about me and what I'm capable of than the last woman I dated." How much more could Avery want from him? "I even shared one of my fears with you."

"Yeah. Just one." She approached him like she wanted to scream at him. Then she stopped. Her face relaxed and she shook her head. Defeat washed over her whole countenance.

"What?" His curiosity got the better of him.

"It's not your fault." She put her hand to her chest. "It's mine. I keep expecting people to rise up to meet my higher standards, and then I get disappointed when that doesn't happen."

"Avery, what do you want from me? Tell me." When she didn't answer, he looked at her apartment door. "Can we go inside and talk, please?"

"I'm just getting off work." She looked down at herself and tugged on her stained coveralls. "I'm not really presentable."

"I think you look, um…" Laz had to pick his words carefully. If he complimented her too much, she might think he wanted another round with her…even though he did. "For talking about business, you look fine."

"Oh. Right. Business." She nodded and kept her gaze away from him. "I'm also really tired. I don't think I should be talking about career moves and contracts right now. I need to be in the right mind. I need to decide whether or not any of this is still worth it."

Laz understood her stance, and he didn't need to push her away. Not again. He didn't like this feeling between the two of them.

"I'll call you when I wake up from my nap." Avery started backing up into her home.

Laz took that opportunity to move forward. "Or I can be here when you wake up." Like he had done the night they had been together, he put his hands on the doorframe over her head. "I only have the best intentions for you. I only want the best for you. May I come in?"

He watched the questions covering her face. She glanced up the stairs to her main apartment.

Avery shook her head. "No. I can't do this again. I keep opening myself up and getting shut down. I can only take so much."

Laz took a deep breath and took a step back. He didn't know how to play this situation. In the past, if he wanted something, he would do what his father would have done and cracked some jokes and made some compliments. Doing that now got him nowhere.

Before Avery could close the door on him, Laz moved forward and put himself in between the door and the frame.

"What are you doing?" She put her hand to his chest. "I told you to go."

Laz kept her hand against his body. "I can't. I need you." If he had any chance of swaying her, Laz would have to be open and honest. "Before I came out here, I lost my job."

He watched Avery's face go blank.

"I quit. I walked away because of a disagreement. I saw myself doing more. I'm spending my own money to realize my dream." He pointed to her. "You are a big part of that. You are my last hope to get back into the business." He glanced back at the rental car he got at the airport. "If you won't let me inside, I'll sleep in my car in front of your apartment. Bottom line, I'm not leaving Virginia without you." He put his hands in prayer form. "I promise you, if you come to New York with me, you will not leave without being signed to a major label."

Avery glared at him for a moment before she spoke. "Are you telling me the truth? You have no job?"

Laz shook his head. "I quit working for Universe."

Her eyes widened. "You worked at Universe? No wonder you didn't want me signing with them."

"You can do much better than them. I know that. I want to give you top dollar because you're worth it." He moved in closer to her. "I called you every day and you ignored them and never called me back."

"Because I thought you had used me. I didn't want to hear you saying that you didn't want to see me again." Her shoulders slumped down.

"I told you I would be back. I told you I would call. You should have believed that."

"I believed a lot of things." She leaned against the doorframe. "My foolish self."

Laz tapped his finger against his watch, still refusing to acknowledge the wedge he had created between the two of them from his actions. "We are wasting time. I'm sure there's a lot we can talk about, but right now, I need to get you to New York so that you can start your career." When she didn't respond, he cleared his throat and lowered his voice. "I never used you. I don't have a secret life back home. No wife. No kids. I made a mistake by leaving so soon. Ordinarily, I would have never done that. While you were in the shower, I had gotten a call from a major label. I don't want to make another mistake by seeing you walk away from this opportunity. May I come inside, please?"

"Why can't I say no to you?" Avery stared at him.

Laz moved in closer to her. "Believe me. You are equally as powerful." He leaned down and got beside her ear. "Let me inside."

Without a word or argument, Avery stepped aside to allow him to come into her place. Laz sighed as he closed and locked the door behind him, and then followed her up the steps to her main apartment.

Laz had planned on only discussing Section Eight news with her. Then he watched her unzipping her coveralls, and his mind went to a fantasy of seeing her naked underneath. Instead, she revealed she wore a T-shirt and jeans. Seeing that still didn't stop his raging heart.

"I know you're tired and want to get some sleep after working all night." Laz made sure to keep a safe buffer of space between the two of them. "I did meet with a record label on your behalf. I do believe in you."

"Then why did you leave out of here the other morning like—" Avery stopped herself from revealing too much, but still avoided looking at him. Then she reconnected her gaze to him to hear his answer.

"The music biz happens fast." He snapped his fingers around her. "When you get the call, you have to move." He shook his head. The more dismissive he sounded, the more he reminded himself of his father. Laz definitely didn't like that feeling. If he wanted this woman to trust him, he had to get her to like him, because right now, he didn't even like himself. "Look. I—" Laz stopped himself. This had nothing to do with him. He needed to concentrate on the woman before him. "Who was it?"

Avery's head rose and she connected her gaze to his. "What?"

"Tell me about the last guy before me who left you."

She moved her bottom lip but nothing came out of her mouth.

Laz scanned her living room area until he found what he sought. "May I?" He pointed to a colorful spiral notebook on her couch.

Avery darted by him and snatched it up. "No. You can't look at these." She glared at him. "Not again."

"I don't want to look through the whole thing. I want you to show me you. Show me one of the songs that best describes how you're feeling."

Avery clutched her notebook to her chest, and Laz completely understood her fear. He strolled over to a chair, figuring it would be less threatening than if he sat on the couch with all its available room. "I have three sisters. One older, and the others are younger, of course. My mom thought it was so cute to get us up in front of her friends and our family during parties for us to sing and dance around. My mom is a frustrated Broadway wannabe. She has always wanted to sing on a stage in front of huge audiences, but never did." Laz snickered. "Despite hating singing in front of a crowd, my mom did give me the love of music." He took a deep breath. "I feel like it frees my soul. I connect to it like nothing else." He stared at Avery and found her looking back at him. "There is one other instance where I connected to something so strongly."

Avery's face transformed into a light blush color. Did it change out of embarrassment or excitement? Either way, Laz found her enticing.

"I know that the words you put on those pages mean a lot to you. They're your babies. I think it would give me a better idea about you and how you feel if you share some of that with me." He sat up taller. "Please."

Avery took a step closer to him. "What makes you think I would write a song about something like that?"

"Because I think you're a songwriter who mines inspiration from her life experiences. You're not looking to write a booty shaker. You have heart. You have a soul."

"What if I'm just like your mother, just another frustrated artist who won't go anywhere?"

"And what if you're not?" Laz scooted to the edge of the chair. "Besides, you have something my mother didn't have."

She snickered. "What? Are you going to say you?"

He nodded. "In a manner of speaking, yes. I'm here to support your dreams. My mother didn't have that."

Avery went over to the couch across from him and sat down slowly. She took a deep breath and flipped through her well-worn pages. Toward the beginning of the notebook, she flipped the pages back and ran her hand over the paper before standing up.

She crossed the room to get to him. "Just read this one and that's it." She handed him the notebook. "I'm going to take a shower and change."

Laz didn't look down at the lyrics until he heard Avery in the bathroom with the door closed and the shower water running. Then he held the book up and read every word.

As he read each lyric of a song called "Sorry, Babe," he gritted his teeth. Avery detailed in a lyrical manner a woman who gave everything to a man only to have him be dismissive to her and giving her the trite, "sorry, babe" line when he moved on to the next conquest.

No wonder she had been upset when he left. Maybe she had written the song about him.

Shit.

He really wanted to flip to the back half of the notebook to see if she had written a new song. He did promise her he would only read the one poem and nothing else.

Laz's thumb brushed over the pages, causing a flipping sound with each pass. He had already disappointed her once. He wouldn't be doing it again. In the meantime, he reread the words she had written over and over again until he had them practically memorized.

He could almost hear the melody in his head. If only he had a piano. Hell, he could even strum out the tune on a guitar if Avery had one. He didn't see one in the living room. He didn't remember seeing one in her bedroom, but at the time, his full concentration had remained on her, her body, and her needs. Laz would have to remember that in negotiating her contract.

After a half hour and a shower later, Avery returned to the living room. Now wearing loose cotton shorts and a pink T-shirt, she looked ready for a softball game rather than an intense sleeping session.

She took the notebook from his hands and retreated to her spot on the couch. "Well? What did you think?"

Laz regarded her for a moment before speaking. "You're a gifted writer. But you're missing something with these lyrics." He rested his hands on his knees. "I also hope that any songs you've written within the last week were kinder." He rubbed his thighs. "Perhaps, instead, you write songs that are happier. Listeners would respond to that more. Not every singer can be Adele."

"Not every singer has been through what I have, either." She shrugged.

"No. But I know the industry. I know what works." He rubbed his hand across the back of his neck. "There are a lot of things I've done in my life, both good and bad. When it comes to business, I'm a straight shooter. I have never crossed the line with a client like I did with you." He should have apologized for breaching her trust. He should have told her that she broke down a wall inside of him, one that kept him from being authentic. "But now I'm focused. I'm here for you and your career."

"Thank you for telling me." She stood.

"Are you going to ask me to leave now?" He started to stand until she put her hand on his shoulder.

"No. I was going to ask if you would feel awkward staying here while I slept."

Laz smiled and shook his head. "No. I can wait."

"Okay. I would tell you that there's food in the fridge. There isn't." She glanced at her TV. "I have Netflix right now until it gets shut off."

"I can keep myself entertained."

When he said that, she licked her lips. "This might help you." She handed him her notebook.

Laz hesitated before accepting it. "It's okay?"

"Cover to cover if you want." She backed up. "It will show you the real me more than I could ever tell you. If you want to know me and know what I'm all about, what's in here will show you." She exhaled. "See you in a few hours."

Avery disappeared into her bedroom, closed the door, and Laz heard her engaging the lock. She let him in, but only so much. He would have to prove himself. Not a problem. He could work hard for this fight.

Laz opened the notebook and, at first, quickly read each and every song Avery wrote. He devoured the words like a kid eating a bag of candy. Then he went back and read each one slowly, absorbing each word and turn of phrase.

Avery showed herself to be a gifted lyrist. What impressed Laz the most had to be how much of her heart and soul she put into each song, whether she talked about wanting to spend the day at the beach, or how much she wanted a fulfilling relationship, she showed herself fully.

The last piece got to him, the one called "Shame." He knew it had to do with him and how he had treated her after they had had sex. He read it over and over again. Each time, it felt like a dagger pierced his heart, but he deserved the pain.

After the last reading, Laz sprang from the couch, ready to go to Avery and hold her. He couldn't. She shut him out in every way, which might have been a good thing. He didn't need to get that close to her again. He had a job to do, not a woman to fall for.

* * * *

Avery stared up at the twirling blades of her ceiling fan. She should have been sleeping. She told Laz she would be doing just that when she sequestered herself in her bedroom. Part of her anxiety had less to do with the fact that Laz had indeed come back for her like he had promised, or the idea that he may have gotten her a recording deal. She allowed someone to read her private thoughts that she created into songs.

At some point during their conversation earlier, she didn't feel like Laz had heard her. Did he really understand her pain?

No longer content to remain in her bedroom, and curious to see Laz, Avery got out of bed and unlocked her door. She took a breath before opening it. She peeked into the living room and found Laz spread out on the couch asleep with her notebook resting on his chest. He had his hand on top of it like he protected it.

She smiled at the sight. He must have understood how much that book meant to her. Before waking him, Avery decided to change her clothes. She closed the door behind herself, but this time she didn't feel the need to lock herself away from Laz.

After stripping out of her pajamas, she opened her closet for an outfit. Before selecting a garment, she heard a knock on the door.

"Come in."

Laz had already seen her naked. No need to have any kind of modesty now.

The door creaked open a hair, but Laz didn't come into the room. That didn't stop her from seeing a bit of him through the crack.

When his gaze connected with hers, he, at first dropped it to the floor, almost in a shy way. Then he slowly brought his head up and reconnected with her. She found it impressive that he didn't look like he scanned her body. His talk of being serious about work and representing her had all been true. That should have made her happy, yet her heartbeat slowed down tremendously.

With his hair ruffled, he looked exhausted but hopeful. "Have you packed? I really do have a contract in line for you."

She pulled out a maxi dress. "No." She almost completed her statement with a "Not yet" but she didn't know if she wanted to make that next step. Everything had happened way too fast. Avery needed to pump the brakes on some aspect of her life.

"Depending on what happens, I won't keep you up there for very long. Maybe three or four days." He cleared his throat. "You can stay with me at my apartment. It's not that big."

She laughed.

Laz felt the need to clarify. "The apartment."

Avery continued laughing.

Laz leaned back to get some eye contact. "What's funny?"

"I'm changing in front of you, but I'm scared of going to New York." Avery didn't mean to, but her body shook when she answered.

With his knuckle, he eased the door open a bit more. "The same fear you had when you sang the second time at Honey's?"

She nodded.

"But you got through that performance. You had a very positive reaction." He cocked a smile at the side of his mouth. "I'm not including me."

"You should include yourself. I wouldn't have gotten through the performance without you there." Although she didn't want to give power over to someone else, she also realized in this realm, she needed the support.

"Then know you will be okay because I'll be there every step of the way." When she looked him in his eyes again, he gave her a thumbs-up sign. "I don't offer this kind of representation to everyone. But I feel different with you."

"I know exactly what you mean."

Silence hung between them until he spoke again. "Did you make a decision? Are you coming back with me to New York?" He glanced down at his watch. "Time is essential. There's lots of ground to cover before the meeting."

"I will if you do three things." If Laz wanted to stick with business, she had to do the same.

"Three? Wow. Okay, shoot." He pushed the door open a bit more.

"I need to see your contract." Enough dancing around the topic. Avery needed to claim her place in her future.

"Done. I have it with me." Laz nodded.

"And I want you to tell me what I should expect from the music business." Avery wanted to know more about the man she just exposed her soul to through her music. She couldn't do that if he kept himself away from her.

"Of course. I'll prepare you as much as I can." He glanced at his watch again. "Actually, I wanted us to hit the road to D.C. tonight. I've gotten some sleep. We can stop somewhere to eat if you're hungry. You weren't kidding about what you had to eat in your kitchen." He chuckled.

"Told you." She slipped the dress over her head and smoothed it out over her body. This time she watched Laz scanning her from head to toe with a few calculated pauses in between. "Not packed. I really wasn't sure what was going on with you, with us." She stared at him as she slipped on a pair of sandals.

"And now?" He grabbed the doorknob and pulled the door closed a little. Damn, he wanted to retreat.

"I'll go. I'm off this weekend. I don't have school next week. What do I have to lose?"

Laz sighed and braced his hands on his knees like he had run a marathon. "Good. Good. I'm glad you're taking this leap with me."

"I am, too. But there's other business between us."

"What's that?"

She opened the door fully and stood in front of him. Standing directly in front of him, she couldn't help but be drawn into his mesmerizing stare, the same one she couldn't break from when he had given her the best sex of her life. Her body tingled as she thought about him, his body, his hands, and the way he kissed.

"My last question is which record label are we going to see? You still haven't said." Avery wanted to be prepared.

"Now I'm going to have to go back on what I just promised. Just like you, I like to have some surprises. I'll tell you when we're on the way to the office."

She felt her bottom jaw drop. "Really? After what we went through, you want to keep something from me?"

He backed away from her. "Would you believe me if I told you that it would be worth it?"

"I would believe you more if you told me the label." She screwed up her lips.

"Then this will be our next test." He swept a tendril from her face. "Yep, a test."

"Maybe I don't like surprises and I definitely don't do well with tests." Although she liked Laz's playful nature, the fact that he kept this information from her reopened that wound.

"Then you'll see how I felt the night you sang that Roberta Flack song." He winked before walking away from her. "I'll wait for you in the living room."

"That ended up being a good surprise, remember?" She immediately recalled how Laz rocked her world after she sang, and wished for that to happen again.

He didn't answer her.

After brushing her teeth, Avery wanted to bring their conversation back around to something tame. "You want to drive all the way to New York?" She had driven to New Jersey one time and had gotten tired of being cooped up in a car for so long.

He shook his head. "We'll stop in D.C. There's something we need to do there. We'll bed down and fly out in the morning."

Avery's silence must have come across as worry to Laz.

"Don't worry. You're in good hands." He smiled before sitting down on her couch again.

Her opened notebook full of her lyrics sat next to him. She stared at it before returning her gaze to him.

"Okay, give me a minute to pack. Then we can go."

Avery didn't worry about much, but this side trip did have her curious about what Laz had planned for her.

Chapter 14

As Laz drove, he let the words to Avery's song, "Shame" roll around in his head. They had tiptoed around the topic, but he knew his lack of communication with Avery hurt her. He started to see himself slipping back to his old ways, the same behavior that got Erin to give up on him and the relationship. If Laz didn't play his cards right, he would lose an amazing client, and the potential of a great woman as a partner.

He gazed over at her on the way to Washington, D.C. Avery hadn't taken her attention away from the contract he had handed her when she left her apartment. She had even canceled on going to her parents' house for dinner on Sunday. Thankfully, she had left his name out of the conversation for the reason why she would be a no-show.

Laz brought his stare back to her when she marked something in the contract with a pen. "What are you doing?"

Without looking at him, she responded. "Making notes. Things I have questions about."

"Oh, okay." At least she had a questioning attitude.

It would have worried him had she signed the contract without really reading it. He wanted her to trust him, but he also wanted her to be smart.

"And there are some things I don't like." She smirked before turning the page.

"Oh, really? Such as?" He had to hear this from this newbie.

"Not now. I want to get through this whole thing first before we talk about this." She rested her hand on her lap. "Should I have an attorney?"

Laz wouldn't lie to her. He couldn't. "It wouldn't be a bad idea. But attorneys cost money. You need to think about what's important to you, though."

She nodded.

"We're not too far." They had already been in the car for nearly four hours.

It didn't escape Laz's attention how much Avery fidgeted in her seat. He had to do something to distract her until he reached his final destination. He leaned forward to turn on the radio when he heard something that sounded way better.

Avery had started humming at first. Then she opened her mouth and sang something so beautiful that Laz almost had to pull over to bask in the glory of it.

For as long as he lived, he would never get tired of listening to Avery's voice. She rivaled any radio or streaming service out there.

Silence hung in the air at the end of her song.

"You can join me, you know."

Laz started to shake his head and disagree with her invitation when she reached out and held his hand. He gazed down at the union before looking at her and then watching the road. D.C. had the market cornered on crazy drivers.

"There's no audience here." Avery squeezed his hand. "It's just me."

He smiled to mask his true feelings. "Just you singing is more than enough for me."

"Maybe it's not all about you. Maybe I need something." She intertwined her fingers with his just as he pulled off the interstate.

Laz didn't have an answer to Avery's statement. He hoped where he had planned on taking her there would be enough distractions to get her off what he could do for her.

He drove through back roads until he pulled up on a cute yellow house with battleship gray accents and jet-black railings.

"I thought we were going to a hotel tonight. Whose place is this?" Avery stared at the house as she asked the question.

"Step out of the car and come up with me." Laz got out first and opened her car door when she seemed reluctant to move.

Even with her door open and his hand out to her, Avery still hesitated. She finally accepted his hand and walked with him to the front door where a colorful wreath hung.

Laz rang the doorbell before knocking on the door.

"This isn't the type of surprise that I like." She pulled her hand out of Laz's grasp. "Whose house is this?"

The door opened before he could answer.

Avery's mouth hung open as she looked at the woman who had answered the door and then Laz. "Is this your girlfriend or wife or something?"

"Yeah. Like anyone would want to marry this guy." The dark-haired beauty slapped Laz on his shoulder. "You could have given me more than a day's notice."

"Where's the fun in that, Stinky?" Laz laughed, and then turned to Avery. "Avery Shields, this is Marissa Kyson, my baby sister."

He could almost see the color returning to Avery's face as she extended her hand to Laz's sister.

"Nice to meet you. Laz has told me so very little about you." Avery shook her hand.

"Same here." Marissa wrapped her arm around Avery's shoulders. "But that's about to change. Come on inside."

"Be nice." Laz followed the duo into his sister's home.

"Hey, you made the first shot when you called me Stinky. Now everything is on the table."

Marissa meant that literally. When Laz scanned the home, he saw his family's photo album sitting on her living room coffee table along with some of his other childhood memorabilia.

"You do not fight fair." Laz shook his head.

"Yeah, but I'm fun."

* * * *

When Avery first saw the tall, thin, young woman when she had opened the front door, she thought Laz wanted to introduce her to his ex-girlfriend. She couldn't see the resemblance since his sister had dark brown hair and odd-colored green eyes, different from Laz's blond hair and blue eyes. The shape of their noses and mouths gave their relationship away.

The inside of the quaint home matched what Avery assessed of Laz's sister. She had every room painted a different color, but somehow it worked. She mixed fabrics and prints, like a strong, hearty black leather couch on top of a fluffy white shag rug.

Even the dinner she had prepared for them had been a hodgepodge of dishes. Indian-inspired sides served alongside Latin cuisine and even sushi with an Italian dessert to follow all of it. Avery would have turned her nose up to all of it if the food didn't all taste delicious.

"Please tell me that you had all of this catered." Avery leaned back in her chair and rubbed her stomach but refused to release her spoon.

By hook or by crook, she would finish this decadent chocolate treat that looked like it came from a five-star restaurant.

"Nope. Cooked it all." Marissa ran her hand back through her shaggy hair, different from Laz's straightlaced hairdo. "I love to cook. Wish I could do it as a profession."

"You don't? That's surprising." She took another bite of her dessert and had to throw in the towel. She tossed her white cloth napkin on the table. "I give. What is this called?" She pointed to the last portion she could not shove into her mouth.

"*Tartufo di Pizzo*. It's just a jazzed-up ice cream. Of course, true Italians would wash my mouth out with soap to hear me call it that." Marissa shoved her sleeves up her thin arms and showed off an array of tattoos.

That view alone made Avery look at Marissa and Laz again to make sure these two could be related.

"So what do you do for a living, since it looks like torturing people with great-tasting food is only your hobby?" Avery smiled before taking another sip of her sweet red wine.

Marissa wagged her finger at her. "I like her." Then she laughed. "I'm a computer geek. I work at the Pentagon."

Avery laughed until she noticed that neither Marissa nor Laz joined her. "Seriously?"

"Yeah. I started under a way different administration. But I'm damn good at what I do, and I make a great living at it."

"She's Dad's favorite." Laz nodded toward his little sister.

Marissa stood and started gathering dirty dishes from the table. "You are so full of it. He loves taking you out with him. His son. His boy." She nudged Laz on his head with her elbow.

Avery started to stand to help Marissa with clearing the dishes.

"Sit. You're my guest here." Marissa reached for Avery's dessert plate when Avery slid it away from her.

Marissa laughed harder. "I get it. Do you at least want me to put it in the freezer for a bit so it doesn't get too runny?"

Avery looked at her partially eaten dish before shaking her head. "I'll keep working on this."

Marissa stopped by Laz before going into the open kitchen area. "Yep, definitely like her more than that other chick."

"Little louder, Stinky. I don't think all of Virginia heard you." Laz shook his head.

At the top of her lungs, Marissa screamed, "Avery is way better for you than the last few chicks you've dated."

"Christ, Stinky. That was a joke, not a dare." He ran his hand over his head. "Besides, we're only working together. I'm trying to represent her and help her singing career."

His sister scraped items into the trash can before rinsing off each dish and putting them into the dishwasher. She looked at Avery. "Do you know he sings?"

Laz huffed. "Not this again."

Avery nodded. "Yes, I've heard him a couple of times."

"Voice like an angel. I'm not sure why he's not a big mega star himself." She snapped her fingers before wiping her hands on a towel. "Be right back." She went to the other side of the kitchen and went down a set of stairs to the basement area.

"You two look nothing alike, but I like her." Avery finished off her wine.

"People used to tell us that I got my looks from our mother, and that Marissa looks more like our father." He shrugged.

"And what about your other sisters?" She twirled her spoon into her dessert and licked her spoon.

When she noticed that Laz hadn't answered, she turned her gaze to him and found him watching her enjoy her sweet treat.

Avery would have stopped but the temptation proved to be too much for her. She slid her tongue up the concave center of the spoon before slithering her tongue into her mouth and following up the taste with a satisfied moan.

She didn't know if the lick or the moan did Laz in, but he grumbled and had to look away from her.

"One sister is a good mix of the two. Really light brown hair and bright green eyes. The third looks a lot like our mother." He ran his hand over his mouth. "Look, I don't know what my sister has planned, but—"

"I don't either, but I know what I want."

Laz said nothing as he stared at her, heavy lidded. His breathing increased as he drummed his fingertips on the table. In the stillness of the room, Avery caught the distinct sound of stomping coming up the steps before Marissa burst into the room.

Her skintight, black skinny jeans looked sprayed onto her body. Avery could tell Marissa didn't wear a bra under her white ribbed tank top with a Guns 'N Roses logo on the front.

"Come on down to the basement. I have something to show you two." She beamed as she led the way.

Laz stood and held his hand out to Avery to get her on her feet. He continued holding her hand as he guided her through the kitchen and down to the finished and brightly lit room. The touch seemed harmless until he brushed his thumb across the back of her hand. The simple move transformed her skin to goose-pimpled flesh in a matter of seconds.

In the wide-open basement with a couple of pillars littering the room, Avery found a few couches, some funky artwork, and an elaborate hookah sitting in the corner of the room.

"Have a seat and enjoy the show." Marissa pointed to the large TV screen mounted on the wall.

Had she set the room up a different way, it could have easily looked like a movie theater. Laz brought Avery to a couch. When he sat, she had expected him to move as far away from her as possible. Instead he positioned himself right next to her.

Feeling emboldened, she rested her hand on his knee as they faced the TV screen.

"Do you remember this?" Marissa clicked a remote.

On the screen popped up an image of a group of kids standing on a deck with a pool in the background.

"Oh, come on, Marissa. Not this." Laz leaped from his seated position.

"Now it's Marissa. Not Stinky anymore?" She giggled. "Enjoy."

"Wait. Laz, is that you?" Avery pointed to a little, fair-haired boy in the center of a gaggle of girls.

"That's my brother all right." Marissa plopped down in a chair and threw her leg over the arm of the chair. "This was either my birthday party or Josie's."

"It was Josie's." Laz resumed his seated position and kept his stare on the floor instead of the screen.

"Oh, yeah. This was at our old house, remember? The one with the pool. I miss having our own pool." Marissa sighed.

"I don't miss these parties." Laz shook his head.

"Why?" Avery didn't understand his disdain for this time in his life.

From what she saw, he looked like an adorable boy who grew up to be a very fine man. In his Superman swim trunks, he looked to be about six or seven years old. Amazing how his scrawny chest transformed into something sleek yet muscular now, a chest worthy of touching.

"Come on, Lazzy. Sing for Mama." A beautiful blond woman scooped up young Laz in her arms and sat him on her lap under a large umbrella.

Laz ducked his head down and nuzzled his face into the side of her neck. His mother giggled.

Even in the video, Avery saw the striking resemblance between Laz and his mother.

"She's beautiful." Avery patted Laz's leg. "Are your parents still together?"

Marissa turned to her. "No. They divorced years ago. Mom lives in Texas now." She brought her attention to Laz. "Have you talked to her recently? She's going to marry that guy she's been dating. She seems really happy now."

"Good for her." He stole glances at the TV.

Young Laz mumbled something into his mother's neck.

"What's that, baby?" She brought his head up. "Speak up so we can all hear you."

"You sing first." He clutched her shirt but kept his gaze on her.

Avery's skin prickled and she sat up taller.

"Us together, okay?" She nodded.

Laz's blue eyes in the video looked huge and cute on him. He nodded to his mother. When she started singing "Walking on Sunshine," it didn't take long for young Laz to join her. Even then, he carried a tune very well.

"Okay, I think we get it." Laz started to stand.

"You know there's more." Marissa clicked something on the remote to cue up another video, this time a group of students stood on tiers like in a chorus recital.

This time the kids looked to be about high school age. Avery searched all the boys' faces until her gaze stopped at one with Laz's same hypnotic blue eyes and boyish face. His body had filled out but not to the magnitude he now reached.

"Shit." Laz shook his head. "Where in the world did you get these? I thought Mom got rid of all this."

"Why would she do that? These are classic." Marissa giggled. "And I begged Mom to let me have them."

This time the students all sang Whitney Houston's "The Greatest Love of All." Almost all the students. Avery couldn't mistake the distinct look of fear in Laz's eyes. She could tell he mouthed the words while his intense stare into the audience became almost uncomfortable to view. His fear leaped off the screen and became so palpable that Avery shifted in her seat watching him.

As soon as the song ended, Laz ran from the stage. On instinct, Avery reached out to grab Laz's hand.

He surprised her by jumping back up again. "I think we've seen enough."

"Aw, come on, Laz. You still can't laugh at this now?" Marissa turned off the video. "You were cute back then."

"Yeah, well, good looks only get you so far, right?" He cut a glance at Avery before turning away.

"Not everyone is cut out to be in front of an audience. That's for sure." Avery stood and strolled over to Laz. "But I think it takes talent to recognize talent." She slid her hand into his. "Thank you for choosing me, and for being a strong enough man to represent me to record execs. I can't do what you do."

He regarded her for a moment. "I will fight for you. You know that, right?"

Avery smiled. "I figured out two important things at dinner tonight." She looked over at Marissa. "Your sister is an amazing cook, and if she would let me, I would live with her just to eat her food."

"Done." Marissa snickered. "I have two extra bedrooms."

"The other thing I learned is that despite how you started, you have a place in the music industry." Avery nodded.

Laz stared at her like he wanted to see if she had given him a line or the truth. When he finally smiled, she exhaled.

Marissa turned off the TV and stood. "I'm taking you two to the airport in the morning, right?"

Laz nodded but kept his stare on Avery. "No, I have the rental. But you can see us off if you want."

"Like I said, I have two extra bedrooms, and there's a pullout down here in the basement." She looked at her oversized watch. "I was going to head out to a club, so you two can have this place to yourselves if you wa—"

"No. We're going to stay at a hotel close by and come back here in the morning for breakfast." Laz held Avery's hand as he went back upstairs.

"We are?" Avery had assumed that with this side trip to his sister's place, and them both being strapped for cash, that Laz would want to stay with family.

Maybe Laz felt the same way Avery did now. Heat radiated through her body, and only one of two things would douse it. Either she needed to take a long, cold shower, or she needed a repeat sexual performance from Laz.

"I thought you were going to stay here. I cleaned out the rooms and everything for you." Marissa followed the two of them up to the main part of the house.

"We don't want to cramp your style." Laz let Avery's hand go long enough to give his baby sister a hug.

"You're not leaving because of the video, are you? I didn't think you would get wound up about that." She held on to her brother.

"Yes and no." He gave her a knowing look and cocked his head.

Marissa split her attention between her brother and Avery. "I'm going out and I won't be back for a while. You two can have the run of the place."

Laz shook his head. "If I know you, you won't be returning here alone." He winked. "I appreciate the offer. Our flight is kind of late, so we'll be here around nine in the morning."

"I'll have breakfast ready." Marissa gave Laz a salute.

"I can hardly wait." Avery hugged her. "Thank you for everything."

"I didn't do anything." When Avery pulled back, Marissa continued talking. "But you could do a lot of great things for this guy. I might give him a hard time, but he's a really good man. If he says he's going to do right by you, believe him." She moved in closer. "And if anything else happens between the two of you, be very, *very* good to him. He's my only brother and I love him to death."

Avery nodded, almost afraid to say anything else.

"See you in the morning." Laz captured Avery's hand again and pulled her out to the rental car.

Once inside, he sped off through back roads, outside of the city until he got to a hotel.

"Wait right here." Laz didn't wait for Avery to respond before he jumped out.

Avery bounced her knee and drummed her hands over her thighs as she waited for him. Even with the air conditioner on full blast, sweat still rolled down the side of her face.

When Laz came back a few minutes later with a small white card holder in his hand, Avery's pulse quickened.

He got in the car and parked it in front of the hotel. When he turned it off, he took that time to address her.

"I got a room for us." He stared at her as though daring her to disagree. "Let's go."

Chapter 15

Laz didn't know what had come over him. He had gone from business-minded to family-oriented to thoroughly embarrassed to horny as hell. After Marissa showed those humiliating videos of him as a kid not being able to perform in front of an audience, he thought Avery would see him as a loser, or worse, a liar. Her show of support made his heart swell.

He didn't wait for the elevator doors to close before he smothered Avery with a kiss. Damn if she still didn't taste like the sweet dessert she'd eaten earlier. Or maybe that sweetness had come from her essence.

He pressed her back against the elevator wall. She held his shoulders and eased her hands down to his waist. When the elevator car stopped on their floor, Laz broke from the kiss to corral their luggage.

"No regrets. I want this. I want you." Avery wrapped her arm around his muscled biceps.

Laz heard every word she'd said. He had been thinking the same thing. When he got to their hotel room, he pressed her back against the door before opening it. Every cell in his body pulsed as he crushed his mouth against hers.

"No talking." He shook his head.

"Get the key." Avery ran her hands down his shirt to his pants.

When she coasted her hand up over the zipper and stroked his erection, he forgot about work and singing and being embarrassed. He had to have this woman. His woman.

Laz retrieved the card key from his pocket. He glanced to the side for a moment when he thought he saw someone else down the hall. His mind played tricks on him.

He unlocked the door and ushered the two of them inside with the luggage. Before closing the door, he put out the *Do Not Disturb* sign and locked it in every way possible.

It didn't matter that he didn't have any lights on in the room. Even if cloaked in pitch darkness, Laz would know every curve, every swell, every place on Avery's body that made her moan for him.

Laz toed out of his shoes as he walked Avery backward toward the bed. When she fell onto it, she wasted no time in reaching for his jeans to undo them. He held her wrists to stop her. He wanted to control this, set the pace, slow them down. If only his body didn't push him to keep going.

Avery gazed up at him, wordlessly willing him to release her, allow her to finish what she started, what she wanted. Laz opened his hands to free her.

She licked her lips as she undid the button fly on his jeans and eased the zipper down. Taking his own advice, Laz said nothing. He removed his T-shirt and tossed it to the floor. When Avery pulled his pants down to his feet, he stepped out of them.

She wrapped her hand around the base of his erect shaft. Thank God he had the forethought to bring condoms even though his rational side told him to carry on a physical relationship with Avery would be a mistake. His heart and body overruled his head, especially when he saw her again.

The first swipe of her tongue across the tip had his knees buckling. He did everything he could not to lean on her shoulders, but when she covered his mushroom-shaped head with her mouth and held him there, he gripped her shoulders. When she moved her mouth down to the base of his cock, he sucked air between his teeth.

As Avery drew her mouth back, Laz growled, "Mmm, good." He swept her hair back from her face.

Avery's tongue curved around his pulsating shaft, making Laz pant hard and fast. He never felt a connection to anyone this fast or this hard. When she stared up at him, he couldn't help but be transfixed in her gaze.

She cradled his balls. At that point, Laz almost dropped to his knees. Avery worked on him for what seemed like hours only because it felt too incredible to be believed. She managed to massage his sac, twist her other hand around the base of his shaft, and lave his penis all at once so in Laz's head, it felt like a million women worked on him at the same time.

He felt his stomach tighten at the same time his legs shook. He knew she had him close to exploding. No way did he want that to happen like this. Not now.

Laz pulled back from her. From her shocked expression, he knew she had more to give him. To give her a better idea of what he wanted, he went to his overnight bag and pulled out a box of condoms.

Once Avery saw that, she stripped out of her maxi dress and sandals. Not content to let her do all the work, Laz helped remove her bra and panties. He hugged her naked body close to his before he kissed her.

Avery leaned her head back and reached for the protection. "Now. I need you." She tore open the box and opened a package at the end of a strand.

This time she had no problem rolling it on him. Laz had no issue getting her against the wall, hooking his arm under her leg before thrusting himself inside her tight, hot channel.

"Oh my God." Avery gripped his shoulders and held on to him as he scooped her other leg over his free arm.

He cradled her rounded ass in his hands as he moved himself in and out of her. "So good."

Avery held on to Laz's shoulders as she squeezed her legs around his waist. The scent of her sweat and essence wafted up to his nose. He couldn't get enough of the smell.

Laz carried her to the bed and held himself inside her while he stared into her soft brown eyes. "Hi."

Avery smiled and nodded. "Hey."

He kept the motion smooth and steady, a perfect way to keep them united. Avery felt soft and firm and hard and everything he wanted. When she leaned her head back, he took the opportunity to lick up her neck and kiss her chin. He curved his hips during one thrust and she tightened her hold on him.

"Yes." She squeezed her eyes shut and nodded her head. "Close."

Laz kept up the motion until Avery broke, moaning and clawing at him until she settled back into the mattress. He cupped her breast and massaged it.

Satisfying her tipped him over the edge. Laz increased his speed until he felt himself shaking again. When he came, he held himself up over her body for as long as he could before collapsing on top of her.

"Do you always travel with condoms?" Avery chuckled as Laz rolled off her body.

Laz pulled out of her and moved off to the side. "Never."

"So why did you have—"

"I was hopeful." No use lying.

Avery turned her head to look at him. "Was it everything you hoped for?"

Before he verbally answered, he kissed her again. "And then some."

"So now what do we do?"

That question couldn't be answered with a simple kiss. Laz didn't know if he had one for her.

* * * *

Avery had to admit that she needed Laz for more than just getting her into the music business. He proved to be good for her soul. Meeting his family further showed her what a good man he'd been.

That still didn't mean she didn't have her head in business. Avery crawled out of bed.

"Where are you going?" Laz sounded like he had woken up from a deep sleep. "Please don't tell me you're taking a shower."

Avery rifled through her overnight bag with her back to him. "Why don't you want me to take a shower?"

"I like the way you smell. You smell like us."

She looked back at him and found him smiling. With only one light on in their cozy hotel room, a dark shadow cast over his face so that his smile became the only thing visible.

"I'm getting your contract." She padded back to the bed and slipped under the covers with him. "I have questions."

Laz ran his hand over his face like he wanted to wake himself up more for her. "Okay. Shoot."

"The contract states that I would have you exclusively for two years. Is that standard?" She felt silly asking Laz about these terms. He could tell her anything.

"For artist management, yes. That's standard. But even after that time, if you came to me for questions, I would still help you." He sat up against the headboard and pulled Avery onto him so that she had her back against his chest.

"Laz, I need the light." Plus she wanted to assert herself as an artist, not a woman completely smitten with him and wanting another round of hot sex.

Laz reached behind himself and turned on the light on the nightstand beside him. "Go on. I saw you mark way more than that."

"Twenty percent."

He wrapped his arms around her, careful to not block the contract in her hands. "That's standard."

She felt him nodding behind her. "Gross, not net?"

He rested his hands just below her breasts. "Great question. It is gross earnings." He kissed her temple. "I'm glad you're looking at things like that."

"Thanks. There's a clause in there about me not being able to work with other artists without your permission. I don't like that." She shook her head.

"And why is that?" He tapped his thumb in the space between her tits.

She couldn't tell if he did that as a distraction or if he did it out of habit. Either way, she had to take a beat before she answered him. "I want to decide that. If all of a sudden Ariana Grande says she wants to do a duet with me, I don't want you saying I can't because of whatever reason." Avery also wanted a say-so in her career.

Laz sighed loudly like a father about to share some bad news. "It's cute that you think that right out of the gate, an artist like that will want to work with you."

"Even though you said I was special?" Had he said what he needed to say to get into her pants?

Avery's head told her no, although she had been known to be a poor judge of character.

"And you are special and talented and beautiful." He held her chin and turned her head so that he could kiss her lips. "Usually as a new artist, you're not going to do collaborations like that. You'll be lucky to get a top producer." He held her tighter.

Maybe Laz felt Avery wanting to pull away from him.

"That doesn't mean you won't be successful. You will, but on your own merit." He stroked her head as he rocked back and forth. "Maybe within your first two years, you let me drive. Then after that, you can branch out. Sound like a good compromise?" He kissed the top of her head.

Enough coddling. At that point, Avery sat up away from him. "No. If I'm going to do this, I want to do it on my own terms. That clause isn't reasonable. I decide what I want to do. Like you said, if I need help or advice, I can ask you."

Laz sat up taller. "Maybe this is a conversation we need to have when we're not naked."

Probably a great suggestion, but Avery wanted to get this out now. "Clothed or not, I won't change my mind on how I feel. My father always said I was a trusting soul to my own detriment. I believed everyone. That's probably how I ended up here with you. I trust you. I believe in you. But at some point, I'm going to have to trust my own instincts." She flipped to the next page of her contract. "I can keep going."

"I'm sure you can."

Avery didn't want to look at Laz at that moment, but a line like that deserved some attention. As she suspected, he smiled at her.

"Why did you bring me to your sister's place?"

Laz pulled the contract down and peered at the paperwork. "I don't think I have that in any of the clauses."

She snickered. "You don't. I want to know the reason."

He interlocked his fingers and rested the back of his head against his joined hands. "It was twofold. My sister had been bugging me to visit her, especially if I came through her town."

"Okay. You two do seem really close." Even with close cousins and her friends from the diner, Avery wished she had siblings, someone to share everything from clothes, if she had had a sister, to secrets.

She created an extended family for herself. Graciela became the sister she had always wanted. Jessie filled in as a brother. Bruno could have been an uncle. Avery loved her parents. Just like with everything else in her life, she wanted more.

"We are close. She's my baby sister. I love her to death, even if she does annoy me." He snickered.

"And your other sisters?" Avery kind of wished she had met them, too.

"One is in California. The other is on the Eastern Shore of Maryland. She has three kids who are all wide open." He smiled to himself. "I wish I could see them more often than I have. Work." He glanced at her. "You know."

She shrugged. "Sure. We all have choices to make." Avery sat on her haunches on the bed and moved in closer to him. "And the other reason for seeing Marissa?"

"I wanted her to meet you. She's always been a good gauge of new people I bring into my life." He drew his feet back to bring his knees up.

"So you bring all of your clients to her?" She watched Laz look a bit uncomfortable for a moment.

"That's a pretty long contract. I'm sure you have other questions for me about it." He plucked the pages.

"I do, but this conversation is way more interesting." She placed the paperwork on the bed next to her and moved in a bit closer. "Where did the stage fright come from?"

"You don't let up, do you?" He unlinked his hands to rest one on her thigh.

She shook her head. "Nope."

Laz sighed. "Isn't it enough that you know I have it?"

Avery shook her head. "I find it hard to believe that a man who is so confident in other areas of his life can be so afraid of performing in front of an audience."

He took a deep breath, and Avery did the same. She knew he would be revealing something heavy. She wanted to be prepared.

"As you saw in the video, I was a shy kid. I had an older sister, so if someone asked me anything, she would answer for me, and I was fine with that until my dad told me to assert myself more. That put into my head that I wasn't good enough, that the way I was wasn't the best. I would withdraw, but as I got older, girls noticed me more. One on one, I was confident with them. But to perform meant you were exposing part of yourself, and I already felt inadequate." He scratched his head. "So I studied really hard. I figured an education would save me, and it did. I could talk music and business because I studied it. But because I couldn't control how people reacted to me, no matter how hard I tried or how well I performed, I would freeze." He shrugged. "I can't shake it."

Avery placed her hand on Laz's chest. "Call me crazy, but I think the opposite. I always feel like the audience is rooting for me the entire time. I never think anyone who is listening to me is against me. Maybe that's my trusting nature again. It gets me on stage. It got me to get in the car with you. It's keeping me from going crazy with not knowing where we're going tomorrow."

Laz smiled. "I'm a protector. I want you to rely on me." He patted his chest.

"You're also protecting yourself too much. I believe you can do anything you want." She leaned forward and kissed him.

"Nice of you to think that." He still looked like he didn't believe in himself as a performer.

Since Avery had him out on this ledge, she thought she might as well keep pushing him. "So tell me about your parents."

"Only if you tell me about school. How's that going?" He kept up the pleasant expression that did disarm her.

"Um, good. It's fine." For a brief moment, she had almost forgotten the assignment her professor had given her.

"That doesn't sound either good or fine. What's the deal?" He squeezed her thigh.

"Why are you trying to change the subject?" As much as she could, she tried looking indignant by putting her fists to her naked hips.

"Why are you doing the same thing?" He cocked his head. "Come on. Show me yours and I'll show you mine."

That line made her laugh. "Fine. I have to do a special project. I have it covered. It'll be fine." She didn't want to delve into too many details. She didn't need saving.

"I'm sure you will be. But I'm here to—"

"I will be fine." She nodded to assure him. "Now tell me about your parents. I know a little about your mother, the Broadway star who never was. What about your father?"

Laz stared at Avery for a moment. "If you were having problems in school, you would tell me, right?"

Avery rolled her eyes and growled. "You're doing it again. School is okay. I have a few more weeks and I'm done." She clapped her hands together. "Now you and your father. What's the scoop?"

This time he shrugged. "No scoop. He's like every other dad out there. He wants me to visit more often. My parents' divorce was surprising. No one saw it coming, especially my mother. But she had managed to move on and find someone who respects her."

"So your dad didn't give your mother any respect?"

Laz shook his head. "I didn't say that."

Avery sighed out loud. "Not this again. Say what you're not saying."

This time he got out of bed and paced. Watching a naked man pace should have been sexy as hell. With Laz, he looked conflicted. He ran his hand over his head, but then stopped to scratch it when he halted his marching.

"I always thought my parents had the perfect relationship." Laz shook his head. "When Marissa graduated college, they told us kids they were separating." He snickered.

"What?" Avery hugged her knees to her chest.

"I should have seen it coming. My dad is a terrible flirt."

"That must be where you get it from." She meant for the joke to lighten the mood.

Instead Laz stood by the window far from her. "I always suspected that my dad cheated on my mom. She never said he did, and my father never admitted that. It's always been in the back of my mind. I was determined not to be anything like him."

Not content to let him stew in his own thoughts, Avery got out of bed and sauntered over to Laz. She stood behind him and interlaced her fingers with his while wrapping her free arm around his waist.

The warmth of his skin soothed her. She hoped holding him calmed him as well. It seemed to have done the trick. Laz patted her arm and even started rocking back and forth.

"I don't know your dad, but I know the kind of man you are to me." She kissed the center of his back. "You haven't steered me wrong yet."

"I can't imagine not being seen as trustworthy, especially by…" Laz stopped.

Avery didn't know what he had planned on saying. She knew holding him tighter worked as the best response. "We can talk about the contract some more in the morning, maybe during breakfast."

Laz laughed. "You talking about the terms in front of my sister? That'll be funny. She'll make you add clauses like foot massages and free ice cream."

Avery walked around his body to face him. Then she wrapped her arms around his waist. "The foot massage thing actually sounds really good."

"You think?" Faster than a blink of an eye, Laz bent over enough to hoist Avery onto his shoulder and carry her back to bed.

Avery squealed. "Laz! Put me down."

As soon as she made the demand, he plopped her down on the mattress. "I think I'm ready to talk about additional perks for you." He straddled her body.

"Ohh, perks. I like the sound of that." She rested her hands on his thick thighs.

"Good. These perks I would like to show you before you agree. Are you game?" He ran his finger over her nose to her lips.

"I can take anything you want to dish out."

Avery meant every word. Laz came from a business where she had every right not to trust him. From the way he treated her, she felt a bond she never had expected to feel in this business. She headed for an adventure that could lead to every dream she'd ever had. Once she made a name for herself, she could tell her parents that she had been right all along.

Sleep came easily, but not quickly. Laz pushed her body to its limit and then some, but Avery enjoyed it all.

Exhaustion filled Avery even as she felt light kisses on her bare shoulder. The sensation reminded her of the first time she and Laz had had sex. She dreamed he kissed down her body, until she opened her eyes and saw she hadn't imagined the sensation.

Although she wanted to prolong the feeling, Avery slowly opened her eyes and turned her head toward the kisses. She found Laz behind her pressing his lips against her bare skin. Until she turned over to take full stock of him, Avery didn't realize that Laz had already dressed.

"You took a shower already?" Avery rubbed her eyes with the heel of her hand.

Laz nodded. "I wanted to wake you up, but you look so tired."

She laughed. "I wonder why."

Feigning surprise, Laz widened his eyes and placed a hand to his chest. "Are you implying that I'm at fault?"

She gave him a quick peck. "You wore me out." Then she slid out of bed.

"Says the woman who said you could take anything I dished out." He got out of bed and followed her to the bathroom.

"I spoke too soon." She turned around in the doorway.

Walking around naked in front of him felt good, natural.

Laz rested his hands on her waist. "As much as I would love to feast on you, we do have to go." He patted her hip.

"I'll take a quick shower and be ready to go in less than thirty minutes, unless—" She let the implication hang in the air as she backed into the bathroom.

She hoped Laz caught the intention in her eyes.

Laz got to the doorway and stopped. "You are very tempting." He kissed her forehead. "Go."

Avery huffed. "This could have been our final moment before things got crazy. You know that's coming, right?"

Laz regarded her for a moment and simply smiled.

Not waiting to hear his assessment of their situation, Avery turned on the shower and got inside. This would be the last day before meeting the label that would, hopefully, sign her. Things would be changing for her, and Avery had to be ready for it.

After getting dressed, Avery and Laz packed up their few belongings and headed back to Marissa's place. On the way to her front door, Laz held Avery's hand.

The intimate touch surprised her, but she liked it. She loved feeling needed.

Laz rang the doorbell and knocked. "If you liked dinner, you're going to love Marissa's breakfast."

The door opened and an older gentleman stood on the other side. When she saw the smile sliding down Laz's face, she suspected she knew the identity of this man with more salt than pepper hair, squinty blue eyes, and a well-manicured beard that matched his hair. He stood eye to eye with Laz.

"There's my favorite son."

Chapter 16

Laz should have expected to see Bradley Kyson at Marissa's place. His sister kept their father in the loop about everything, just like she did as a child. She would have told their dad about Laz's trip and his subsequent return.

Laz had hoped he kept his true feelings in check. From Avery's rosy cheeks, he suspected she felt embarrassed for him.

To lighten his mood, Laz smiled and embraced his father. "Hey, Dad."

Bradley hugged him back. "What happened to you calling me when you came to town?"

"I got busy." Laz pulled back from the hug in time to catch Bradley staring at Avery.

"I'm sure you did." Bradley's comment only came off as charming because of his heavy Southern accent.

Otherwise the comment would sound as lecherous as his old man had meant it.

Marissa moved from her stove top to her double oven. "Breakfast will be ready soon, but coffee is ready, and I have juice."

Laz cleared his throat.

"Oh, yeah." Marissa nodded her head back. "A pack of tea bags are up in the cabinet. Help yourself."

"Before anyone moves, I need to introduce myself to this lovely woman." Bradley held his hand out to Avery, who smiled and politely accepted it. "Bradley Kyson. And you are…?"

"Avery." She peered at Laz. "Avery Shields."

"What an interesting name. Powerful." He winked at her, and then turned her hand over so that he could kiss the back of it. "Very nice to meet you. My son is a little slow on his manners."

"I was going to introduce you. You're just a little faster with other women." Laz let the implications of his statement hang between the two of them. When his father gave him a cutting look, Laz continued. "I'm working on getting Avery a record deal." He put his arm around her shoulders, which he hoped would have encouraged his father to release her hand. "She's a very talented singer."

"Very good." Bradley bowed his head. "Do you know that Laz has a wonderful voice, too?"

Avery nodded. "I've heard him."

"He should be the one out there filling arenas." Bradley followed Laz and Avery into the dining room area.

"Nice of you to say, Dad, but I know what I bring to the table." He turned to Marissa. "Speaking of which, anything I can put on the table to get this meal going?"

"In a rush to go somewhere?" His father stood next to him in the kitchen area.

"Yes." He looked at Bradley. "Going back to New York."

"And Avery is going with you." Bradley glanced at her.

"Of course." Laz placed a bowl of fresh, hot biscuits on the table, and then returned to the kitchen. "She's coming with me to meet the label owner."

"I'm sensing something here." His dad put his finger to his lips in a pensive manner.

"Probably my frustration from not eating anything yet." Laz glared at his baby sister. "You know how I get when I'm starving."

"And horny." Bradley laughed. "I swear. That summer I grounded you after you took that trip to Florida, you were fit to be—"

"Dad."

"What? I'm just talking about the good ol' days. I thought you like reminiscing." Bradley shrugged.

"Maybe not in front of company." Laz gripped the back of a chair. "Marissa went through all this trouble to make this happen."

When Bradley had his attention diverted and Laz kept his gaze on Marissa, she stuck out her tongue. She looked like her younger, brattier self.

"Son, I rarely get to see you. And your calls have been very infrequent." Bradley turned to Avery. "I hope you treat your parents a little bit better than this one."

Avery flashed a very polite if not tight smile. "They probably feel the same way you do. I don't call enough. I don't visit enough. I don't do enough." She rested her hand on top of his. "When is enough enough?"

Bradley volleyed his attention between the two of them. "Good answer." He kept his stare on Laz. "And you're right. Marissa made us a great breakfast. We should all enjoy it." He started to come around to pull out Avery's chair when Laz beat him to the punch.

Marissa came to the table with the rest of the food and assumed a chair next to Bradley instead of the head of the table. So Laz sat there and hoped the position spoke volumes to the group.

The meal started off in silence. Laz watched as each person served themselves a little bit of everything Marissa had prepared. The scent of bacon caught Laz's attention. The sweet meat became a treat to him as he chewed on a strip while he observed the group.

"So, Mr. Kyson—"

Bradley put his hand on top of Avery's, a move that made Laz bristle. "Please call me Bradley. Mr. Kyson is my son." To punctuate his joke, he winked at Laz.

"Okay. Bradley, what was Laz like as a kid?" Avery smiled at Laz.

"You didn't get enough stories from Marissa last night?" Laz shook his head.

"Nope." She giggled. "He told me about his spur-of-the-moment Florida trip. And I saw videos of him singing."

"Or trying to sing." Marissa snickered before taking a big chomp from a fluffy biscuit.

"Don't tease your brother." Bradley wagged his finger at Marissa. "Laz was a great baby." He stared at Laz for far too long.

Laz had to lower his gaze to his plate of food that he now found impossible to swallow.

"He rarely cried." Bradley wiped his mouth. "Only when he needed something, but that's it. He was an incredibly shy kid. I remember it took two summers for you to ask out the neighbor girl."

Marissa had to cover her mouth when she started to laugh. "That's right. I had forgotten about Amy."

Laz wished they had all forgotten about that time in his life where he didn't feel worthy. "It wasn't exactly two years. And I was seeing someone else at the time."

Bradley cocked his head. "Dorinda was simply a friend, and you know it. Besides, nothing wrong with dating around. Life is too short to stay saddled with one person."

Laz wiped his mouth and put his napkin on the table. "That's it. I'm done." He looked at Avery. "Are you ready to go?"

"What's wrong with you?" Bradley wiped his fingers before resting his hands on the table.

"Yeah, we were just teasing you. You used to be able to take a joke." Marissa leaned back in her seat and ran her tongue over the ring pierced through her lower lip.

"A joke I can take. I can't take advice from someone who thinks it's okay to cheat when you have a committed partner." Laz stood.

Bradley stood with him. "I asked you nicely not to bring up things you know nothing about between me and your mother. What you think you know, you have no idea." He kept his stare on Laz.

As a young child, the look used to reduce Laz to a puddle. Today, he stood strong.

"I don't? Why don't you school me?" Laz put his fists to his hips.

"Laz, not the time or place, man." Marissa shook her head. "Why don't you take a walk and cool your head?"

"No." He shook his head. "I want Dad to explain to me how beneficial it was to him to date around while Mom cried each night."

"That's enough." Bradley came around from his side of the table to get into Laz's face. "I don't owe you any explanations about my past relationships, and that includes the one with your mother. But I will tell you this. People don't only cry for pain. There could be other reasons."

Laz studied his father's eyes. Although Bradley could be a terrible flirt, Laz always found truth in his father's stare.

"What other reasons could there be?" Laz didn't want his voice to come out so hushed, but he didn't think the thought he had rolling in his head would materialize.

Bradley didn't answer. Or maybe he did with his steely stare. His eyes gave a full story of hurt and pain that Laz wanted to delve into more. Then he felt a hand on his arm. He peered down and saw Avery touching him.

"Maybe we should go." Avery's eyes carried a pleading look to them, one that screamed she didn't want to get in the middle of his family drama.

Laz gave her a solid head nod as his answer.

Avery turned to Marissa, who stood. "Thank you so much for dinner last night and breakfast." She hugged her. "You're an amazing hostess."

"Thanks." She patted Avery's shoulder. "You need to come when I have game night."

"I would love that, but I'm super competitive." She released Marissa.

"Good. You'll fit right in."

Avery stepped over to Bradley when Laz went to his sister.

"Thanks for everything." Laz kissed Marissa's cheek.

Marissa hugged Laz, but held on to him and whispered in his ear. "Cut Dad a break. You don't know everything, okay?"

Laz pulled back and looked back at his father, who now hugged Avery. "I know enough."

Marissa shook her head. "You don't. You really don't." She guided him to the front door away from Bradley and Avery. "When you come through again without Avery, talk to Dad. I mean really talk to him."

Laz couldn't imagine taking time out to discuss anything with his father. "Thanks for everything, including setting me up."

"I didn't think bringing family together would be seen as a setup." Marissa shook her head. "Take care."

Avery strolled over to the duo. "I'm ready. Aren't you going to say goodbye to your father?"

Laz looked back at Bradley. He wanted to say so many things to the man. He finally uttered the only thing that came to his mind. "Goodbye."

* * * *

Avery didn't expect to be put in the middle of a family feud. Since leaving Marissa's place, Laz had remained quiet. He said nothing during the drive to the airport. He didn't say a word as they waited to board. He had even stayed quiet on the cab ride to his apartment.

Avery glanced up at the building before stepping inside the place. She started to haul her luggage up the steps but Laz grabbed her suitcase handle and carried his bag and hers up the steps.

"Home sweet home." He opened the door and allowed her to go inside first.

Hearing him speak finally had a calming effect on her. She exhaled like she had been holding her breath since breakfast.

Avery glanced around the apartment. Although small, he kept the place sparsely decorated.

"Nice." She nodded. She turned to him. "Want to talk about—"

"You hungry?" He placed their bags in the middle of the living room and ducked into his galley-style kitchen. "I don't have much. Crackers, chips, soup." He opened the refrigerator door. "This Chinese takeout is only a few days old."

"No thank you. I wanted to know if you want to talk about what happened with you and your Dad back at—"

"The bathroom is here." He pointed to a door on the other side of the living room wall. "My bedroom is across the hall. You want to lie down for a bit?"

She shook her head. "No, I—"

"Or you can watch TV. I can—"

Avery held up her hands. "Stop it. Why won't you talk about what happened with you and your father?"

He joined his hands together and rested them on top of his head. "No one wants to reveal the moment their hero disappoints them." He shook his head. "Growing up, the man could do no wrong in my eyes...until he did. Now I don't feel like I can forgive him."

"What if you were wrong?" Avery put her hand to his shoulder. "If my parents never gave me a second chance, I don't know where I would be right now." She looked at her watch. "Speaking of which, I need to call them."

"You need some privacy?" Laz started to push her toward his bedroom.

"No. I'm fine here." She pulled her phone from her purse and called her parents' number.

Good or bad, she wanted Laz to hear her conversation.

"I'm going to get something to drink." He sauntered into his kitchen out of her view. "You want something?"

Avery shook her head when she heard her parents' phone ringing on the other end. When she heard the line click, her back stiffened.

"Yes?" Her mother's curt answer chilled Avery's body.

"Hi, Mom. Sorry I missed church." Avery slipped out of her sandals and padded over the hardwood floor.

"It's okay. You are still coming over for dinner, right?" Hope filled Hazel's tone.

"Um, no." Avery leaned against the wall that led into the kitchen. "I told Dad that I was going out of town."

"Out of town? Why?" Her mother's tone rose to that level of frustration that Avery remembered. "Is there something wrong?"

"No. I hope not." Avery took a deep breath. Like she did when she performed the second time at Honey's, she stared at Laz for strength. "It's for work."

Laz gazed up at her when Avery stretched her truth.

"Work? Are you working at another diner for Uncle Pig? Your father is here taking a nap, and I know he doesn't have work elsewhere." Hazel huffed. "What's going on with you? Is it some late-term internship or something?"

No time like the present. Avery had to admit her feelings and, most importantly, her plan. "I'm in New York with Laz. You remember him. He was at my place when you and Dad—"

"I remember. Why are you in New York?"

Laz approached Avery and kept his stare connected to hers.

"I'm trying to get my music career started again." Avery held her head up high. "Laz is trying to help me. We're going to be meeting with a label tomorrow. Hopefully, it'll all go well."

Silence met Avery after her admission, which did not seem like her mother at all. Even when Avery had complained about not liking a shrimp dish at her mother's favorite restaurant, Hazel had spent the next thirty minutes telling Avery why she had been mistaken.

Avery had to break up the silence. "Mom?"

"And school?" Hazel's voice came out low, almost like she didn't want Avery's father to hear her.

"I've got a few weeks left. I'll still finish." Avery pushed herself away from the wall and stood on her own two feet. "This is my time. If I don't do this now, I may never get another chance."

Avery heard rustling on the other end of the phone before she heard her mother say, "Talk to your father."

For this conversation, Avery wanted to take a seat. She backed up out of the kitchen area and padded over to the living room where she took a seat on a bright green couch that definitely did not match Laz's tastes.

"What's going on? Avery, is that you?" Clinton's stern voice would have bowled Avery down had she still been standing.

"Hey, Dad. Look, I won't be at work for the next couple of days." She glanced up at Laz for confirmation.

With a glass of water in hand, he didn't agree or disagree with her. He sat on a chair opposite from her and took a drink.

"Why is that? Are you in trouble again?" He sniffed. "Why does your mother look so upset?"

Avery closed her eyes at that bit of news. She didn't want to distress her mother or anyone. "I told her that I was in New York with Laz to hopefully jumpstart my music career."

Clinton sighed. "God help you. You're not on this again."

She heard drawers opening and being slammed closed.

"Tell me where you are and I'll come up and get you."

"Dad, no. This time around, I'm fine. I didn't call to ask for help." She scratched her head. "It would have been nice if you would support me and my decision."

"No parent wants to see their child disappointed or hurt. Going down this path will only lead to failure."

Avery's heart stopped at that proclamation. "Thanks, Dad."

"If you aren't at work tomorrow night, I'll have to let you go." The frustrated tone left his voice. Now he sounded saddened and pissed.

Avery took a deep breath to keep herself from breaking down over the phone. "Fine. As always, thanks for the support. Glad you believe in me."

"I do, but—"

"Tell Mom I love her." Avery disconnected the call and tossed her phone to the empty space next to her.

She tried hard not to break down. When she gazed up at Laz, the tears came flooding down. Had she just made a colossal mistake by choosing to be selfish?

Laz sprang from his chair and came over to her. "What's wrong? What did he say?" He handed her a handkerchief from his pocket.

Of course he would have a handkerchief on him.

"They were not happy about me coming out here and doing this." Avery wiped her eyes and under her nose. "He said if I'm not home in time for work tomorrow, I'll be out of a job." She cried harder again. "I can't win. Every time I think I'm okay, something happens."

Laz drew her into his arms. "We can't always be the light in our parents' eyes. You saw that with me."

Avery pulled back from him. "No. Your situation was different. You're disappointed with your dad. He, however, thinks the world of you. You can see the pride he has for you in his eyes. My parents see me as a disaster. I can never do anything right." She pointed down. "This time, though, it all feels right. I don't know if it's the timing or the feedback to my singing." She paused and stared at Laz. "Or you. I want it this time. I want to make it so badly."

"I know. I'm here for you." He hugged her again. "Maybe if you go back home with a signed contract, they'll feel different." He kissed the side of her face. "And speaking of signed contracts, since I'm home, I'll look over your proposed changes. We can talk about them and iron some things out. Then, before tomorrow, you can officially be my first client."

Avery nodded.

"Good. Now, what do you want to do?" He rubbed his hands together.

"A tour. Give me a tour of your place." She looked around the small room and had a feeling the tour wouldn't last very long.

"Sure." Laz stood and held out his hand to help her to her feet. "This is the living room slash dining room slash entertaining area."

Avery glanced back at the couch. "And this?"

Laz smiled. "A gift from Marissa. You couldn't tell?"

"I could tell it wasn't your style."

He held her hand and led her to a small alcove where a piano sat. "This is where I relax. Playing music allows me to think or sometimes not think. I can be myself."

"I know what you mean." Music had done a lot for Avery in her life.

He pulled her over to a door on the other side of the piano. After flipping a light switch and standing off to the side, he said, "Bathroom."

The small space had a black-and-white checkered floor that matched the white tiles surrounding a white claw-foot tub. He went against the whole black-and-white theme by hanging bright red washcloths and towels in the space.

"And..." He walked backward to a room across from the bathroom. "My bedroom."

Avery looked around the space. She had to admit. He kept the place clean and neat, nothing like her place. The dark colors he used to decorate the room gave it a dour demeanor, nothing like the man who had managed to curl her toes and step outside of her comfort zone.

"Nice." She turned to him. "Would I stay in here?"

"Of course." He cocked a smile. "I can take the couch."

She shook her head. "Why would I want you on the couch after everything we've done and been through?"

"Because I don't want you thinking that I would bring you here only for one thing."

Avery put her fingers to her lips. "Because of what I can do with my mouth?"

Laz smiled.

She dragged her fingers down her chin to her throat. "Or maybe it's because of what I can do here."

He wrapped his arms around her waist and pulled her close. He pressed his lips against her forehead and temple before kissing her cheek and going to her ear.

After swiping the shell of it with his tongue and making her shiver, he whispered, "I'm going to work on that contract."

Avery groaned. "Such a tease."

Laz laughed as he backed away from her. "You relax, write, watch TV, take a bath, whatever." He glanced at his watch. "I can take you to my favorite Italian place for dinner later. And then we can come up with a game plan for tomorrow." He backed up to the doorway. "Basically the plan is that I talk, you don't."

Avery blinked.

"I'll secure that deal." He winked at her.

An uneasy tickle went up the back of her neck. "Wait. Are you going to tell me the name of the label now that we're here in New York?"

"Tomorrow. It'll all be revealed tomorrow."

The more time Avery spent with Laz, the more he revealed himself to her. Some parts she liked. Others made her question her place there. Did he really think she would want to start her career with someone else pulling all her strings?

Avery mulled over several things in the hours before they walked down a few blocks to dinner. The hole-in-the-wall place didn't look impressive from the outside, not even the couple of wrought iron tables and chairs that decorated the place. She did note the A rating on the window, so she knew it had to be a good spot.

Laz's recommendation hadn't disappointed her. All the food tasted fresh and homemade. It helped that the place looked like the inside of someone's home, complete with an open kitchen.

Laz held Avery's hand on the walk back to his apartment. The intimate touch felt so right with him. She almost felt invincible.

"Will you tell me something?" Avery squeezed his hand.

"Anything." He held up his other hand. "Open book here."

"You heard my demo. You said you liked my voice."

"I did." He pulled her closer to him. "I do."

"What did you like about my voice?" Avery's question had less to do with fishing for compliments and more to do with getting constructive feedback. "I've been looking at the comments on my video."

Laz groaned. "I wish you wouldn't do that."

Avery grabbed his arm and tugged on it. "Why? I want to know what people like and don't like so I can improve."

"Most people who comment come from a real, legitimate place to say something constructive. Others are only interested in a few minutes of infamy to be that disparaging comment that will give them attention. It's comments like those that I'm afraid will get in your head and stay there. I want you how you are now. Untouched. Pure. Raw. Trust me. Once you get into the business, you will get your fill of becoming jaded. I don't want that for you now." He kissed the back of her hand.

"Okay, fine. I'll try to stay off." Avery thought about some of the comments. "Overall, though, they have been positive. There's this one commenter named Kitty Girl who has been my biggest champion. If anyone says anything negative, she shoots them down quick."

"Great. Your first stalker." As though one stood a few feet away from them, Laz wrapped his arm around her waist and pulled her close.

"Not stalker. Advocate." She leaned into him.

Back at his apartment, he took off his shoes and placed them neatly in his closet. Avery stepped out of her sandals and sauntered to the couch where her notebook sat. Even in her thinnest sundress and Laz with his air-conditioning window unit blasting, she couldn't lower her overheated body temperature.

Laz must have felt the same way. He tweaked a knob on his unit and then stripped out of his T-shirt so he walked around in only shorts. The view made Avery lick her lips. Damn, he looked good.

He looked even better after he sat at his piano by a small window. As soon as he touched the keys, he made beautiful music.

Laz played something jazzy that she didn't recognize at first. When Avery stood and strolled toward him, she recognized the Stevie Wonder song that he had arranged differently. She didn't think anyone could perfect something Stevie had created. That alone gave him cool points.

When she sang along with the melody, he kept his stare on her as he played. She leaned on the piano while she sang about everlasting love to him. At the end of the song, he reached for her hand and pulled her forward to kiss her.

"I want to play something else for you. You haven't heard this song before, but you know the words." Laz smiled and started playing something mid-tempo.

Avery hadn't heard this tune before, but she liked it. With the right accompaniment and lyrics, it would be a great radio hit and dance track. When Laz started singing, she realized why he said she would know the words. He sang her song "Secret Wish" to her.

It overwhelmed her to hear her words with music that she had to sit on the piano bench next to him. Content to let him sing the whole song, Avery at first didn't join in with him. At the chorus, she couldn't let him go at it alone. She sang along with him.

At the end of the song, he rested his hands on the keys before looking at her. "What did you think?"

Avery couldn't speak, mainly because her throat started to close.

"When I read the lyrics, I heard the music in my head. I hope you don't mind."

"And you remember my words. You didn't miss one word." She looked at the stand in front of him, the empty stand.

Laz didn't go by her notebook to recall the lyrics. He knew them by heart. "What can I say? I know what I like." He stared into her eyes.

Avery knew what she liked, too. She caressed his cheek before bringing his face down to hers to kiss him. He still tasted of the dessert he had had at the restaurant. Sugary, decadent, delicious.

As soon as she slipped her tongue into his mouth, his needs must have taken over his senses. Laz held her waist and guided her up so that he could position her on his lap facing him while she straddled him. He broke from the kiss long enough to douse the light in that area, although the living room light remained lit.

The backlight gave her enough illumination to see him, all of him. She trailed her fingers down his strong neck to his chest where she circled his nipple, making it harder with each of her passes. Then she eased her hand down his body to his growing erection through his shorts. She rubbed it as she stared into his eyes.

That must have been enough for Laz. She felt him reaching under her dress and grabbing the side of her panties. As she started to stand so that she could shimmy out of them, she heard a distinct rip and felt the fabric cut into her hip.

Ordinarily, she would have been pissed. Considering she wanted this man just as desperately as he wanted her, she worked on getting his hard penis freed from his shorts. She undid the fly and unzipped him at the same time Laz pushed what remained of her undergarments to the side.

As soon as she touched his shaft, Laz stopped her by slipping one finger inside her.

Avery gripped his shoulders as she rode him, slowly at first. The intense connection between them added to the fervor.

Laz wrapped one arm around her waist before slipping a second finger inside her. "That's it." He nodded. "So good."

Avery held on to his shoulders while she leaned her head back. "My God." She rode him faster and faster.

Sweat trickled down between her shoulder blades and between her breasts. She wrapped her legs around him tighter to bring him in deeper into her channel. Her body trembled.

Laz must have known what that meant. "Come on, baby. Do it. Do it."

Avery nodded before sitting up straight and moaning while she came. Every muscle in her body tightened to an almost painful degree until the climax subsided.

Laz unfastened a few buttons on her dress before pulling it over her head. Then, like before, he undid her bra from behind her with only one hand and without looking. He pulled it down her arms and tossed it to the side.

"You. I want you inside me." She kissed him lightly. "Please."

She felt him doing something with his feet under her before he stood with her still on him. He carried her to the couch and placed her on her back. Then he dove into his carryon bag for the condoms he had with him at the hotel.

Laz opened a package and rolled the protection on himself. He kissed her all over her face before finally connecting with her lips. In one stroke, he plunged himself in her.

He cupped her breast and squeezed it, massaging it while making slow, easy thrusts in her. Then he twirled her nipple with his long thumb.

This time, when she felt his muscled thighs shaking, she held him down. Avery gripped his shoulders while moving her hips to meet his thrusts.

"Perfect. Perfect." Laz gritted his teeth like he didn't want to come. He even shook his head.

Avery needed this man. She pinched his nipple at the same time she squeezed his ass cheek with her free hand.

Laz nodded. "Yes!"

Avery felt his hot seed bathing her insides as he held himself in her.

He looked down at her, panting and sweaty. "The next time you see Marissa, you cannot tell her what we did on this couch."

Avery laughed. "Just tell me that your bed wasn't a gift from anyone."

"Only to you." He winked before laughing.

"You almost said that with a straight face." She kissed him. "Let's go to bed before our lives change tomorrow."

"Everything will change." He nodded. "Are you ready for it?"

Avery didn't know about that. For now, she would smile and hope for the best.

Chapter 17

Laz gripped the woman's hand who had changed his life since the first moment he listened to her over a year ago. Each time he stole glances at Avery on their trek to Section Eight he found her beaming as though she knew a secret that she desperately wanted to share but didn't, or maybe couldn't.

He had been holding in a secret, too. No matter what happened today, he had fallen in love with this woman. Everything about her, from her drive to her creativity to her passion, both in the bedroom and out, had him in every way, shape, and form. The fact that they both enjoyed music cemented his love for her. After this meeting, he would share his secret.

"Are you ready?" Laz squeezed Avery's hand.

"I think so." Avery took a deep breath. "Yes, I'm ready. I've wanted this forever."

Laz stopped, which made Avery stop in her tracks. He stood in front of her. "Now remember, even if you get signed, it may take a while to get your album out, if you even get to record an album."

Avery rolled her eyes. "I know. I get it. It's a hurry-up-and-wait kind of business."

He held her hands and looked at her to make sure she understood every word he said. "It can also be a ruthless business if you let it. I don't want to see you get hurt."

She put her hand on his cheek. "I would only get hurt if you didn't believe in me or my talent. But you do, right?"

He took her hand off his cheek and kissed the back of it. "Of course I do. I wouldn't have gone through everything I have if I didn't think you were worth it."

"Then everything will be fine. I feel the same way about you." She opened her mouth like she wanted to say something else.

Laz's heart started pounding. He squeezed her hands, trying to call some strength to reveal his true heart.

Avery laughed a little. "If it doesn't work out, I will have lost two jobs because of you. I could write a song about that."

Laz smiled. "I'll look out for you. I promise. I won't let you go through all this for nothing."

"Great. Now will you *finally* tell me where we're going?" She peered around the big buildings in Manhattan. "This is your city. Not mine. I don't know where we're at."

"We're here." He stopped her in front of the doors to the Section Eight office.

Avery looked up at the steel-and-glass structure. Her smile melted the higher her gaze got. "I see the symbol at the top, but I don't think I know this company."

"They're called Section Eight, and it's run by Sanaa Farook. They mainly do rap acts." Laz had his hand at the small of Avery's back when he felt her take a large step back.

"I don't rap." She shook her head.

"I know. They're looking to expand, and they're wanting a flagship, unknown artist to kick off their new brand. That could be you." He stood in front of her and stared into her eyes. "This could be your big break."

She stared back at him for a moment before gazing up at the building again. "What about Charisma? I mean they're local, well, for me. And they seem to do the kind of music that I—"

"Maybe as a Plan B. But this Plan A one is damn near a surefire bet." He wrapped his arm around her waist. "Come on. Let's go in and wow these people. If it doesn't work out, we'll Plan B it."

Avery took a deep breath and nodded. "Okay. I'm ready."

Laz opened the front door for her and walked in behind her. Avery stopped in her tracks at the security desk.

"Oh, wow." She said the utterance in a low tone but still audible enough for Laz to catch it.

"Standard. There are a lot of wackos out there." He stood behind Avery and rubbed her shoulders.

"I don't remember seeing anything like this at Charisma." She slowly stepped forward toward the security checkpoint area.

"It's okay. You're here to sing. Let's get through this and start your destiny." Laz helped her load her metal items into a dish.

Once she got through the detector unscathed, her shoulders dropped down. Laz joined her on the other side and walked with her to the receptionist desk. Stone Face kept her demeanor stoic until Laz got close to her desk. Then she had a slight hitch at the corner of her mouth.

"Hi, Laz Kyson and Avery to see Ms. Farook." He smiled to keep up the professional demeanor.

The receptionist cut her gaze away from Avery. "You two can have a seat. I'll let Ms. Farook know that you're here."

"Thank you." Laz started to turn when he felt a hand on top of his at the counter.

The young woman with the stick-straight hair had his hand pinned down and had herself positioned halfway out of her seat. "Are you still thirsty? I could quench it for you."

Laz glanced at Avery, who looked stunned, confused, and a bit pissed, before he brought his attention back to Stone Face. He slipped his hand from under hers. "No. We're fine." He made sure to point to the two of them. "We'll wait for Ms. Farook."

Laz followed Avery to the waiting area. He sat next to her and draped his arm across the back of the chair behind her, to which she responded by sitting up straight and away from him.

"She seemed very eager to please you." Avery crossed her legs.

"She's a receptionist. She's supposed to make guests feel comfortable." That reasoning sounded plausible.

Guilt plagued him that he had flirted his way to change that woman's demeanor.

"I don't know her. I've been here a couple of times." He braced his elbows on his knees and lowered his head.

"Okay." Avery picked up a magazine on the coffee table in front of her and absentmindedly flipped through pages.

He shook his head. "I think she must have mistook a couple of compliments as something more."

Avery nodded and remained quiet, but her crossed leg and swinging foot spoke volumes. After a beat she slammed the magazine closed. "So you didn't like it when your dad was a little flirtatious during breakfast, but it's okay for you?"

Laz definitely didn't see the comparison. "Hold on. There's a huge difference between me and my father."

"What's that?" She stiffened up her back.

"He was married when he stepped out of line. We're…" He stopped himself from going any further.

"We're what?" Avery glared at him. "Look. I understand. I get that we're going to have a working relationship. You said from the beginning that we shouldn't cross the line." She glanced at the young, Asian woman behind the receptionist desk. "What we did, we did out of fun. If you want to date other people—"

"I don't." Damn it. If he had any chance of swaying her, he had to do it now. "And I want us to be more than exclusive besides you signing that contract and being my client."

"Laz, I—"

"Mr. Kyson!"

Laz turned when he heard his name coming from someone with a booming voice. The guard that had taken him up each time he had been to the label called to him from in front of the private elevator.

"Ms. Farook will see you now." He clasped his hands in front of his body as he waited for Laz and Avery to approach him.

Laz stood first and held out his hand to her. Avery got up on her own accord and walked ahead of him.

Shit. He really fucked this up big time. Laz had to make this right.

Like before, the guard got them up to the top floor, entered his security credentials, and ushered them in the room. Inside, Sanaa sat behind her massive desk. She didn't bother standing when Laz and Avery entered the room. Why should she? She owned this castle.

The same three stooges that had stood off to the side of her during Laz's last visit assumed their same position this time. When Laz noticed Avery walking slower and slower next to him until she now walked behind him, he stopped until she could catch up. Trying to give her a bit of his strength, he held her hand.

Avery felt like she wanted to jerk out of his grasp, but he held her tighter.

"You got this." He nodded to her.

"Have a seat." Sanaa pointed to two chairs in front of her. Then she looked at Avery. "Allow me to introduce myself." She stood from her desk finally and made her way around it to stand in front of Avery. "I'm Sanaa Farook. I own Section Eight." She glanced over at her team. "These are my employees who help me with business deals."

Sanaa's monochromatic theme continued. Today she wore all black from head to toe. Damn. Did the woman have to look like she was headed to a funeral? The look couldn't have given Avery a positive outlook on her chances there.

Sanaa extended her hand to Avery, who shook it tentatively.

"Nice to meet you. My name is Avery Shields." Avery drew her hand back.

"Mr. Kyson is one of your biggest cheerleaders." Sanaa walked back to her seat. "I didn't believe him when he said he had someone special in mind for my burgeoning R&B and pop line." She shook her head. "I saw the video of you." She clicked a button on a remote, populating a video on a large screen in the room.

The video showed Avery singing "Make You Feel My Love" during her first night at Honey's. Laz couldn't tear his attention away from the beauty on the screen. If only she had opened her eyes, he could have experienced her full soul then. Since that moment, he had bonded with her in a real way. He wanted more. This misunderstanding couldn't tear them apart.

Sanaa's loud clapping startled Avery enough that she gasped and put her hand to her chest.

"Amazing. Beautiful." Sanaa smiled and pointed to the screen. "That's the type of artist I need here at Section Eight."

"Thank you." Avery tucked her hair behind her ear. "I have a question for you."

A couple of people in Sanaa's team shuffled as though asking Sanaa a question went beyond what a mere mortal could do.

"Go ahead. Is it about the contract?" Sanaa glanced at Laz. "He showed it to you, right?"

Avery didn't look at him. "No. He said he would review it for me."

Sanaa shook her head and tsked. "Not good. Sounds like he's trying to control you and stifle your voice."

"Not true and not fair. I had questions about a lot of the terms that I wanted to discuss with your attorneys first. Nothing's getting signed today." Laz waved his hands in the air.

"Don't be so sure about that." Avery didn't look at him when she responded. She kept her full attention on Sanaa. "Why do you call this place Section Eight?"

Sanaa leaned back. "I feel like I've answered this in interviews time and time again."

"Unfortunately, I didn't know which label I would be seeing today until I stood outside of your doors this morning." Avery crossed her arms over her chest and crossed her legs.

"Wow. More controlling tactics." Sanaa winced. "As a businessperson, I can respect your need to have a handle on everything. But you have to listen to your artist and let them be."

This meeting started to feel like his last meeting at Universe. Laz couldn't take another character assassination. "I wanted to surprise Avery, not withhold anything from her."

"Sure." Sanaa shook her head at Laz. "Anyway, I wanted a name that was tough but showed some resilience. To be in section-eight housing means you are down on your luck, but you haven't given up. You're asking for help to make your life and your family's life better."

Avery nodded.

"Plus Death Row and Murder were already taken." Sanaa shrugged and chuckled, which made her team laugh as well.

"Oh. For a short time, my family was on public assistance." Avery kept her stare directly on Sanaa.

Laz blinked at her admission. He wanted so much to hold her, but the strength in her words almost put an invisible barrier around her. Avery didn't need protection. She needed to be understood.

"You're right. Hitting rock bottom like that did make my family fight for a better life." She glanced down at her watch. "I work with my father in his janitorial business. If I'm not there tonight to help him, he's going to fire me, and I'll be out of work."

Sanaa shook her head. "No, you won't dear." She snapped her fingers. "I'm prepared to offer you a contract, a recording contract. Not an artist grooming one. I want you to hit the ground running."

The big man in the track suit stepped forward with another leather-bound journal that Laz suspected had another boilerplate contract inside. He couldn't let Avery sign it. The terms asked for everything short of her first-born child.

Avery's eyes widened. "Are you serious?"

Laz furrowed his brows. "Wait. Hold on. Let's talk about this." He had never known a label lately to be this aggressive on a new artist. Usually, they had to prove themselves with writing hits and singing background before making their own mark.

Sanaa ignored Laz. "I'm serious. I liked what I heard." She scanned Avery up and down. "And I like what I see. You're pretty and sexy but talented. Lately, it's been a crapshoot."

Avery reached for the contract until Sanaa raised her hand in the air.

"But there is one thing I need. Actually, two things." She held up her index finger. "The first thing is I need to see and hear for myself that you're the real deal." She sat back in her chair.

"What does that mean?" Avery's attention went from Sanaa to Laz and back to Sanaa.

"Sing. I want you to stand right here and belt out a tune for me right now." She pointed down. Then she tapped on her watch full of diamonds. "And my time is precious so don't keep me waiting."

"Um, okay." Avery stood, which, again, startled the group next to Sanaa until the woman held up her hand.

"Wait. She hasn't prepared a song. She hasn't warmed up." Laz did everything he could to save his client, his woman. "This isn't really fair to—"

He stopped talking as soon as Avery started to sing. The air went out of the room. Or maybe it existed in the space only for Avery to sing. What surprised him had to be her song choice. Out of the millions of songs she could have chosen, she sang her song, "Secret Wish" with the same arrangement he had come up with and played on his piano last night.

At the end of the song, Sanaa applauded again. "Don't know that tune, but it was excellent."

Avery beamed. "Thank you. It's one of my originals. You think I'll be able to sing all of my own songs for my album?"

"Sure…eventually." Sanaa signaled for her attorney to resume his spot next to her other employees.

"Eventually?" Avery furrowed her eyebrows.

"Yes. First album, I'll pair you up with a known songwriter. What's that one chick's name? She does a lot for Charisma. Tessa? Teresa?"

The skittish, sweaty short man in a suit spoke up first. "Tassia Hogan, ma'am."

Sanaa nodded. "That's it. Thank you. I'll see if she's done sucking on Charisma's teat to do some tunes for us. She sang on that ooh-wee nasty song not too long ago. What was that hook?" She snapped her fingers. "Yeah, I remember. 'Baby, let's get naked and let me ride on you all day.' Not sure if she wrote that, but that was the song of the summer."

"I remember it. Not sure if that's my type of music." Avery resumed her seat again. "I like writing. I want to express myself through my own music. That's what I was hoping."

"Probably for your next album." Sanaa picked up her tablet and started tapping over the screen. "Or you can be backup for a year before your album drops. That's guaranteed money right now." She flipped her tablet around. "I'm prepared to offer you that for that plan of singing backing vocals and then dropping an album."

For an unheard of artist without any experience, the amount looked insane. As her manager, Laz would be set. If only his conscious would allow her to sign that contract.

"All of that sounds great, but—"

Sanaa interrupted Laz. "And we would have a stylist assigned to you. I'm thinking a bit of Ri-Ri with a lot of Nicki Minaj. I want her tits and ass out."

"Excuse me?" As though some of her body parts now showed, Avery tugged down on her skirt and pulled her top up. "My father is a pastor, and my mother—"

"Will be proud of you pulling in millions and millions of dollars." Sanaa rubbed her thumb against the pads of her index and middle finger to signal all the cash she would be earning. "Besides, you're an adult. You are over twenty-one, right?" She glared at Laz.

"Of course. That doesn't mean I want the world to see me half naked and gyrating on a stage."

As though something Avery had said triggered something, she snapped her fingers again. "That's the other thing. Dance lessons. I'll do you like Beyoncé's daddy did her and make you run in stilettos to get you in shape to doing a full set in high heels."

"But that's not what I want to do. That's not how I saw myself." She stared at Laz with a pleading look in her eyes.

This meeting had spun out of control. Laz did not see it turning out this way. He had expected Avery to be excited about the label. The more questions she asked and the more items Sanaa wanted to change about her, the more he realized that going for the low-hanging fruit this time didn't work.

Avery looked as uncomfortable as he felt. Signing a record deal at a major label shouldn't have been set up as a surprise. He should have told Avery about Section Eight. He should have shown her the contract. He should have let Avery be instrumental in her career decisions. From what Laz heard and saw, no way could he allow Avery to be a part of this operation.

"Thank you for your time, Ms. Farook. I want to be able to discuss all of this with Avery and get back to you." Laz stood.

"Before you go, I have another perk for you. You know most new artists get their big break by singing with an established and popular singer." She clicked something on her tablet. "Bring her in." Then she looked at Avery. "What if I were to entice you with singing with one of the hottest stars out there?"

Laz got an uneasy feeling in his belly as soon as the door behind them opened. He turned around in time to see Kat strolling in with a Cheshire cat grin gracing her face.

"Hi, all." In a tight, knee-length red pencil skirt and a black button-up top, she looked like a true rockabilly chick, complete with her raven hair in soft waves. "Am I late to the party?" She stood by Laz. "Hey, you." She bent over and kissed his cheek, then whispered in his ear, "Since you didn't fuck me, I'm going to fuck you."

Damn.

Chapter 18

Avery could barely believe her day. First she sat in a record label's office talking to the owner of it about her potential career there. Then Kat the superstar showed up, and Avery could possibly sing a song with her. The idea blew her mind.

She wanted to thank Laz, but the whole thing seemed off to her. Why didn't he show her Section Eight's contract? Why had he kept her in the dark about so many things? Why the hell was Avery even considering signing with a label that she knew her parents would hate? Why did it seem like Kat and Laz knew each other?

Kat sauntered to Avery, complete with an obvious sway in her hips. "Hi, I'm Kat." She extended her hand.

"Um, Avery." For whatever reason, Avery felt compelled to stand when she shook Kat's hand.

Now Avery had listened and danced to a lot of Kat's music. The poppy sound didn't overshadow some well-written songs. She did go overboard with using auto-tune, but what star nowadays didn't use that device?

"I saw your video. Whenever someone said something negative, I put them in their place." Kat nodded defiantly.

"You did?" Avery had to sit down again. She couldn't take any more surprises.

"Yep. Between you and me, I'm Kitty Girl." Kat winked at her.

Laz lowered his head.

"No way." Avery shook her head. "That's insane. I can't believe someone like you even found my video to make a comment on it."

"Talent finds talent."

That comment made Laz lift his head up.

"Laz, did you want to say something?" Kat cocked her head. "No? Pity." She sauntered around the desk to stand next to Sanaa. "I've never done this before, but I want to make you my protégé, like what Usher did for Justin Bieber or T.I. did with Iggy Azalea or Akon and Lady Gaga. I want to be in on the ground floor of your success." She rested her hand on the back of Sanaa's chair. "When I told Sanaa about my plan, she was all for it. But she found one problem."

Avery's gut tightened. "What's that?"

"Who you had listed as your manager." Kat pointed to Laz. "I warned Sanaa that he might pose an issue."

"An issue? What do you mean?" Avery looked at the man who she had shared not only her body but also her soul in the form of her lyrics.

"A couple of videos I saw." Kat nodded to Sanaa.

"You mean when I sang at Honey's?"

"No. Other videos." Kat faced the large screen.

In one shot taken from the end of a hotel hallway, it showed Laz kissing Avery against a hotel room door. It had to have been when Avery left with Laz from Marissa's place after dinner.

"How did you get this video?" Avery covered her mouth with her hand.

"I have my ways." Sanaa looked at the quiet young woman that stood between the short man in the suit and the big man in the track suit.

"You had us followed." Laz's voice sounded gravelly like he wanted to scream at any moment.

"It's what I do before I make a deal with anyone. Don't take it personally." Sanaa shrugged like this invasion of privacy shouldn't be a big deal.

"Personally, this other video is my favorite." Kat pointed to the screen.

It showed Avery straddling Laz's lap while he sat at his piano in his apartment. The night vision camera caught their images through the window despite the lights being off and them sitting in the dark.

"Okay, turn this off." Laz stood. "This is a joke."

"Really?" Kat crossed her arms. "Wasn't a joke when you took a video of me, right?"

Laz squeezed his eyes shut as Avery rose to her feet.

"You and Kat were together?" Avery didn't want to be that woman that got caught off guard by her man, but the fact that he said nothing about them floored her.

Kat came around the desk. "Did he tell you that he regularly records his meetings?"

Avery didn't answer. She couldn't. The words choked in her throat while she stared at the man who had started to look like Mr. Perfect to her. Now he came off as Mr. Predator.

"Did he tell you that he normally doesn't sleep with people he works with but he loves your talent?" Kat nudged her elbow into Avery's side.

Laz glared at Kat and shook his head. "Don't do this."

"Don't do what?" Kat blinked. "Is there something you want to say?"

He exhaled through his nose. "You know I can't."

Kat shrugged. "That's a shame."

"It is." Laz nodded. "Avery signed my management contract. I don't want her working with you." He reached for Avery's arm.

She ducked out of his grasp. "I—I didn't sign your contract."

Kat laughed and then covered her mouth. "Burn. That's got to sting."

Laz faced her. "What are you talking about? We talked about the changes. I made them and printed it out. I saw you with a pen reading it over in my living room."

Avery nodded. "I was reading it. I did have a pen. I was ready to sign. But I wanted to read it over one more time first. I still want an attorney to review it. That's what I was trying to tell you in the lobby before we came up."

"You know we have an excellent management team here at Section Eight." Sanaa raised her hands up like a game-show beauty.

Laz shook his head. "You don't want to do that. Think about Pebbles and TLC. You will get the short-end of the stick in this deal." He glanced at Sanaa. "Think of this as a casino. The house always wins."

Avery moved away from Laz. "What I'm thinking about is myself. I believed every word you told me. Turns out, you're just..." She shook her head. "You're not the man I thought you were."

Laz shrugged out of one of the guards' grasp before they forcefully escorted him from the premises. "I'll wait for you outside. I waited forever for someone like you. I can sure as hell stay for a meeting."

"Come on, Casanova." The other guard grabbed Laz behind his neck.

The move triggered Laz to take the man's hand and wrench it behind his back like he had done with Uncle Pig. Avery didn't know what else Laz had done with his hand behind his back, but the big man screamed and stood on his tiptoes.

"I'll go. Just let me say something first." Laz turned to the other guard. "Don't make a move or something is going to get broken."

"Shit. I thought *I* was gangster." Sanaa snickered. "Say what you have to say and let my man go."

Laz stared at Avery. "Don't sign anything."

Avery shook her head. "I'll do what I want. You don't control me. Don't say anything else to me."

Laz continued. "Don't sign anything, understand? I'm sure you find all this incredible. The fame, the money, the opportunity. You're talented. You can have this at other places if you just believe in me and wait."

Avery considered his words as she approached him and the man Laz had in a precarious position. "Before we walked into this building, I would have listened to everything you said. Now I don't even trust you. I don't believe you." She took several steps back from him. "I'll finish my business here, go to your place, get my things, and go home. I have enough on me to take the train home."

"No, I flew you out. I can fly you back." Laz placed his hand on the guard's shoulder that he controlled.

"Better yet, Avery. I'll have my personal jet fly you home whether you sign with us or not." Sanaa smiled. "Good day, Mr. Kyson."

Laz scanned everyone in the room before he finally let the guard go. The big man twirled his arm around to get some feeling back into it. Then he turned to land a punch on Laz's jaw.

Laz managed to miss the intended hit, and instead cracked his fist against the man's face, knocking him to the floor where he groaned and remained.

Laz looked up at Avery. "I'll wait for you."

Then without another fight, he went to the elevator and waited for the other guard to escort him back down.

"Good. Now that he's gone, let's talk about your future." Kat rubbed her hands together.

"Yeah, my future." Avery had envisioned it with Laz.

Now she had no idea what to do and who to trust. The fact that her heart felt broken into a million pieces didn't help. She didn't want to talk business. She wanted to crawl in bed and throw the covers over her head.

After her meeting, and with the contract in her hand, Avery stepped outside of the Section Eight building. True to his word, Laz stood on the sidewalk in front of the building. He had probably been told to stay off company property.

Although Avery's heart pounded seeing him waiting for her after a couple of hours in the office with Sanaa, Kat, and Sanaa's staff, she couldn't forget everything Kat had said about Laz recording her.

Avery stayed on the Section Eight plaza area until she had to hit the sidewalk. At that point, Laz caught up to her.

"Avery, please listen to me." He tried standing in her path, but she got around him.

"I need to catch a cab and get my stuff." She stood at the side of the street and raised her hand in the air like she had seen on TV and in movies.

"You don't know how to get back to my place." He whistled and held his hand up, too. At that point, a bright yellow cab pulled over to the side. "I'll take you back to my place."

"Fine. I'll need to go to the airport. I'm taking Ms. Farook up on her offer to take the jet back home." She climbed into the backseat, and Laz followed her.

After giving the driver his address, he turned to Avery. "I didn't mean to hurt you by not sharing the contract details. I wanted to do what's best for you."

She snickered. "I wanted to sign with Charisma. You ignored that request. I wanted to sing my own songs. I guess I'll do that eventually. I wanted to be instrumental in my career, and you shut me out." She clutched the contract closer to her chest. "I'm more than just a voice. I wanted a man who wouldn't treat me like I don't matter, like a means to an end." She turned away from Laz. "I need to stop doing this to myself. I need to realize my worth. I need to be a star in my own production."

"Why do you sound like a little bit of Sanaa and a little bit of Kat?" Laz attempted to put his hand on Avery's knee.

"Don't touch me." She pushed his hand away. "I have my own mind. I don't need to listen to you or anyone else." She rubbed her forehead.

"Avery, I wanted to tell you the situation with me and Kat, but I couldn't."

"Couldn't or wouldn't?" She looked at him to gauge his response. "Never mind. It doesn't matter. What matters is that I get my stuff and get as far away from you as possible. I don't want to hear about you or anything else related to you again." When the images of them kissing in the video and the sex they had had in his apartment played in her head, she couldn't stop the tears from flowing. "They saw me. They saw us. My dad will…"

Laz held Avery's hand. She tried hard to pull it away but couldn't. "You're a grown woman. We did nothing wrong." He moved in closer to her. "*I* did nothing wrong. You have to believe me."

She removed her hand from his. "I don't."

"Avery. I love you."

She couldn't look at him. The last bit of her heart cracked. "People who love each other don't keep secrets. They don't hide things. They don't shut people out like you're doing with your dad, and how you're treating me." She wiped her hand under her nose. "Please leave me alone for the rest of the ride home. I can't deal with you right now."

Laz moved away from her. "I'm not giving up on you, on us."

"There is no us."

Laz shook his head. "I'll figure out how to make this work."

A small part of Avery wanted that, wanted someone to fight for her. The other part reminded her that Laz tried controlling her, controlling her career and situation. She couldn't have that.

After they arrived at the apartment, Avery slammed her items into her overnight bag along with her notebook full of songs. Getting that had been her main concern. Since she didn't take it with her to the meeting, she had to come back to Laz's place.

A car horn outside grabbed Avery's attention.

Laz looked out of his front window. "That's right. They do know where I live." He shook his head. "Black stretch out there. I guess that's your ride."

Avery said nothing as she headed to the door. Laz stopped her, wrapped his arm around her waist, and kissed her.

She wanted to claw his eyes out, slap him, tell him that everything she had done with him had been a mistake. Instead her body melded into his. She moaned a little when he rubbed his hand up and down her back.

As soon as he broke from the kiss, the car horn sounded again.

"Goodbye." Avery left the apartment with the words "I love you" stuck in her throat.

She made it to the car and found herself with her knees drawn up to her chest on the ride to the airport. The car took her to the section with private planes.

Did Avery really want this life? She did, but with the right partner. The whole thing felt so wrong, so contrived.

As soon as she had gotten home in the early evening, she wasted no time in jetting over to her parents' house. Avery rang the doorbell and knocked on the door until it opened.

"My God, girl, what is wrong with you?" Hazel asked as she held the door.

Avery couldn't speak. She wrapped her arms around her mother's neck and cried.

"Oh, Avery. What's wrong?" Hazel pulled her child into the house and closed the door behind her. She sat her down on the couch and made her place next to her. "Tell me what's going on?"

"Mom, I should have listened to you and Dad." Avery wiped her eyes with her hands until Hazel gave her some facial tissue to do the job. "Thanks. I went to a label called Section Eight."

"Section Eight? What kind of music would they do?" Hazel shook her head.

"They mainly do rap, but they want to branch out and do more. The problem is that the person I trusted to get me a great deal was not who

I thought he was. This whole experience was not what I expected." Her bottom lip quivered. "Now Dad's going to fire me and I won't have any jobs." She looked at her mom. "I was let go from Uncle Pig's diner a couple of weeks ago."

Hazel sighed. "Avery. Why didn't you tell us?"

"I know you and Dad worry about me. I really was trying to be responsible, do the right thing. I'm not perfect. I make a lot of mistakes. This one is pretty big." Avery looked around. "Where's Dad?"

"Out running errands before work tonight." Hazel patted Avery's hand. "Might be a good thing." She stood and grabbed her daughter's hand. "Come with me."

Hazel took Avery to the den and picked up a remote to the mounted TV over the fireplace. She clicked a couple of buttons until something popped up on the screen. It looked like a video from the 80s, complete with big hair, fluorescent clothing, and shoulder pads.

"Mom, is there a reason you're showing me this?" Avery blew her nose.

"Are you watching the video?" Her mother nodded toward the screen.

Avery cocked her head and looked at the image. After a few seconds, she had to blink. The woman with the biggest hair in the middle of the trio looked exactly like her mother. She stared at the screen and then looked at her mother several times.

"No matter how many times you look, it'll still be me." She pointed to the screen. "In both places."

"Mom! You were a singer in a girl group?" Avery had to sit down.

"Yes. Where do you think your talent came from? Your father?" She laughed and sat next to her.

"How do I not know any of this? How did you and Dad keep this a secret?" Avery kept her full attention on the screen.

"It was something I did when I was a little younger than you. Me and my two best friends at the time used to sing at small clubs and stuff. We always talked about making it big." Hazel shook her head.

"What happened? Why aren't you singing now?"

"Life happened. One member wanted to stop to start a family. The other, well, she got caught up in the bad side of the business. Eventually, the drugs she got hooked on took her life. I met your father. He was supportive of me getting into the business. We did everything we could. For a short while, we even lived in his car. When I got pregnant with you, we stopped. We realized that my singing career was a pipe dream." She held Avery's hand. "This is the reason we don't want you trying to get into the business. It's hard. There are many pitfalls. You're doing the right thing by getting your education. That will help you. It'll give you stability."

No wonder her parents encouraged her to get her degree. Avery hugged her mother for a different reason this time. "I didn't know."

"I know. We didn't want you to know. We didn't want you hanging out with that Laz dude. Where is he?" Hazel grumbled.

"Still in New York, I guess." Avery sat back. "I found out some things about him that made me rethink everything." She would leave out the fact that he admitted he loved her.

She wanted to say the same to him at one point, but not after what Kat had revealed.

"Are you okay?" Hazel framed Avery's face in her hands.

Avery nodded. "I'm home. I can focus on what's important." She exhaled. "Do you think Dad was serious about letting me go?"

Before Hazel could answer, the front door slammed. Probably sensing Avery's nerves, Hazel patted the back of Avery's hand.

Clinton appeared in the doorway to the den area. "What are you doing here? I thought you were in New York."

Avery stood from the couch and approached her father. "Can we talk, please?"

Clinton remained quiet before peering over her shoulder. He must have seen Hazel's video. He sighed and screwed up his lips before he brought his attention back to her. "Come on to the living room."

Avery followed him and sat in the chair that her mother normally occupied. Clinton sat in his usual cobalt-blue upholstered chair.

"What's going on? I don't have a lot of time." Clinton leaned forward and joined his hands together.

Several things went through Avery's head. She had to reveal to her father that she had almost made a couple of huge mistakes. The first being signing a management deal with Laz. The other being signing an artist deal with Section Eight. Before she could address all that, she had to clear the air.

"Dad, I'm an adult." Avery took a deep breath.

Clinton scratched his head. "Considering you're my child, I know how old you are."

She nodded. "You know my age, but you and Mom still treat me like I'm a child. That has to stop." She pointed in the direction of the family room. "All this time, you two have been telling me not to go for my dream without a real reason why."

"Because it's a volatile business." Clinton's eyes widened.

"So is being a police officer or an FBI agent or president of the United States. I don't hear you telling me not to go for those dreams. Why didn't you tell me about Mom?" She scooted to the edge of her seat. "You say that I trust everyone. Did you bank on my trusting nature to keep information from me? If that's the case, then that's just wrong."

Clinton glared at her for a moment before he dropped his gaze. "Hazel is the only woman I loved." He brought his head up. "You are my only child. I want to make sure both of you are happy."

"If that's the case, treat me like an adult. Guide me. Don't lie to me or withhold information. That's a surefire way to lose me." She crossed her legs and her arms over her chest.

Clinton exhaled. "Did Laz hurt you? Did he lie?"

Avery thought carefully about her answer. "He did to me what you and Mom did to me." She shook her head. "I'm starting to see that it's not okay."

Clinton nodded but kept quiet.

Avery exhaled. She had been wanting to get that off her chest for a long, long time. "If you need me tonight, I want to work."

Clinton studied her for a moment. "Have you gotten any sleep?"

She shook her head. "But I'll be fine after a quick nap."

"You're not going to be any good to me if you don't get enough sleep."

Avery stood from the chair and hugged her father. "Sorry I didn't listen to you. I was so stupid."

Clinton hugged her back. "Don't call yourself that."

"From now on, I'm going to stick to what's real." She pulled back from him and decided to tell them what they wanted to hear. "What's real is that I'll graduate in a few weeks and get a real job. I don't need to think about singing as a career."

Clinton tilted his head as he looked at her. "Your mother and I did what was right for us at the time because we had you on the way. We were afraid that you would get hurt in this business. If you really want to walk away, you know I'll support that. That's what you really want, right?"

Avery nodded, unable to say the words out loud. "Can I sleep here before we go in tonight? And will you wake me when we're ready to go?"

Clinton smiled. "Yes and yes. You know where your old bedroom is." He pointed down the hall.

Avery kissed his cheek and walked down the long hallway to her old bedroom. The trek shouldn't have made her feel defeated. Too bad it did. She finally figured out her place. It would be without Laz Kyson.

Chapter 19

That damn gag order. Laz wanted to punch something, someone. Seeing Kat again, he knew something bad would happen. Guess that gag order applied to him but not her. Had he said anything though and Avery admitted she knew Laz hadn't slept with Kat, he could have been sued. Then again, he would still have Avery.

Being without her for a week crushed his soul. Laz found himself watching her video over and over again. He missed Avery. He craved her.

Now with all his free time, he needed to do something to occupy himself.

Laz knocked on Marissa's door and waited. It didn't take long for it to be answered. Too bad his sister hadn't opened the door. A voluptuous African-American woman adjusted her off-shoulder top.

"Marissa here?" He stood off to the side while she exited.

"Late for work." She fluffed her big, curly hair. "Yeah, she's in there, but you are definitely not her type." She snickered.

Laz walked inside of his sister's home. "Stinky?"

Marissa strolled out of the bedroom area, adjusting her shirt as well. "Perfect timing as usual." She continued into the kitchen area. "Tea?"

"Of course." He sat at one of the barstools at the breakfast bar.

"Two visits in a month. To what do I owe the pleasure of your company?" She popped a tea container in her machine to brew him a cup of tea.

"I fucked up. I really fucked up." He shook his head.

"You mean with Avery, at work, or with Dad?" She braced her hands on the counter.

"For one, I lost my job weeks ago." He figured he should come clean to someone. Staying holed up in his apartment left him lonely and frustrated.

"Holy shit. Did you tell Mom and Dad?" Marissa ran her hand over her shaggy hair. "Wait. Have we established yet if your fuck-up also involves Dad?"

Laz couldn't even enjoy the scent of the hot tea coming to him as he thought about Marissa's question. "I don't understand why you're so forgiving? He broke Mom's heart and broke up our family."

Marissa handed him his tea. "What do you think you know about their separation?"

He sighed. "Give me a break. I was there. You were still too young. I saw Mom crying."

"Yeah, but do you know what she was crying for?" She scratched the back of her neck.

Laz blew his breath over the hot beverage. He didn't answer her, knowing the obvious answer.

"Let me tell you a story." She came around the breakfast bar and sat next to him. "When I was four, Mom used to take me to the country club she and Dad were members of. They had an onsite daycare. The daycare teacher said that Mom was having a tennis lesson." She chuckled. "I know. So cliché."

Laz set his tea down to hear the rest of this story.

"One day, I decided to sneak out of the daycare area to find Mom. I was still a bit clingy then. I found her. She was in the dirty towel room getting served from behind by her instructor, and I don't mean a backhand."

Thank God Laz didn't have a drink in his mouth. "You're lying. You were four. What did you know?"

"I know I saw her do that with that guy, her personal trainer, and the UPS man. Each time, she would tell me that they're friends, but I shouldn't tell Daddy. I believed her, until I heard other women talking about her. But then Mom couldn't help herself. She had her flings at the house. Dad finally walked in on her."

Laz gave his full attention to his sister. "So her crying?"

"Guilt."

"Why wouldn't Dad tell us that?" He wiped his hands over his face. "All this time, I thought Dad, with his flirting and stuff—"

"That was on me. I told him that a man who had only been with one woman since high school deserved to get out there and see as many women as possible. I thought you would help him." Marissa patted his back. "Plus, if I hadn't have said something to Dad about what I knew, he wouldn't have told me. He always wanted to protect us. He loves us."

Laz leaned back. "Shit. All this time…" He stared at Marissa. "Why didn't you say something when they first broke up if you knew? Here I thought Dad had cheated on Mom."

"I was embarrassed for Dad. His wife of twenty-five years had been cheating on him, and you saw him as your hero. I didn't realize how deep you let the rumors about Dad's supposed infidelity get into your head until recently. I thought the comments about him flirting were just about how bad of a flirt he was." Marissa laughed. "I really wanted to tell you during breakfast the last time you were here, but Dad was adamant about you not knowing."

Because of his need to control all aspects of his life, Laz ruined his relationship with his father and Avery. Now that he knew his mother's past, he started to envision her differently, too. How could she hurt his father like that?

Marissa wagged her finger in Laz's face. "I know that expression. Don't think that it's cool to shut your Mom out of your life now."

Laz braced his hands on the bar. "Why not? She hurt Dad and didn't tell us the truth. Every time I talked to her and made comments about Dad cheating on her, she never corrected me. Not once."

Marissa shook her head. "Dude, it's none of your damn business why our parents split. You're a grown-ass man. They're adults." She held her arms out like an eagle in flight. "Nobody is fucking perfect. Not me. And especially not you." She punched him on his arm. "So what did you do to mess it up with that special girl? I liked her."

"I did, too." He thought about Avery. "I do." He pushed his tea away from him. "I love her."

Marissa's bottom jaw unhinged. "Bro, are you serious? I didn't even hear you say the L word when you were with your last girl. Does she know?"

Laz nodded. "She also knows part of the reason why I no longer work at Universe."

His sister wagged his finger at him. "See. That's part of your problem. You don't know how to communicate, and you are too controlling."

He sighed. "I think I've heard that before."

Marissa hugged her brother. "Grilled cheese?"

He chuckled. "You can't fix all of my problems with food."

"But it doesn't hurt, right?" She kissed his cheek. "You want my advice?"

Laz released an exaggerated sigh. "I guess since Josie isn't here."

"Dick." She picked up a banana from the bar and threw it at him. "Don't call Dad."

Laz felt his eyebrows rutting together. "I thought you would want me to—"

"Go to him. Talk to him face-to-face." She grabbed a cast-iron skillet from overhead and placed it on the stove. "Then you need to do the same for your girl if you truly love her and want her back."

"But if I tell her the truth—"

"What? Are you going to jail or Hell? If she feels the same way, she'll hold you and the secret. If not, I'll bail you out." She winked at him. "I saw the way she looked at you, especially when you two tore out of here after dinner. I think she loves you, too."

"I'll see Dad. Um..." He drummed his thumbs on the bar.

"Need a place to stay?" Marissa took out the ingredients she needed for her dish. "Of course you can stay here. Just keep out of my way if I bring someone over."

"You mean like that young lady that left out of here this morning?"

Marissa fanned her face. "Hot, right? I could see her again."

Laz covered his mouth in surprise. "Two dates? Are frogs going to fall from the sky at any moment?"

"Have I called you a *dick* this morning already?"

"You have. But I deserve that."

After eating his sister's awesome grilled cheese sandwich, Laz had to do something. He couldn't travel to Texas right now. If he could have, he would.

He called his mother's number and waited for her to answer.

"Laz, it's good to hear from you."

As always, Jocelyn's voice sounded light and bubbly.

"Hey, Mom. I need to talk to you."

Marissa allowed Laz to make the call from her home. She let him sit in the kitchen to talk while she kept herself busy in the basement.

"Of course. What is it?"

Laz would start off positive. "I heard you're getting remarried."

Jocelyn laughed. "Yes. Sorry I didn't tell you personally. Donald just asked me a week or so ago. You should see the ring. I'll take a picture of it and send it to you. I think it looks like one of Elizabeth Taylor's rings."

He imagined his mother holding her left hand out to admire the piece. "That's nice, Mom." He tapped his foot against the base of the breakfast bar. "Tell me something. Whenever I talk to you about Dad and how you two split up, why didn't you ever correct me?"

A pause lingered before Jocelyn spoke. "What do you mean?"

Laz felt the fire building up inside of himself. He hoped his mother hadn't planned on lying, but he had a feeling she would to save face. "When I would say that I couldn't believe Dad cheated on you, you never said he didn't."

"Of course I didn't. I don't know if he remained faithful to me or not." Indignation filled her tone.

"Did you cheat on him?"

This second pause lasted longer than the first. "Where is all this coming from?"

"I'm here in D.C. visiting Marissa. I'm about to go see Dad soon. Until a week ago, I wouldn't have done that. I thought when you two split that Dad stepped out on you, and you never corrected my assumption. You never said that you were the one who had been unfaithful to him. That's wrong."

"Laz, you have no right to—"

"I stuck up for you. I believed you. As a result, I pushed my father away. That wasn't right for me to do, and I wished you could have been honest with me." Laz thought about the full picture. "You need to be honest with yourself. If you don't fix the reason why you cheated on Dad, your relationship with Donald will be doomed."

"Don't say that. That's not fair." Jocelyn's voice broke. "Your father worked a lot. I felt ignored."

"Did you tell your fiancé the real reason your marriage fell apart? He might need to know that. Trust me. If he finds out later on, it could destroy the trust he has in you."

Laz heard his mother sobbing a little. "Is that what I did with you? Did I push you away? I didn't mean to. I—"

"I know. No one is perfect." Laz looked up at the doorway that went down to the basement area. Marissa poked her head up and smiled. "I learned that from my baby sister." He winked at her. "If you start with a foundation of trust, you'll have a strong relationship."

Jocelyn sniffed. "I have to go. Tell Marissa hi from me, and that I love her." Then she quickly added, "I love you, too, Laz. I love my Lazzy."

He nodded. "I know, Mom." He disconnected the call, but the news he had learned and this conversation still weighed him down.

* * * *

Laz made a special trip to D.C. from Maryland. He pulled up to his father's place and hoped he hadn't missed him. The entire trip there, Laz's gut tightened. He couldn't believe all this time, he assumed his father had stepped out on his mother. He protected his mother's image. For that reason, Laz should have been better to Bradley.

Laz went to the door and knocked. When he waited for what he thought had been a bit too long, he started to knock again when the door opened. Bradley stood on the other side looking just like the hero he remembered. The extra bits of gray in his hair and lines around his eyes didn't take away from his appeal.

"Laz, my boy. What are you doing here?" Bradley hugged Laz.

Laz didn't want to let his father go.

"Hey, what's going on with you?" His father patted Laz's back. "Everything going okay?"

"Yeah, sure." Laz finally let his father go. "Can we go in?"

"Sure. Sorry. Come in." Bradley stood off to the side to let Laz come into his home. "You want something to eat or drink?"

"No. I'm good. I stopped off at Marissa's first." Laz waited to go anywhere in his father's home to see where he wanted to go. He had to learn not to control every situation.

"She is an excellent cook. I think she got that from—"

"You?" Laz remembered his father manning the barbeque grill whenever his family held a cookout.

"No. I'm great at warming up food." He shook his head. "No, your mother was, well, is a great cook. She could transform anything into something special."

Laz smiled. This man could be bitter about the dissolution of his marriage, but he chose to take the high road. Laz could learn a lot from him.

"So what's going on with you? What brings you down here? Looking for more talent?" Bradley sat down on a brown leather couch in the living room.

Laz sat on the other side. "No. I've made some mistakes."

"Ah. Just like when you were little, you come home to heal. I like that about you." Bradley knocked his hand against Laz's. "What mistakes did you make this time?"

Laz took a moment before blurting his recent news. "I lost my job recently."

"Oh, wow. Was that since looking for a singer to represent?" Bradley leaned his head on his propped up fist.

"Actually before. I didn't tell you all because I really thought I could turn my life around." He rubbed his hand over his mouth. "I'm sorry."

Bradley furrowed his eyebrows. "Why would you be apologizing to me? Wait. Are you moving back in?"

Laz laughed. "Not yet. I'm not that bad off yet."

"You know you could. I'm in this place all by myself. I could use the company." He looked around his modest home.

"I think I might cramp your style when you bring dates back here." Laz's subtle comment hopefully let his father know that he approved of him moving on with his life without mentioning that Marissa told him what had happened between him and Laz's mother.

That couldn't be enough. So much had been left unsaid between him and his father in the past few years. Marissa could hold on to a secret. Laz couldn't.

Bradley smiled at him. "I appreciate you thinking about my romantic needs. Speaking of romance, what about you and that beautiful young lady I saw you with? I know you said she was a client. I got a different vibe from her when I saw you two together."

Laz rested his ankle on his knee. "That's my other screwup. She thought I had done something inappropriate with another woman." He glanced at his father now that he knew about his romantic past.

"But you didn't, right?" Bradley sat up straight like he prepared to argue with him if Laz said he had.

"No. But because of who the person is, I'm not really allowed to talk about what happened with Avery."

Bradley shook his head. "No. If you care about her, you tell her everything. Rules are for other people. You stay transparent to the ones you care about."

"Dad?" Laz had to be careful and present the question in a way that gave his father some dignity. "Infidelity is serious." He stared at his father. "Once you lose that trust, it's hard to get it back, right?"

Bradley regarded his son for a while. "Being cheated on is a hard pill to swallow. It absolutely, positively destroys trust. Sometimes, if both people are willing, you can seek counseling. Even that may not work."

Laz started to get a picture of what happened between his parents without asking the question outright. "I didn't cheat on her."

"Then you'll have to fight for her." Bradley pumped his fist in the air. "Don't go in with charm. Do it with honesty. Lay your heart on the line. Expose your true feelings. If you go in completely vulnerable, she'll have to listen."

Laz rubbed his hands over his thighs before he spoke. "I know about you and Mom." He peered up at his father. "I made a snap judgment about you without proof, and I am so, so sorry."

Bradley held up his hand. "I wish Marissa hadn't said anything. It's not something a man should talk about with his children, especially his son." He shook his head.

"Why?"

"I don't want to talk about this, Lazarus." Bradley's eyes narrowed.

"Dad, talk to me. Don't you know that each time you tell me something, I take it to heart and it affects my life? I don't perform in front of people because you said I should assert myself. That made me think that I wasn't doing that enough, so I withdrew. I thought withholding information and only sharing what I needed to with Avery would make us both happy . I ended up pushing her away when I did that. I don't know how to open myself up to let someone in."

Bradley stared at Laz until a smile stretched across his face. "Looks like you're doing a pretty damn good job right now. I think this is the most you've ever said to me since your mother and I announced our split." He cleared his throat. "I don't want to go into details about what caused your mother and me to divorce. I will say that trust was lost, and in our situation, it could not be repaired. That's not to say that all situations like that are lost. I know you. I know your heart. You can win her back if you do to her what you just did to me."

"And what's that?" Laz shrugged.

"Bare your soul."

Laz didn't know if he could do that, especially since Avery avoided his calls. He couldn't blame her considering what she must have thought of him. He just hoped Avery didn't sign that contract.

"So what are you going to do about work?" Bradley now sounded like a dad.

"The same thing I'm going to do to get Avery to talk to me again. I'm finally learning to listen and relax a little." Laz took a deep breath and smiled at his father. "Before that though, you want to go out and get a drink or something? Maybe you can find someone nice."

Bradley stood. He patted Laz's knee. "Let's have a couple of beers here so that we can do some talking. How's that sound?"

Laz stood and put his arm around his father's shoulders. "Sounds like a perfect plan."

"And maybe I can help you with your other problems."

"I'll take all the help I can get from you."

Chapter 20

By the time Avery looked up from writing her final notes, she noticed that she sat alone in the class and Professor Klein watched her. Her mind had been on Laz and her recent decisions. She had almost had Laz making all of her decisions. Too bad at one point, she would have done anything he had asked of her.

She gathered her things and headed up to see her professor. "Did you get my report?"

He nodded. "I did. Interesting take on making it in the music industry."

Avery had no idea what to do for her report until it came to her. Studying the probability of her making a mark in the music industry got her thinking about a lot of things. Did she still have a song in her heart without Laz?

"So is that what you want to do, be a singer?" Her professor cocked his head.

Avery didn't know how to answer, or that she even wanted to answer that question. Each time she started to talk about walking away from her dream, she wanted to cry.

"You know when I was a kid, maybe a little younger than you, I wanted to be a cowboy. My mother saw another life for me." He chuckled. "You know you define your own life."

She shook her head. "That sounds nice, but my parents are just like your mother. They see a different life for me." She hoisted her bag on her shoulder.

"You only have one life. Live it the way you want or you'll have so many regrets."

Her professor looked like he wanted to touch her shoulder, but she shrugged away from him.

"Thanks. I can't wait until I graduate in a couple of weeks. I can really get my life going." She headed to the door.

"And here I thought I was the only one obsessed with education." He chuckled.

Avery wanted to smile with him but her heart wouldn't let her. She did what she normally did for the last couple of weeks since leaving New York and Laz. She went straight back to her apartment, opened her notebook, and stared at a blank page. She found that she no longer felt inspired.

It didn't help that her heart remained with Laz. He understood her. At least she thought he did. Her mind tripped over imagining Laz doing the same thing he'd done with her with Kat. Superstar, mega-rich, ultra-famous Kat. Why would he want Avery? Oh yeah. Work. She would have been a money earner for him. He would have used her. Her heart didn't believe that.

Avery's phone rang. Her body tightened, thinking that it might be Laz again. He regularly called or sent her a text message, usually with an apology. Her favorite messages, the ones she kept and listened to often, had to be the messages where he played piano for her and not said anything.

The memory of their time at his piano would forever be burned in her mind. Then she replayed the moment Sanaa and Kat played the video of them during a meeting. A stranger recorded her and Laz, and strangers watched them. Embarrassed heat filled her cheeks as she reached for her phone.

When she saw Graciela's name across the screen, she smiled. "Hey."

"How did your exams go?" Graciela sounded more excited than Avery.

"Okay, I guess. I'm finally done with them all. It's now just a wait-and-see situation." Avery shrugged.

"And what about you and Mr. Perfect?" Her friend made an obscene growling noise.

"Not so perfect." Avery sighed.

"Oh, no. What happened? Do I need to beat someone up?"

Avery could imagine Graciela grabbing the bat her friend normally kept by her bed and heading over to see Avery to pummel all who dared to hurt her friend.

"He was supposed to help me get into the music business. It had all gone wrong. Bad contracts, wrong label, possible past relationships." Avery shook her head.

"Relationships? Why would that bother you?" When Avery didn't answer right away, Graciela filled in the blanks. "Just admit you two had a thing for each other."

"Fine. Yes, we did. Now we don't." Avery would have to learn to move on, both from her dream and from that man.

"Don't get testy. So you have no record deal and no man?"

"The record deal is still a maybe only because I owe Section Eight Records an answer." She did promise Sanaa Farook that she would get back to her by the end of the month.

Avery hadn't bothered to have anyone review the contracts since she hadn't planned on signing anything. She didn't have the heart to do so.

"Section Eight? Isn't that the same label of Murder Man and Lil Chop? That's hardcore. Are you doing that now?" Graciela's voice rose.

"No. They're planning on expanding to R&B. They wanted an unknown to start off the label." The thought of that still flattered Avery. She didn't see herself with that company.

"That sounds ideal. You would be the template. You would set the standard. You don't want that?"

Right now, Avery had no idea what she wanted. Her phone beeped, indicating she had another call.

The name "Unknown Caller" flashed across the screen. For that reason, she didn't bother answering it. Either the caller had to be a telemarketer or Laz being sneaky...again.

A beat after the phone stopped ringing, it chimed to signal that the caller left a voicemail message.

"You want me to come by?" Graciela offered.

Normally, Avery would have said no. This time she didn't want to be sitting there alone with her thoughts. "Yes. Bring wine and spirits. I'm ready for a girls' night."

Graciela squealed. "I'll be there in thirty minutes. I'll have wine and chocolates."

Avery smiled. "Sounds perfect."

After disconnecting the call, Avery saw that she had a voicemail message waiting for her. She sighed before listening to it. The last thing she needed would be another piano recital from Laz. Her heart wouldn't be able to take it.

She put her phone on speaker and played the message.

"Hey, Avie. It's your Kitty Girl, Kat." Kat completed her introduction with a giggle.

Avery sat up taller, mainly because Kat had called her "Avie." No one had done that before.

"Haven't seen you since New York, and I'm back in your town tonight. I have a show and I would love to talk to you about the next step in our relationship. I'll leave your name at the door for you to come backstage so that we can talk." Kat left the information about the club on the message. "See you there."

Avery stood and looked at herself in the mirror across the room. Would she even go? Her report findings showed that she won't make it. Maybe she could flip that script.

Before she did anything, Avery called her friend back.

"Please don't tell me you've changed your mind about me coming over." Exhaustion filled Graciela's voice.

"Yes and no." Avery headed to her bedroom. "Want to see a show tonight instead?"

If Kat wanted to see Avery, she would have to do it with Graciela in tow. At this point, Avery could use all the backup she could get.

Hours later, Avery sat in the dressing room of a star who had performed for royalty. Getting Graciela into the show had been a bonus, but they wouldn't let her into Kat's dressing room. She would have to wait backstage with the rest of the groupies.

Avery couldn't believe her luck. She strolled around Kat's dressing room where her makeup and wardrobe stylists waited for the star.

Moments later, the door flew open and ushered in loud, clamorous shouting and screams from the audience. Kat strolled in wearing thigh-high white boots and a sparkly leotard.

"Whew, what a show." Kat's gaze connected with Avery's. "You made it." She squealed and galloped over to her. She pulled Avery into a hug. "So glad you're here. I've been thinking about you and your voice for a while." She pointed to the couch to request Avery have a seat.

"Thank you. That's very nice for you to say." Avery did sit and watch Kat get attended to by three different people.

Each person took control of some aspect of Kat's look. One person worked on removing her boots. Another got her out of her jewelry. The third undid her outfit.

"Thank you for coming out. Did you enjoy the show?" Kat ducked behind a partition.

"Yes, I did. I can't imagine commanding a room like that." Avery crossed her legs.

"You have to see it to believe it." Kat giggled. When she reemerged, she had on a pink flower-embroidered silk robe. "Everyone, get out." She pointed to the door, and then sat down next to Avery. When her team exited, Kat continued. "I wanted the opportunity to talk to you by yourself." She scooted closer to Avery. "So, Sanaa tells me you still haven't signed their contract. What's wrong? Is the money not enough?"

Avery put her hand to her chest. "Oh, gosh no."

If Sanaa really wanted to pay her that amount of money for doing what she loved, she would be a fool to turn it down. Too bad Laz's final words and his actions still powered her decisions.

When he appealed to her during their meeting with Sanaa to not sign the contract, she had listened. He seemed so passionate about her not making a critical mistake. Then when he punched out that big guard, it made her look at him differently. Now sitting across from Kat, she only saw him bringing her to an orgasm, too.

"So what's the deal? I really want to work with you." Kat epitomized her name by curling her legs up on the couch.

"I would love that, too. It's just I don't know if this is the life I want."

"What? Are you kidding? Money, travel, men." Kat raised her eyebrows. "Girl, I still look at that video of you and Laz."

Hearing that didn't sound like the compliment Kat had intended. Avery tried smiling through the comment, but her stomach lurched.

Kat scooted closer to Avery. "Tell me something, just between the two of us."

"Oh, okay. Sure."

"What's he like? Laz Kyson. I imagine his dick is huge." Kat licked her lips.

Avery's stomach unknotted. "What do you mean? I thought you two had done something. You said—"

"Pfft." Kat waved her hand to Avery. "I just said that to piss him off because I knew he couldn't say anything about it. Gag order." She winked. "So? Spill it. And are you two an item or do I have a chance?"

"A chance? Are you serious?" Avery watched Kat's face go somber.

"What are you talking about?"

"I turned my back on Laz because I questioned his integrity." Avery hoped Kat took that to mean his business acumen and not on an intimate level. "You made it seem like he slept with you."

"So?" She crossed her arms over her chest. "Why would that bother you?" Her eyes widened. "You did fuck him, didn't you?"

Avery picked up her purse and stood. "I'm going to go."

Kat's smile melted. "What? Are you a prude or something? Too good to talk about sex?"

Avery nodded. "I am. I'm also glad I didn't sign that contract." She headed to the door. "If working with you and working under Section Eight mean I can never trust anyone, I would rather clean toilets for the rest of my life. You're a piece of work. I hope someone does to you what you did to Laz and me."

Kat bolted to her feet. "He did do that to me. I tried to fuck him, and he recorded the whole thing and showed it to the head of Universe, my manager, and my attorney. He humiliated me." She stomped her feet. "He deserved to be embarrassed and penniless. I hate him."

Avery never struck anyone in her life, but at that moment, she wanted to slap Kat so hard. "Have a good life."

"Leave. You won't make it in this business."

"That's okay. I'll have my education to fall back on." Avery opened the door but turned back to Kat. "Thanks for the opportunity."

Avery wanted to yell at the woman for making her doubt Laz. No, she had herself to blame for that. She should have trusted him. Now she had to figure out a way to get him back. Would he even take her phone call?

Chapter 21

Laz waited outside the back door of the studio he knew Chantel and Truman Woodley would be emerging from after they did their performance and interview. One great thing about being in New York had to be the access to a lot of the talk shows and news programs filmed there. With the help of some old connections who tipped him off on the Woodleys' whereabouts, he kept himself poised close to a stretch black limousine but out of obvious view.

When the door burst open, his heart raced. He saw two big men come out first before Truman walked out with Chantel following behind him. Chantel no longer looked like that diva in long, slinky ball gowns and high heels. With her brown hair in soft waves and her long, flowered dress, she looked like the perfect earth mother.

"Chantel! Truman!" Laz approached the car.

Truman looked over, but Chantel kept her head down and continued to the car.

One of the big men approached Laz. "No autographs today."

"Wait. I need to talk to Chantel." Laz continued forward. "Chantel, I don't know if you remember me. I'm Laz Kyson. I worked at Universe."

At that admission, she finally stopped and looked over at him. She started to walk toward him with Truman by her side.

By that point, the guard secured Laz by his shoulders as he faced him. Laz looked around the man with a long ponytail to make eye contact with Chantel. He had to make the appeal to her.

"I saw you that night of that show." Laz wouldn't go into great detail. He knew it had to have been a low, dark moment of her life. "I also went to bat for you with Zinner when you came to Universe."

"Mr. Kyson, I would suggest you go back to Universe." Chantel shook her head. "There's nothing for me there."

"Or me." Laz waited until she regained eye contact with him again. "I quit working there a couple of months ago."

"Why are you here then?" Truman positioned his body in front of Chantel. "We've all moved on with our lives."

"I know. It's one of your moves I wanted to talk to you about." Laz pushed the guard's hands off his shoulders. "I know of a great artist who would be perfect for your label."

"Not looking." Truman turned and wrapped his arm around Chantel's waist, surprisingly thin considering she had given birth to twins not too long ago.

"Avery is amazing. You don't want to pass her up."

Chantel pushed passed Truman. "Wait. Did you say Avery?"

The guard stood next to Laz as he moved a bit closer to the Woodleys. Laz nodded. "Yes. She's an incredible singer and songwriter."

"I know, if it's the same woman from that viral video." Chantel held Truman's arm.

"Probably the same woman. She sang that Bob Dylan song."

Truman smiled. "Now you have my attention since you attributed the song to Bob Dylan and not Bryan Ferry or Adele."

"And you know this singer?" Chantel moved closer to Truman.

Laz nodded. "And you do, too. Or maybe you do. She and her father clean your office building."

Chantel covered her mouth. "Are you kidding me?"

"It's where I found her. I tried telling you about her but I couldn't get a meeting." Laz held his hand up. "I get it. It's the reason I had to meet you this way."

"Why are you going out of your way for her? Are you two dating?" Chantel asked.

Laz shook his head. "I'm not that lucky. I've made a lot of mistakes in my life." He clasped his hands together. "I always regretted not fighting hard enough to get you the money you deserved from Universe. And I really regret staying at Universe after you left. I got comfortable. I got complacent, until that wasn't good enough for me anymore, and I couldn't take the b.s. there."

Since he couldn't mention the situation with Kat, he wouldn't bring it up.

"It's okay." Chantel backed up. "I'm exactly where I need to be. Controlling my art gives me freedom."

Laz saw her retreating. He couldn't let her go. "I'm sure it does. I would love for you to give that kind of love and freedom to Avery. She's special. She's very special. I have one of her songs here." He reached into his pocket, which made the guard nervous, understandably so.

For all the guard knew, Laz could have been reaching for a gun. He pulled out his phone.

"I don't represent her. I offered to represent her as her manager. She never signed the contract." Laz had to learn to be okay with that.

"So you don't have a financial stake in her. Why are you here on her behalf?" Chantel leaned her head on her husband's shoulder.

"I love her. Like with you, though, I didn't fight hard enough. She had shared with me that Charisma was her dream label. Instead, I went to a label I felt was a sure thing. But the place was not the right fit." Laz shook his head. "I hope she didn't sign with them. If she didn't, I need to make my pitch for her for Charisma."

Chantel and Truman stared at Laz like they had to make their assessment. Laz placed his heart on the line. If nothing else, even if he couldn't get Avery back in his life, he would do what he could to help her realize her dream.

"Oh my God! It's Shauna Stellar!" The scream at the end of the alley echoed between the walls.

"Come on. Get into the car with us. We can talk about this new talent." Chantel went to the backseat door and got inside along with Truman and Laz.

Laz had gotten this far. He would have to do more for Avery. He owed her that. He loved her enough to put himself on the line.

* * * *

Avery looked at herself in the mirror and adjusted her graduation cap on her head in the conference center bathroom. After today, she would put in applications to get a real job. Yep. She would integrate herself into the workforce and be happy about it.

"There's my smarty pants!" Graciela pinched Avery's ass cheek.

When Avery squealed and turned around, her friend embraced her.

"I'm so proud of you." Graciela kissed her cheek. "I knew you could do it."

"I'm glad someone did. I wasn't sure sometimes." Avery wiped fake sweat from her brow.

"Hey, Avery." Jessie came from behind Graciela and hugged her. "Looking good."

"You, too. Still driving all the women wild?" Avery nudged her arm against his.

"Maybe one." He gave a quick glance to Graciela, who did her best not to return the stare. "I'm going to find us some seats. I'll see you in there." He took Avery's hand and kissed the back of it. "Congratulations, again."

"Thanks." Avery waved at him as he walked off. When she knew he wouldn't be able to hear her, she turned to Graciela. "He's in love with you."

Graciela sighed. "I know. And you know what the bad part about all that is?"

Avery shrugged.

"I think I love him, too." Graciela hung her head down. "Girl, help me."

Avery laughed. "I'm the last person you should ask for help. Remember, I'm the one who let a good one go when a skank made me believe her lies." She quickly burned every Kat CD she had and secretly wished that Kat felt the pain. "But I'm happy for you as long as you're happy."

"I don't know what I am. But I guess we'll see." Graciela looked behind Avery. "I'll see you marching soon. You have company."

Hazel came up behind Avery as soon as Graciela walked away. "You look great." She smiled and put her hands on Avery's shoulders as she stood behind her. "Are you ready?"

Avery plastered a smile on her face before she turned around. "I am. Are you proud of me?"

Hazel smiled while fighting back tears. "Of course, dear. I knew you would get to this point eventually."

Avery held her mother's hand as they walked out of the bathroom. Avery's father waited in the bustling atrium area, wringing his hands.

She approached her father and hugged him. "Thanks for everything."

Clinton hugged her back. "You did all the work. I'm just glad you did all of this on your own."

"I couldn't have done this without your support. You employed me." Avery let her father go. "I'm forever grateful."

Clinton looked at Avery but remained silent for a while. Then he turned to his wife. "Honey, go in and get us our seats. I need to talk to Avery for a minute.

Hazel kissed Clinton and Avery before walking away.

Clinton turned to his daughter. "I'm very proud of you."

Hearing those words finally from her father allowed Avery to exhale. "Thanks, Dad. That's all I ever wanted."

"That's not true. There's something else you want." Clinton held Avery's hands. "You want to sing professionally."

Avery dropped her gaze and shook her head. "Stupid dreams now. I've learned my lesson after my trip to New York. I'm grounded now."

"But are you happy?"

That question stopped Avery cold. "Sure. I'm getting my degree soon. I'll get a great-paying job. I'll be a responsible grownup." She laughed.

Clinton remained quiet. He studied Avery.

"Dad, don't make this weird. I'm good." She noticed the other students lining up to march inside of the convention center room.

"I'm not trying to make this strange for you. I just noticed in the last few weeks how the light in your eyes has gone out since you made your decision not to pursue your dream. I don't want to see you get disappointed like your mother had been." He removed his hat and held it. "I don't want you living your life wishing you could have done more. Singing gave you life. I want you to live."

"I don't need to sing to get my life." Avery started to go to the lineup but Clinton held her arm.

"You don't need to sing. You *have* to sing. You should sing." He hugged her again. "I really hope you rediscover your passion again. If you get a second chance, take it."

"Fine, Dad." She kissed his cheek. "Go and sit with Mom. All of this will be over soon."

Clinton nodded and went into the large room while Avery got in line with the other students.

"Did you hear who was doing the commencement speech?" Avery overheard one of the students around her asking another.

"Comedian or politician?" the other student asked.

"Neither. Chantel Woodley. Can you believe that?"

Avery couldn't believe it. Although she wanted to work for this woman at one time, she would at least absorb her words of wisdom about working in the real world.

After marching into the crowded room and assuming her seat, the graduation proceedings started with various speeches from the university deans and president. Then they introduced their commencement speaker. True to the rumors, Chantel Woodley walked out on the stage.

She looked so different from her glamorous image. Even in her cap and gown, she still looked gorgeous. Chantel had the life she had wanted.

"Good afternoon, students, faculty, family, and friends of Old Dominion University. Welcome to the spring graduation ceremonies." Chantel smiled after her opening.

Avery applauded along with the rest of the audience.

Chantel gave a very moving speech about perseverance and facing adversity, both she did publicly.

"Please always remember that inner strength shows through every success. And there is always an opportunity for forgiveness and second chances. With that said, I have a friend who would like to close out this ceremony." Chantel stood off to the side.

Avery peered over to the side of stage and stopped breathing when she saw Laz Kyson crossing the stage to the podium.

"Thank you, Chantel." Laz kissed her cheek. "And thank you for letting me share this stage. This is something I normally would not do because performing in public scares the hell out of me."

Laughter filled the large conference center room.

"As I have been told by my family and friends, if I want to get anywhere in life and in love, I need to learn to let go and open my heart." He took a deep breath. "I want to do something for someone special, graduating student Avery Shields. She told me that in doing a performance, the audience is on my side. I really hope she's right about that."

Someone pushed a small keyboard out on stage along with a chair. Laz sat behind the keyboard and started playing a tune that Avery didn't recognize. When he started singing, she exhaled and had to put her hand to her chest as he sang her song "Love Like Crazy."

Avery couldn't believe he remembered all the words to it and created a melody behind it. What really stunned her had to be the fact that he sang in public, something he said he would never do. He pushed himself out of his comfort zone and sounded great doing so.

Avery stood and moved out to the open aisle area to watch him. She crept closer to the stage until he got to the end of the song where he belted out a long note that she never thought about for the song but that worked perfectly. At the end, she ran up on stage and wrapped her arms around him while he sat on the chair.

"That was beautiful." She kissed him. "I can't believe you did this. I'm so sorry I didn't believe you."

"I should have told you about the situation." Laz smoothed her hair back from her face.

"I understood why you didn't. I'm sorry I didn't sign your contract. I should have."

Laz shook his head. "It's okay."

"No. I didn't trust myself and I projected. But know this. I didn't sign with Section Eight, and I'm not going to sing with Kat. I've missed you so much." She kissed him again.

"I love you. I would do anything for you." Laz held her around her waist. "As a matter of fact." He stood and got down on one knee. "Would you do me the honor of being my wife?"

The crowd screamed and applauded.

Avery nodded. "Yes. I would love to be your wife."

"Good. I already asked your parents for permission first." He slid the ring on her finger.

The president of the university went to the microphone. "So that we can get this graduation going, let's award Ms. Shields her diploma now." He handed the rolled paper wrapped in blue ribbon to her.

At that point, Laz led her off the stage to a back hallway area. There Chantel joined them.

"Congratulations." Chantel hugged Avery.

"Oh my God. I can't believe you're here and you're talking to me." Avery held on to her idol until Chantel had to pull back first. She looked at Laz. "So you really did know her?"

Laz shook his head. "No. I had to track her and her husband down. I begged for an opportunity for you."

"For me?" Avery turned to Chantel.

"I heard you sing. I think you're incredible." Chantel smiled. "If you're interested, I would like to sign you to a development deal with Charisma. I want to see where you go with your songwriting." She peered at Laz. "The great thing is that when you're ready to record, you'll have a great producer."

Avery looked up at Laz.

He nodded. "I'll be producing music, which is great. If I can't develop talent, I would like to help artists in other ways."

"Me, too. If you're not too busy with your day job, I would love for you to sing with me on a track for an upcoming album." Chantel held Avery's hands as she spoke to her.

"Uh, hell yes!" Avery hugged Chantel again. "Thank you. What a wonderful day."

Chantel peered over when Truman Woodley and a security team headed her way. "I have to go. Come by the office on Monday to discuss the contract." She leaned closer to Avery. "No more cleaning floors and toilets for you." She winked and left with her husband.

Chantel hugged Laz again. "I still can't believe you're here. I've missed you so much." She kissed him and slid her tongue in his mouth.

Laz held her close to his body.

When she pulled back from the kiss, she rested her hands on his chest. "Think we can find a broom closet somewhere? I've missed you."

"Missed you, too, babe. But your parents are here. I think we should at least see them." He patted her backside. "Besides, we have the rest of our lives to make beautiful music together. I love you."

"I love you, too." Avery couldn't wait for her life to begin with love, music and Laz.

Don't miss Crystal B. Bright's next book in the Love & Harmony series,

Crazy on You

Available soon!

Chapter One

"Baby, let's get naked and let me ride on you all day." As soon as Tassia Hogan sang the infamous hook in the popular song by Aaron, another Charisma artist, her stomach knotted despite the smile on her face.

The large crowd in the open arena area at the Virginia Beach Amphitheater screamed as soon as she sang that line. Some of the fans even sang with her. Tassia danced around on stage while Aaron commanded the crowd. One day, the roles would be reversed. She would be the lead and she would have others backing her. Hopefully, she would sing something better than songs like "Ride Me."

When her part of the song came up again, Tassia steeled her nerves, smiled, and sang her heart out. When she noticed small, preteen kids in front of the stage singing that same titillating line, she had to look away.

Singing this damaging line did, at least, put her out there in front of audiences. She had spent years in the background singing backup for lots of singers including Chantel Woodley when she used to be known as Shauna Stellar. Since the song landed in the number one spot on several music charts, she had gotten paid handsomely. She knew she wanted more.

"Thank you, everyone!" Aaron raised his hand in the air. When Tassia came down to the front next to him to bow alongside with him, he immediately said, "Good night!" He walked off without her allowing her to bow alongside with him.

Embarrassed heat flamed her cheeks as she walked off the stage behind Aaron. The singer who had a lighter skin tone than Tassia's chestnut-colored one paced offstage as though waiting for something.

Tassia listened to the crowd and heard them screaming, "Encore! Encore!"

Aaron clapped his hands and skipped around. "They want more of the kid. Let's go." He ran back out on the stage.

One of the backup singers in all black held Tassia's arm. "You going?"

Tassia shrugged. "Why? He's not doing 'Ride Me' again, and I'm done doing the backup thing." She saw Aaron jumping around on the stage. "You had better get out there."

Tassia continued on to her dressing room, one she shared with the other backup singers. She didn't mind that. She like talking and laughing along with the other men and women who stood only a few feet from stardom. She did wonder when her time would be coming.

Tassia took the opportunity to get in a shower before the other singers came to the room to strip and do the same. She washed off all the glitter and makeup. As she stood under the hot streaming water, she let everything go down the drain. She would forget about the state of her career or the types of songs she sang for the moment.

When she heard a door closing, she assumed the other singers had finished their work and had come back to the room. She finished up her cleansing shower and turned off the water.

"Hey, how was the encore?" Tassia opened the curtain as she waited for the answer.

To her surprise, Dorian stood in the room with his phone pointed in her direction. Thankfully, she didn't open the curtain all the way so that he caught her nude body.

"What the hell?" Tassia held the thick tan curtain in front of her body so that only her angry face could be visible. "What are you doing?"

"Say hi, baby." Dorian got in the camera view. "Standing here with this hot lady after a great set with Aaron here in Virginia Beach."

Tassia shook her head. "Turn it off and get out."

Dorian covered his mouth. "Oops. Looks like the show is over. Bye, world." He clicked something on the screen and lowered the phone. "Great show."

"Get out and close the door behind you." Tassia didn't believe Dorian when he looked like he had stopped recording.

"What? Fans want to see you." He crept up to her. "Hell, *I* want to see you."

Tassia pointed to the door while keeping the curtain wrapped around her body. "Get out."

Dorian raised his hands in the air in surrender. "All right. All right. I'll see you out there." He brought his face forward like he wanted to kiss her.

She closed the curtain on him and stayed in the stall until she heard the door close. With great caution, Tassia pulled the curtain back again and peeked out into the all-white bathroom. Finding it empty, she stepped out and quickly picked up a bath sheet to wrap around her body. She tucked the additional fabric in front and also slipped on a thick, blue terrycloth robe.

She wiped her hand down over the frosted mirror to see her reflection. Through the water droplets on the reflective glass, she found that she looked exhausted. Dark circles ringed her eyes. Despite working out every day and keeping to a strict diet to keep fit for this tour, her face look puffy. After removing her bright red lipstick, her lips appeared chapped.

This life didn't suffer fools or weaklings. At least tonight would end a six-month-long stateside tour. She could now relax. Her relaxation would involve a beach somewhere where no one knew that damn song or the part she played in it. For as childish as Dorian could be, he at least provided a great distraction for her. He could turn a root canal into a party. She would need that fun energy.

She got dressed in leggings and an oversized T-shirt in time for the other background singers to arrive to the room. Along with them came Dorian. In his oversized button-down plaid shirt and baggy jeans, he looked like he wanted to look like a teenager. It didn't help that he kept his Afro cut in a high-top fade.

When she first met the roadie, she thought the African-American man looked cute. He made her laugh, and was down to have fun at all times. He made her remember that she should still have fun in her life.

"You've gotten so many hits on your video." He held up his phone to her.

"Not a great thing." Tassia shook her head.

Dorian shrugged. "Why not? You want your fans to see you, right? The real you?" He wiggled his eyebrows in a comical way.

"Right now, I just want to see the insides of my eyelids until I can take a long vacation." She grabbed her suitcases and dragged them out the door.

She would have thought Dorian would have helped her. He followed her out to the tour buses. Gentleman all the way.

Tassia stopped next to the bus. "Look. We've had a lot of fun on this tour."

Dorian reached for her. "Yeah, girl. In the hotel, in the bathroom, on the stage." He licked his lips and leaned down like he wanted to kiss her neck.

"Yes." She smiled despite the public display of affection. Never her thing, but with Dorian, she would roll with it. "Now we can go off and do that secluded island thing. I know of a great spot in—"

"Whoa, whoa, whoa." Dorian held Tassia's shoulders and pushed her back. "Secluded island? That sounds like we would be alone."

Tassia fought hard not to laugh in his face. "That's the whole point of a vacation."

He shook his head. "That doesn't sound cool to me."

She blinked. "So vacationing on an island with me doesn't sound like a good thing to you?"

He snickered and stumbled back from her. "Nope. To be on an island with just you would make me feel like my parents or something, like we should be playing shuffleboard or bingo." He laughed.

Tassia didn't. "We're both twenty-three. We're young."

"Yep. Young, black, and gifted." He nodded while keeping his hands on her hips.

"So we can walk around on a beach and wear bathing suits all day if we want. And now that the tour is over—"

"Yeah, now that the tour is done, we can go off and do our own thing...with other people." Dorian's face became solemn. "This was all for fun, right?"

Tassia stared at Dorian. How could she miss seeing that he hadn't taken her or what they did together seriously? "You don't want to keep seeing me?"

Dorian shrugged. "I just see two different things for us. I'm working on my career."

"As a roadie? That's your career?" She put her hand to her head.

He nodded. "It's what I want to do, babe. You'll be going on other tours. We'll split up. A relationship like that won't work." He pulled a joint from his pocket along with a lighter. "I'm sorry if you felt like this would go somewhere."

"Thanks." She started loading her luggage on the bus by herself. "I can't believe this is happening. You used me."

He snapped the lighter before dousing it. "Don't be all like that. We used each other. You needed a distraction on the tour." He licked his lips. "I wanted the 'Ride Me' chick."

Tassia could have reminded him that the few times she did have sex with him, it had felt more like a chore than pleasure. She wouldn't stoop to that level. She still had to leave this situation with her head held high, and she had a good opportunity for that as long as Dorian kept his attention on his drugs and not her.

"Fine. Have a nice life, Dorian." Tassia headed to the open door of the bus.

"See you, hotness. Hope you're not simply a hook girl." Dorian sneered at her before he walked away.

Damn. Dorian voiced a concern that she had had. Would her mark in music be reduced to a line she hated singing night after night? Something would have to change.

Once Tassia got back home to Virginia Beach, she visited Charisma Music to pick up some of her stuff and for a meeting. It still felt good to visit the place. Her shoulders relaxed when she walked in the doors. This place felt like home.

In the open lobby area hung artwork done by musicians. No pictures of current Charisma artists to show anyone favoritism. The cozy furniture and plethora of plants gave the place a homey feel.

Never did Tassia regret signing her development deal with Charisma five years ago. She certainly had a lot of great opportunities since then. If she didn't have this meeting, she would take advantage of the end of the summer season and enjoy the local beach before going to a more exotic on out of the country. Greece would be nice.

Tassia peeked her head into Chantel's office. Finding it empty except for two high chairs and toys littering the floor, she went to a nearby conference room where she found Chantel's assistant cleaning up what looked like cereal from the long conference day.

"The twins took over." The mature man scraped the strewn pieces into a trashcan. "Looking for Mrs. Woodley?"

Tassia smiled at Earvin. "Meeting. I thought she would be in her office."

He pointed down. "In the studio. Meet her and the mister there."

She raised her eyebrows. "Truman is here, too?"

Tassia shouldn't have been worried. She had done great work for the company. She also knew how volatile and fickle the business could be. One day she could be up. The next day she could be out the door. She hoped the latter didn't apply to her.

She got to the studio and heard some tunes coming from the space. It helped that the door had been left open. Had it been closed, she wouldn't have heard anything.

Tassia stepped inside and saw a familiar face behind the boards.

"Hey, superstar." Super producer Laz Kyson nodded to her as he turned off the music. "I thought you were still on tour with Aaron." He stood and hugged her.

"Ended yesterday." She sat down next to him.

The tall blond-haired, blue-eyed hottie didn't look like he would fit at a record label run by the R&B Princess of Love Ballads. Then again, Chantel's country-singing husband flipped the perception of the recording studio. The music that came out of the place could best be defined as eclectic. Pop, rock, R&B, country, indie. That variety attracted Tassia to the label.

"You just got off tour and you're already working?" He nodded at her.

"Not by choice." She crossed her legs. "I would much rather be lounging on a beach somewhere."

"I hear you."

"Speaking of hearing, what were you playing before? Sounded good." She looked in the studio area and didn't see anyone in there recording.

"You like that?" He hit a button on the panel and played a song from beginning to end. "It's called 'Shame' by singer/songwriter Avery."

"Sounds incredible." Tassia nodded.

"It better. If I didn't make my wife sound good, she would never forgive me." Laz chuckled.

Tassia found hope to see so many successful couples in the business. She didn't see that happening to her, especially if her last relationship meant anything.

"By the way, the bosses are in the conference room down the hall." Laz nodded his head forward.

She stood. "Do you know what it's about?"

Laz shrugged. "Not sure. But I'm sure you'll be fine."

"We'll see." Tassia hung her purse on her shoulder as she walked down the hallway.

She arrived at the conference room and found Chantel and Truman Woodley sitting at the conference room table. Chantel had her feet up on her husband's lap. He rubbed her bare feet. The romantic gesture brought a smile to Tassia's face.

"Hi." Tassia stepped into the room. "Is this a bad time?"

Chantel removed her feet from her husband's lap. "Of course not." She padded over to Tassia. "So great to see you again." She gave her a hug.

"Yep. Welcome back." Truman stood and hugged Tassia also. "Please have a seat."

Like a gentleman, he pulled out Tassia's chair and did the same for his wife. Looked like Chantel found the last of the good ones.

"I know what it's like to just get off tour. I know all you want to do is rest and relax." Chantel smiled as she spoke to Tassia.

Chantel and Truman sat at one end of the table. To not make the meeting seem so official, Tassia sat on one side of the table instead of the end and positioned herself as close to the duo as she could.

"You're right about that. I feel like I've been running for years." Tassia noticed the slightly concerned looks covering her bosses' faces. "But you know me. I never turn down work. Bring it on."

"That's good to hear." Truman nodded.

"But I am concerned about something. Since I have you two here, there's no better time than the present to discuss it." Tassia sat up taller.

"Sure. What's on your mind?" Chantel leaned forward.

"When I signed my development deal five years ago, I knew that I wouldn't be banging out albums right away. I knew it would take time and I would have to work hard." Tassia had to frame this right. She had to show her appreciation.

"And you have worked very hard. Don't think we haven't noticed." Chantel put her hand on top of Tassia.

It still blew her mind that this multi-platinum artist could be this kind and personable with people who worked for her.

"Thank you." Tassia patted Chantel's hand. "I hope with all the work I've done that I've finally earned my spot. I've written hits for you, Truman, for you, Chantel, for the two of you as a duo, and more. And I've sang backup for a lot of artists."

"And let's not forget that incredible hit song." Truman wagged his finger at her.

Tassia tried so hard not to roll her eyes, but it happened.

"What's that look about?" Chantel cocked her head.

"I'm not ungrateful about that opportunity. Aaron is a hot artist out right now. I was able to be on a successful track. People know me more."

"But?" Truman adjusted his baseball cap on his head.

Tassia took a deep breath. "I don't want to be known as only a 'hook girl.' I'm more than that."

"You are right about that." Chantel held Truman's hand. "My husband and I recognize that. We also know that you've paid your dues. For that reason, we have an opportunity for you."

Tassia felt the tide turning. Since she no longer had any kind of relationship now, she could concentrate on herself.

"Have you heard of Hyde Love?" Truman picked up a remote.

"Hiding love?" Tassia almost thought the two of them got into her thoughts.

She hadn't planned on turning her back on the idea of love. She wouldn't be seeking it while going to the next level. Relationships, sex, and love would only slow her down. The little fling she'd had with the roadie had to hold her for a while.

"No. Hyde Love, an artist." Truman hit a button on a remote. "A country artist."

Tassia focused on the screen. A tall, incredibly good-looking man – emphasis on man – populated the screen. He looked tall on the screen, but that could have been due to camera angles. Through his backward baseball cap, she spotted his light brown hair. His scruffy beard kept him from looking like a teenager like Dorian. At one point, Hyde looked directly into the camera. Tassia had been told that for an African-American woman, her green eyes looked hypnotic. She didn't see it. Now looking at Hyde's eyes, she understood.

Tassia looked away from the screen before she got sucked in even more. "Looks like he's a good performer."

"And the singing. What did you think about his singing and the song?" Chantel grabbed the remote and turned up the song.

Tassia brought her attention back to the screen. She hadn't been a big fan of country music, even the crossover version. Hyde sang a song about finding the one when a person figured out and fixed their flaws, kind of deep for what Tassia imagined for country songs.

"He sounds good." She shrugged. "Song sounds good. I like that he's singing about more than beer and hayrides."

Truman cleared his throat. "Nothing wrong with songs about beer and maybe more beer."

Damn. Tassia had a feeling she would have to do her research about her boss. She knew Chantel's catalogue. As a fan, she devoured her music. Despite Truman marrying her idol and being her boss, she didn't listen to a lot of his music. She knew that any song she had given him, he killed it.

"So what's the deal with him?" Tassia crossed her legs. "Is he a Charisma artist?"

"Not really. We're trying something new. We want to try something new. We've met with his management, and we want to do another album of duets where we cross genres." Truman stopped the video.

Oh, no. Tassia saw the writing on the wall.

"We want you to do an album with Hyde." Chantel beamed. "Bring your soul edge along with his country flavor to make something groundbreaking."

Tassia volleyed her attention between Truman and Chantel. "Like what you two did."

Chantel glanced at Truman. "Something like that. We think that now is the time to cross boundaries, show people that being different doesn't mean you can't work together."

Tassia had to wrap her mind around several concepts. Her first album would be a duet with a country singer she didn't know. It sounded like Chantel and Truman saw this as some sort of political statement.

"I don't know." Tassia shook her head. "I envisioned my first album having my own sound."

Chantel sat up straighter. "It still will. Truman and I want you and Hyde to write all of the music on the album."

"Does the album have to have a political slant? I don't think I want my brand to be that." Tassia tried hard to get out of this situation as tactfully as possible.

Chantel furrowed her eyebrows. "So you hate being called a 'hook girl,' but given the opportunity to do something substantial, you don't want to do that?"

Tassia didn't want to seem ungrateful. She had to turn this around and put this in her favor. "I truly appreciate you two thinking about me for this special project. I can tell it means a lot to you. I don't know if I can give this project the right flavor it needs." She grabbed her purse strap to signal she wanted to go.

Chantel looked at Truman before dropping her gaze for a beat. "I understand. I'm sure you're exhausted. We are asking for a lot from you."

"Thank you for understanding." Tassia stood.

"We do. I hope you understand that right now work at Charisma has slowed. Lots of tours are ending, so not a lot of work for backup singers. Christmas albums have wrapped for the upcoming season. And no need for studio work." Chantel stood. "Enjoy your time off." She put her hand out. "If you decide that you change your mind about recording, let us know."

Shit.

Tassia smiled as she shook Chantel's hand. In a nutshell, her boss laid out Tassia's financial future at the label. Do the duets album and get paid, or do nothing and have no work.

She had a lot to mull over and not a lot of time. So much for a summer vacation.

* * * *

"I love you, Hyde!" A female fan screamed through the darkened window of his limousine.

Thankfully the fan couldn't see Hyde's expression. He rubbed his eyes while hanging his head down. "Can we go, please?"

"What? You don't like this attention?" Hyde's manager looked at the chaos happening around the car. Abe enjoyed this attention more than Hyde, especially when the young women pulled their tops up and pressed their naked breasts against the glass.

The first time he saw that, Hyde couldn't believe his luck. Of course, he saw his first set of naked boobs when he started in the business at eleven. Fifteen years later, the allure of this strange unconditional love from strangers all seemed foreign, unreal, unnatural. After all this time, Hyde longed for something real, something substantial.

The limo eased up a little before finally pulling away from the ravenous crowd. Once on the interstate, Hyde removed his cap, now an unexpected signature trademark, and tossed it on the seat next to him.

"Great show." Abe pulled out his phone and started typing over the screen. "Put the hat back on and smile." He held his phone up to Hyde's face.

"Will you give me a break? No photos right now, all right? I just want to chill. Can't I just…" He leaned back, kicking his legs out front of him and crossing them at the ankles.

"Your fans want to know all about you." Even with his eyes closed in the darkened ride, he saw through his eyelids a bright flash. "They'll have to accept a picture of you sleeping."

"Damn it." Hyde shook his head. "Does every part of me have to be for sale?"

"If you want to sell records and sell out arenas, yeah. You have to give up a bit of yourself. Besides, you have more sales that that Justin kid out right now doing the pop thing. That's unheard of in country. Not since Garth Brooks and Tim McGraw." Abe knocked his foot against Hyde's. "You have broken barriers." He cleared his throat. "That reminds me. Are you awake enough to discuss business?"

"No," Hyde replied flatly.

He really didn't want to talk about anything except for maybe a scheduled break. He hadn't had one of those in several years. Between recording, touring, interviews, and other appearances, Hyde's life no longer belonged to him. Record labels and fans dictated every part of his existence.

"Okay, I'll talk. If you fall asleep and miss what I'm saying, I'll tell it to you again later." Abe clicked the overhead light in the limo.

"Light off." Hyde didn't ask for much, and he couldn't really be qualified as a diva. Quiet and silence came at a premium. Whenever he could get it, he demanded it.

"Fine." Abe turned the light back off. "So I had an interesting conversation with Truman Woodley."

Hyde lifted his head and tried looking at his manager in the darkened car. Although Truman started recording professionally only a few years ago, Hyde liked his style. He especially liked the fact that Truman recorded songs with heart and substance, post "Beer and More Beer." Being married to Shauna Stellar must have changed his whole perspective.

Hyde almost wished he could find a true love like that. In his business, he didn't know who wanted what from him. Fans wanted his time. Some women who went after him wanted his money. Other artists, especially the newer ones, wanted his fame. Truman didn't seem to fit in any of those categories. He married the most famous woman in music.

"What did Truman say?" Hyde hated that Abe baited him into this conversation. His curiosity got the better of him.

"Truman and Chantel are looking to do an album of duets. They checked out your catalogue of music, and they like your style. They want to know if you want in." Even in the darkness, Abe's teeth shined brightly.

"Are you serious? Truman wants do an album of duets with me, not his ultra-famous wife? Doesn't make sense." Hyde sat up and drew his feet back.

"The duets wouldn't be with Truman or Shauna or Chantel or whatever she's calling herself nowadays. It would be with you and one of their artists." Abe looked at his screen and started typing something over it.

"Do you know who? They have lots of different artists signed to them."

"So you're interested." Abe rubbed his hands together like he wanted money.

"I'm curious. There's a distinct difference." Hyde scratched the back of his head.

"We're in North Carolina. It's a hop, skip, and a jump to Virginia. I can set up a meeting with Truman and his wife. That is if you're still curious." Abe had a playful lilt to his voice.

Hyde thought about the possibilities. Lately he had lost the love he had with country music. Maybe this would give him the boost he needed.

"Set it up." Hyde settled back in the seat.

"Done."

Hyde would see if this new project would give him the love that he lost in music. If it didn't, he had to reevaluate his desire to stay in the business.

Meet the Author

Crystal B. Bright graduated with a B.A. from Old Dominion University with a major in Creative Writing and a minor in Communications with an emphasis on Public Relations. She earned her M.A. from Seton Hill University in Writing Popular Fiction. For more information about Crystal and her writing, please visit her website at www.CrystalBrightWriter.com. You can also find her at https://www.facebook.com/crystal.bright.397, or follow her on Twitter @CrystalBBright.